Prisoner of Thian

Book 3 of Shields of seiflands

Jay Roshni

Prisoner of Thian

Copyright © 2024 by Jay Roshni

All rights reserved.

No part of this publication may be reproduced, distributed, or transmitted in any form or by any means, including photocopying, recording, or other electronic or mechanical methods, without written permission of the publisher.

Book Cover by Getcovers.com

Contents

Map of Greylan — V

PROLOGUE — 1

1. Chapter 1 — 4
2. Chapter 2 — 15
3. Chapter 3 — 23
4. Chapter 4 — 34
5. Chapter 5 — 47
6. Chapter 6 — 60
7. Chapter 7 — 68
8. Chapter 8 — 81
9. Chapter 9 — 91
10. Chapter 10 — 101
11. Chapter 11 — 109
12. Chapter 12 — 117
13. Chapter 13 — 128

14.	Chapter 14	137
15.	Chapter 15	146
16.	Chapter 16	159
17.	Chapter 17	174
18.	Chapter 18	184
19.	Chapter 19	193
20.	Chapter 20	205
21.	Chapter 21	217
22.	Chapter 22	224
23.	Chapter 23	236
24.	Chapter 24	246
25.	Chapter 25	257
26.	Chapter 26	268
27.	Chapter 27	277
28.	Chapter 28	286
29.	Chapter 29	296
30.	Chapter 30	303
31.	Chapter 31	312
32.	Chapter 32	320

PROLOGUE

Mentra had patiently bided her time. Three months were a mere speck in the over seven centuries she had existed in this world, out of which forty miserable years were spent on this continent. She didn't mind waiting, not when the fruit would be the sweetest in the bunch. Downfall of Niferon, the god—no, the man who had slayed her child and husband.

The coldness of the tear that escaped her tightly closed eyes jerked her out of that painful memory.

Thili could go on believing that her warning had an effect, that Mentra had retreated into her shell because she feared Thili would expose her location to Niferon. That was why she had waited three months for her next step—to give Thili the false hope that Mentra would not act because of fear.

It had always been one of her strengths—everyone believing that she was less powerful than she really was. What could an enchantress do other than seduce her victims and leech powers out of them, only to submit those powers at the feet of the king of the gods? No one, not even Niferon, had realized that the enchantress could keep a part of that power for herself. And he called himself the king of the gods.

Thili should have known better. After all, it had been her idea to accumulate power and break free from Niferon. That was what both of them had done—break free from being in the service of the gods.

Gods. Mentra chuckled through her tears.

Niferon and his cohorts could fool the whole of humanity by pretending to be something they were not. But she knew they were not even immortal. All they had was power—power that anyone could hold if one could obtain their scrolls.

The *gods* knew that death would come for them too—maybe not as quickly as it did for the rest of the world, but even Kalantra, who called herself the goddess of death, would one day decay, and Zesta, the goddess of life, would have to give up breathing. When that time came, their seat of power should not lie vacant and the scrolls would find their successor.

A successor. That was the tricky part that Mentra did not understand. Everyone had always believed that only a worthy successor could read the scrolls, but she had grasped the contents of Varys's scroll and mastered the manipulation of water.

Other scrolls would be no different. They would also open up their secrets to her. It was just a matter of time before she found all the six remaining scrolls, and then nothing would stop her from bringing Niferon to his knees.

But for the time being, she had to leave Prithi's scroll where it was—under the hills of the Western Frontier. Thili had played that game well. The hills were currently under the direct scrutiny of

Coraen. Thili knew Mentra would do nothing that would harm her own son.

Her chest clenched for a moment. What she was planning to do could not but have some effect on Coraen, even if it did not harm him. It would shake up the entire continent. For a moment, her resolution faltered. Was the dead child dearer to her than the living one?

She roughly wiped away the tears that had never ceased to be her constant companion in the past forty years. No, both were equal to her, but Coraen was a grown man who could take care of himself, while her daughter had never crossed the threshold of infancy. It was that child who was depending on her for justice to be served. And now it was time to act. Now it was time to go to the seifland of Thian.

1

Deena dashed past the terrace, jumped over the vine-covered balustrade, and lay with her stomach pressed to the wet, muddy ground. The puddle formed after the evening's rain seeped into her shirt, and an involuntary shiver ran down her spine. It was not from the coldness of the water or the night air. She was familiar with earth and mud and water. She could easily wade deep into ponds in the middle of the night to pluck the leaves of amaran or invade the thorny bushes of jaira to collect its petals. What she wasn't used to was being followed by armed soldiers.

Her pursuers took the steps down the terrace and paused.

"Where did he go?" a woman yelled from the terrace.

"Was it a *he*?" a man asked. "The thief surely had feminine . . . curves." He giggled.

"You must go back to your training barracks," the woman said. "I am sure you will when Mother Len learns about your incompetency. The gender of the thief doesn't matter. Find him or her before they get away."

The two soldiers examined the grounds, and Deena tried to squeeze herself into the vines that spilled down from the railing.

The swollen leaves of the vine squished, and a pungent sap trickled down her neck.

She muttered a curse. It was pulitra leaves—a natural pest killer that was also good for inducing itchy rashes, if anyone wanted that. She scrubbed the sap from her skin with her sleeve, succeeding only in spreading it further.

A pair of boots stopped a few feet from her.

Her scramble must have alerted the soldier. The owner of the boots advanced one step toward her.

Thump.

Something hit the soldier on the back of his head, and he tumbled forward. The sound of his fall brought forth his companion. Out of the shadows, an inky figure emerged with a sword held aloft. It was a broad-shouldered man covered in a black cloak and mask, but Deena knew who it was. She would either get caught by the soldiers of Thian tonight or have a lot of explaining to do to her cousin and foster brother, Kran. The latter seemed more probable.

Metal clanged against each other as Kran crossed his sword with those of the other two. With a powerful push, he sent the soldiers reeling backward. In the time it took them to regain their balance, he turned his head and spoke one word.

"Go."

Deena got onto all fours, her hair choosing that inopportune moment to break free of its bun. Her fingers got tangled in her tresses as she lifted them up to avoid tripping on them.

Kran parried the soldiers who had returned to attack him. She was losing precious moments. She wound her hair around her neck like a stole and ran to the gate leading out of the garden.

A gasp from one soldier made her wince. She did not desire anyone to get hurt. That was not her intention at all. Harming a life went against all her beliefs and oaths as a healer. But if she stopped now, it would put Kran at risk of capture as well.

The guards at the gate whom she had earlier disabled lay supine on the ground—unconscious and unharmed. But she couldn't say the same for the soldiers who were now fighting Kran. With the tiny pebbles pricking through her wicker sandals and the guilt having the same effect on her conscience, she lost herself in the darkness of the streets of Thian.

At her hut, Deena drank five tumblers of water before her heart slowed down to a normal pace. It did not last long because as soon as she lit a candle and sat on the wooden tripod stool behind her worktable that was cluttered with bottles and tubes, the door slammed open and Kran walked in. Her heart began racing again as she anticipated what was about to come.

Of all her foster family members, only Kran ever gave her fearsome reprimands. When she'd wandered off into the woods as a kid or had swum in the river without notifying anyone, he would be present at the doorstep to welcome her back home with a scowl marring his otherwise kind face. It didn't matter that he was only five years older than her. He considered himself a parental figure and would list the severe repercussions her actions would have invited—like getting eaten by a wolf or getting eaten by a crocodile. Now that she thought about it, it had always been about getting eaten by something.

"I should never have left you alone here." Kran dropped his cloak on the floor, untied the mask that covered his square jaw, and went to the water pot. It was empty.

She got up to refill the pot, plotting an escape route.

"Sit." Kran scowled, the sinister effect deepened by his shoulder-length hair that fell in black curtains around his face. "I can get it." He didn't go out to get the water, though. "What were you thinking? If Lord Alayster or Lord Thian finds out that you or I were involved in tonight's break-in, it would destroy a lot of relationships."

"Was anybody hurt?"

"If you had cared about people getting hurt, you wouldn't have gone there."

"You didn't have to come and attack the soldiers." It was an ungrateful thing to say. If not for Kran, she would be languishing in a prison right then, awaiting her punishment. "I had planned on getting in and out quietly without alerting the guards. And I wouldn't have harmed anyone. I had put the guards to sleep with oaflin smoke. Those two soldiers came out of nowhere. Oh, I would never forgive myself if they were hurt."

"No one suffered any injury that a good healer can't rectify in a day. I promise. Although a good healer wouldn't have acted in such a way as to cause injuries to others."

He didn't have to tell her that. She had thought she had everything under control. It hadn't seemed so risky when she had planned it. After all, the garden itself was open to the public during the day, and she had scouted it several times to get an idea of the premises.

Both the conservatory and the shrine of Zesta behind it were out of bounds, but guards were present only at the main gate. Once she had put those guards to sleep using the smoke of oaflin leaves, her path should have been clear, and she should have been able to find out the secrets hidden in Lord Thian's private greenhouse, alerting no one.

That family controlled the supply of various rare herbs and plants without making it available to the public. She had only wanted to gather enough evidence to take the case to the healers' guild and to force the family of Thian to share the herbs with everyone.

"Don't look so sullen," Kran said when she remained quiet for a few moments. "I am tempted to complain to Mother about your behavior, although she would just hug you and send you off to bed instead of giving you an effective reprimand."

Kran was not wrong. His mother—her aunt and foster mother—had only ever showered her with love and warmth. But that hadn't prevented Kran from often complaining to her about Deena's lawless behavior, as he put it.

"Well, you are here to reprimand me, but I only did it to help my patients." She struggled against the pout that was forming on her face. She was no longer a child who didn't know which risks were worth taking. This must be dealt with like an adult. It was not fair that even at twenty-six she could be made to feel like a petulant child by Kran.

"The garden you entered tonight is considered sacred by the mother of Lord Thian." Kran loosened his belt, from which hung his sword. "That should have been enough to show you the error of your ways. You don't enter other people's land, especially when it is prohibited."

"What made you return to Thian?" Deena didn't bother to keep the irritation out of her voice. The angry blister developing behind her neck did not help. Soon it would itch.

"I knew you'd pull something like this after your constant grumbling about the rarity of heliatin."

"If you know me that well, you'd also know that I can distinguish right from wrong."

Kran shook his head as though he had given up all hope of instilling sense into her. He then kneeled beside her. "I am indebted to Lord Thian for letting you use heliatin to save Sheila. How can we be ungrateful to such a man?"

"How is Sheila?" She knew what the answer would be. She had taken care of her little niece and had been thrilled to take her to the path of recovery from her congenital disease. But she wanted to hear it from Kran.

"She is doing great. She doesn't get tired until her normal sleeping hour. That is such a relief."

"It is, isn't it?" she asked pointedly.

"What are you getting at?" Kran released a frustrated sigh.

"I am treating another child now, a boy this time. He gets seizures quite unexpectedly. His parents are scared out of their wits, but I know he can be cured. Only thing, the eela root needed to prepare that concoction is not available anywhere. I have written to healers as far as Alayster, Kendrek, and Rothshire. Now, if you are best friends with the lord of Alayster or the cousin of Lord Rothshire, you stand a good chance of getting rare ingredients from Thian. But common folk must wait for months to even get news about where the herbs and roots are available. All these rare herbs come from Lady Len's private cultivation. And I need to know why she is having a firm grip over these rare plants, which should be freely available to all. In the end, Lord Thian gave you free access to the herb only because you are Lord Alayster's friend. Isn't that true? Why should other children suffer because they are unknown to seif lords?"

"I don't deny the truth of your words." Kran stood up. "I need that water after all." He picked up the pot and went out of the hut to the well.

He was taking time to think. Let him. She was not in the wrong. Tonight would have gone well had she been a little more careful, a little less excited. But seeing all those plants flourishing in their cases was exhilarating. There was no scarcity. She even spotted some herbs that she had only ever seen in drawings in ancient scrolls.

Stealing one plant was not her motive. She had to find which plants were being cultivated in the greenhouse and take those records to the healers' guild. Together, they could protest against Lady Len's iron grip over the herbs. For that she had to pluck leaves and petals as samples.

That was when things went wrong. She had spotted the very eela plant that she needed for her patient, and in her excitement, she had forgotten to check her surroundings before hurrying to the plant. A soldier had spotted her and raised the alarm.

"I understand the validity of your words, Deena." Kran had returned with the empty pot. He hadn't filled it or drunk water from the looks of it. "But I can't help but feel I have to protect you. When my parents brought you in as a wee baby, they made me promise I would be your elder brother."

"Being an elder brother doesn't mean you have to always stand between me and danger." She stood up and immediately wished she hadn't. At her fullest height, she only reached Kran's chest and had to look up to see his face. It made her feel like a child again.

"Return to Alayster with me. I will talk to Lord Alayster, and maybe he can negotiate with Lord Thian and Lady Len about the rare herbs, but I can't do that if you are caught. It is enough if one soldier recognized you. You could end up in prison for a long time, and then neither Lord Alayster nor I can get involved. Come, Deena. How will I console Mother if something happens to you? You must listen to me."

He didn't wait to check if she did. Instead, he rewound the belt around his vest and gathered up some of her clothes, stuffing them into a sack. Then he went to fill a pouch with water. As far as he was concerned, they were leaving Thian, and as much as she hated running away, being thrown into prison wouldn't serve her patients. She would run now, only to return later.

The shadows thrown by the houses gave them ample cover, even though the moon chose this night to appear at her illuminated best. It would have been the perfect night to collect the dryfly flower or to crush mehua bark. But not tonight. Tonight, Deena had no option but to abandon her patient and run away from the promise of getting him a cure.

She stubbed her toe on an uneven plank of wood on the paved road and cried out in pain. Kran skidded to a stop and looked around for possible chasers.

"I thought you got hit by an arrow," he said.

"Just stubbed a toe."

Kran heaved an exaggerated sigh and restarted jogging. "We can't afford to stop for stubbed toes."

Easy for him to say, as he was wearing leather boots designed for a soldier. She had to depend on her wicker sandals even on a night in which she had to run for her life.

The houses became more widely spaced as they approached the outskirts of the city. They had fewer covers and, if anything, it only increased Kran's speed. Deena clutched the stitch at her side and bent low, blowing into her tunic top, under which sweat had pooled.

"Please stop. Can't we pause for a while?" She panted.

Kran took out the water pouch from his bundle. "Drink. But we can't pause."

"Aren't we safe now?"

As if in answer to her question, a horse neighed in the distance and hooves clopped closer and closer.

Kran took her hand and pulled her forward, the water pouch splattering on the ground. They left the road and ran across a field. If Kran hadn't been dragging her behind him, Deena would have found herself mired in the clayey soil that now filled the legs of her loose trousers.

A bridge led to another field, but instead of crossing it, Kran helped her slide down its steep side to the canal underneath. They stood half-submerged in the sinisterly smooth water, waiting for the horse and rider to reach them and pass along the road. Peace reigned for a while, rendering false solace, and a lonesome owl hooted in the distance, breaking the silence.

Deena whispered, "If there is any chance of us getting caught, you must get away. Don't get into a fight. I am sure trespassing is not as great a crime as attacking the soldiers. And your daughter's need is greater than mine. It wouldn't do if you were stuck in a jail in Thian."

"How do you talk so much when you don't have the breath to run?"

"I manage."

"My daughter needs me, but so do you. I will not abandon you."

"Not abandon. You can help me more by being out of prison. Maybe request Lord Alayster to put in a good word for me."

Deena didn't have to see Kran's expression to know what his reaction to that was. She could feel him bristling up next to her. There was no way he would drag Lord Alayster into justifying an act of trespass.

"I . . ."

A massive splash that sprayed them with water prevented whatever he was about to say. Something or someone had landed in the canal. The shadowy figure rose, water dripping from their form. A band of light extended from them—a sword made from their life force. And in the sword's light, a gruff-faced man glared at them from under impressively thick eyebrows.

2

"Fires of Kalantra," Kran cursed, hastily pulling up his scarf to cover his face. He did not want to be recognized. That much was clear. But his continued muttered curses indicated that he'd rather not face this opponent, whoever he was.

The sword bearer advanced, manifesting a rope made of light in his free hand. "Surrender. There's nowhere to run."

A sentar warrior.

But that couldn't be the reason for Kran's hesitation. He was no coward. Yet he dragged her a few steps into the underbelly of the bridge, where they were enveloped in the leafy smell of a cluster of algae. Before Deena realized what he was doing, he drew his sword.

"I won't harm him," Kran said, "but I will buy you some time."

"No," Deena cried, moving forward with him. Any further attack would only worsen the situation, and she would not run away, leaving Kran to deal with the mess she had created.

But Kran had already hurtled himself toward the sentar warrior, only to crash into a shield of senria that was not there a moment ago. The oval block of light illuminated the black water, the surface of which was occasionally broken by mullets coming up for air.

The warrior released the shield and pirouetted low, swinging his sword at Kran's legs. Kran leaped into the air and aimed a kick at the warrior's shoulder that was parried by another shield.

Kran lost his balance and fell in a heap into the canal, the cold water slapping Deena's face. If she had had a moment to think, she wouldn't have acted. She would have gone down on her knees in surrender and begged to end the fight, but the blade of the warrior's sword was already descending on Kran, who was spluttering and choking as he raised himself out of the water.

Bending low, she ran into the warrior's solar plexus, knocking the wind out of him and also interrupting the flow of his senria. His sword slipped from his hand and his rope flickered as he fell back into the water with Deena on top of him. The sword brushed her fingers as it sank into the water. She could have picked it up by a mere stretch and held it to the man's throat, but she let it sink out of sight.

"Run," she yelled to Kran.

She couldn't hold the warrior down for long, but she fervently hoped it would give Kran enough time to get away. Her prayer was answered as she heard Kran heave himself up the bridge. He must have realized that fighting would only worsen their situation, and if he was caught along with her, the breach of the palace would be considered political violence, as Kran was a soldier of Alayster.

The warrior overturned her and bound her wrists with the rope as a horse rode away on the bridge. He seemed to have realized that Kran had stolen his horse because the knots around her wrists became excessively tight.

"He won't get away," he said with barely controlled fury. "My soldiers have surrounded the area."

"I am the only one you need. He is not involved in any way. I confess to having entered Lord Thian's garden earlier."

"So you confess to the crime?"

"Yes, but I was acting alone."

"You were by no means alone. A masked man helped you back in the palace, the same as now." The man half carried her out of the water and up the path leading to the bridge. It lay desolate, with vast fields stretching in either direction, showing no sign of soldiers or horses.

The sky grew paler, revealing a row of trees on the horizon. Kran would have ridden into the woods, and since he was alone, he had a better chance of evading the soldiers who would follow him. She must not reveal his identity, whatever might happen, and she had to plead his innocence.

"He only helped me because he thought you were attacking me. It was solely my decision to enter the garden tonight. No one helped me do it."

The man scoffed and pushed damp, curly hair away from his forehead. He wore riding breeches and a dusty black jacket that were now soaking wet like her clothes, although she would have been grateful to have the protection of a jacket against the night breeze. The absence of the silver armor of Thian struck her for the first time, and she wondered why she was confessing her crime to a stranger.

"Who are you, by the way? Do you have the authority to hold me and ask these questions?"

"I asked you no question until now. And what are you going to do if I don't have the authority to hold you?"

"Request you to let me go." She struggled against the ropes.

He cast a derisive glance at her attempt. "The rope won't budge until I release it."

"I did nothing wrong." She ran behind him because the pull of the rope forced her to do so. "I am a healer and I was only trying to expose the unjust control that your lord and his mother have over some of the rarest of herbs. Someday even your loved ones might need one of those medicines, and no healer could help you without special permission from Lady Len."

"I am sure I can easily acquire a special permit from her, as I am her only son."

Deena staggered to a stop but was tugged forward by the rope. "Lord Thian."

"No need to curtsy."

She shouldn't be needled by his mocking tone. If there was a time to hold back her tongue, it was now. Yet the words slipped out. "I wasn't going to."

No wonder Kran decided to finally abandon her. He wouldn't fight Lord Thian after all that the latter had done for him, and she had teetered on the verge of insulting the lord and his mother. She tried to replay her words in her head but could recollect nothing.

"I did not mean to be disrespectful," she said reluctantly. Her future would depend on the mercy of this man.

"Do you think being disrespectful to my family is a more severe crime than what you committed at my palace tonight?"

She didn't get the time to respond as they heard horses in the distance. Lord Thian held up his hand and let out a whistle. Within a few moments, three horses and their riders approached them.

"My lord," a woman addressed him, patting her over-energetic horse. "I will take her."

"No, I will do it," Lord Thian said. "The three of you must go toward Feryar. Her accomplice stole my horse and went that way."

"Yes, my lord." The three soldiers went after Kran.

No sooner had they left than three more came by. This time, Lord Thian made her ride with one soldier, and he shared the horse with another. Even though she was on her way to the prison, Deena was relieved at not having to walk anymore. If only she could confirm that Kran was safely out of Thian, she would have gladly resigned to her fate of having to live out the rest of her days in a dungeon in this foreign seifland.

A possible stint in prison did not frighten Deena, but the piercing eyes staring at her did. She got the feeling that trespassing was not a crime that the lord of Thian easily forgave. He sat motionless like a terracotta idol, and the resentment etched on his face promised her that the consequence of her action wouldn't be pleasant.

Behind Lord Thian's chair was a wall marked by the insignia of the seifland—a lightning bolt nocked to a bow. The room was designed to welcome visitors who weren't expected to sit, for Lord Thian's was the only chair under the barrel-vaulted ceiling. The three soldiers who had ridden with them stood behind her.

Muted paintings of the goddess of life, prosperity, and justice, Zesta, adorned the walls and ceilings—in some she wielded the scales of justice, and in others she pronounced judgments or dragged the indicted to the pits of Kalantra. The large oval windows were closed, shutting out the dawn and making the atmosphere stuffy.

"Do you know why you were brought here?" Lord Thian's voice was calmer than she'd expected.

"Yes, my lord."

"So, you don't deny you were in our garden earlier in the night?"

"No, my lord." There was no point in lying. She wouldn't have been caught if someone hadn't recognized her. It had to be the soldiers whom Kran attacked in the garden.

"So you are just a burglar, not a liar."

"I am neither, but merely a trespasser." She scratched the itch behind her neck. If one of her patients had done it, she would have scolded them. Nails were no friends of blisters.

"Why were you in the shrine if not to steal?"

"In the shrine? No, I wasn't—"

"And who was with you? Who helped you break our soldiers?"

"No one." The last thing she would do was give up Kran. She wouldn't mind lying for his sake, but this wasn't a lie. Kran did nothing to harm the soldiers.

"It must be the same man who was with you. Give up his name if you want to be shown the least of mercies."

"I have told you, my lord, that I acted on my own."

"Two of them might not survive until daybreak. Are you telling me you single-handedly destroyed two soldiers?" His eyes swept to her feet and back.

"What?"

"I am witness to the fact that you had a helper tonight. There is no point denying it."

"You must listen to me, my lord. I was only ever in the greenhouse, and the security guards outside the garden were disabled only for about an hour by using the smoke of oaflin leaves. They should have recovered from their sleep-like state by now. I was nowhere near the shrine." She looked behind her at the soldiers who had captured her, as though they would jump to her defense. They didn't.

"What business did you have in our greenhouse?"

"I wanted to know why there is a scarcity of much-needed medicine. And in your greenhouse, I learned the herbs are readily available, even though we don't have access to them to treat the needy. The worst I would have done is organize a protest against your mother."

Lord Thian's eyes glinted with amusement, but he did not smile. "As much as I would have liked to see you protesting against my mother, you have graver things to worry about."

"You said someone was hurt. Take me to them, my lord. I have experience tending to battle wounds."

He snorted. "You want to heal the people you attacked?"

"I attacked no one."

"Your friend, then."

"I came with no one, and I needed no one's help to just take a look in your conservatory."

A murmur from the soldiers behind her was followed by a tinkling of bangles. An elegant, lithe middle-aged woman swept into the room, decked in her fineries as though she were attending a royal parade. Not a strand of her tightly curled black hair escaped its severe bun. Hooped earrings grazed her shoulders, and a matching, though smaller, ring adorned her right nostril.

"Mother, I promised to send word as soon as I obtained more information." Lord Thian stood up.

The lady did not respond. Instead, she grabbed a dagger from the belt of one of the soldiers and held it to Deena's neck, drawing blood.

3

It was not the first time Horace had witnessed his mother's rage. Tonight, however, her anger was tinged with fear, and her knuckles were pale as she held the dagger to the healer's throat. Reason wouldn't work with her at this moment. He commanded his life force to extend as a shield in front of him, and that was what his senria did. The shield pushed his mother away from the disheveled girl, and both fell to the floor, the latter clutching her neck from where blood trickled through her fingers.

"How dare you use your sentar weapon against me?" His mother turned to him, gathering her heavily pleated sapphire-blue skirt. Her stormy eyes looked at him as though he was an erring child.

But he was not. "You are forgetting yourself, Mother," Horace said with as much calm as he could muster. "This is my court of justice, and I am still questioning the suspect."

"I was doing the same, but my method would have elicited an answer by now." She got up and glared at the healer, who was still separated from her by Horace's shield.

"But it is not your place to question her." He turned to the healer. "What is your name?"

"Deena."

"Deena, tonight you trespassed into our private land, and a witness saw you entering our shrine."

"What witness?"

"One of the soldiers who was on patrol."

"Then take me to him, my lord. He could tell you it wasn't me."

"Unfortunately, he has grievous injuries—"

"Inflicted by you," Lady Len exclaimed.

"No. No. I couldn't. I wouldn't." Deena shook her head vigorously. "How did he recognize me?"

"The same way the soldier outside the conservatory did. Both of their descriptions were the same. 'Black hair extending to the ankles.' That is what he said before he passed out. Your hair is quite distinct." He eyed the single plait of raven hair that was draped over her shoulder in a loop and ran down the front of her body to the silver anklet that shined on her ankle.

"But . . . but . . ."

"And it wasn't hard to find someone who fits the description—the new healer from Alayster who had been given special permission by the palace of Thian to practice her treatments in our city has not only fashioned elixirs to promote hair growth but also has hair to prove her skills."

Deena touched her hair as though in a daze and again shook her head, a tear sliding down her round cheek.

"Horace, you know what to do." His mother dropped the dagger with a loud *clang*. "I could arrange to administer wija in an hour, and then she would spill out all her truths."

"No." Horace's protest was louder than he'd intended. He must talk to his mother before she did something foolish.

"I will not vouch for its efficacy, my lady," Deena said hesitantly. "The pain will drive one to one's death. How can it elicit any truth from a dead person?"

"You know about wija?" His mother's eyes widened and then rapidly narrowed.

"Yes, I have read about—"

"Wija is not used in my land." Horace felt the need to restate that before his mother was tempted to test its efficacy. "Pari." He turned to the soldiers.

They were pretending not to listen to the ruckus caused by his mother. He had expected at least Pari to react and contribute with a shield of her own to stop his mother's attack on the healer. It was not like her to stand by and let matters get out of hand. Yet, the sentar warrior had just stood stoically, watching the scene.

"Yes, my lord." Pari stepped forward, looking more resplendent than any of the other soldiers, standing head and shoulders over them. Wariness clouded her kohl-lined eyes.

"Take the prisoner to the healers' residence. Don't enter until I come. The three of you must wait outside with her."

Pari bowed, her intelligent hazel eyes not meeting his. He would have to talk to her later. There was something weighing on her mind. It was unlike her to glance away from him as he spoke.

As a sentar warrior, her experience was only a couple of years lesser than his own, and he had entrusted her with the safety of his seifland in his absence. There were few threats these days, but whenever he'd had to travel to the Western Frontier, he had been at peace knowing that Pari stood guard on his land. But she mustn't blame herself for what had happened in the garden. No one could have foreseen such a break-in.

Deena accompanied the soldiers without protest. Now it was time to deal with his mother. He retracted his shield and offered his chair to her with a hand gesture. She declined with a curt show of her palm. He remained standing, although he would have much preferred to sit or even lie down. It had been a rough ride in from the Western Frontier, and the breaks he had taken were short. But it was lucky that he arrived this night—lucky for the healer. Heaven knew what his mother would have done to her in his absence.

"Why can't we administer wija to her?" she asked as soon as the door was closed behind the soldiers.

He could stare down his mother even if no one else could. "I won't agree to give that torturous potion to even hardened criminals."

"Then you are a lesser man than your father."

"You do know that I am proud of having fewer violent tendencies than Father." His eyes involuntarily went to the panoramic painting stretched over the arched doorway. The artist had skillfully captured the movement and the sinewy muscles of the horses as they leaped over headless human torsos, considering he would have received only a few moments to observe the complete scene during one of the famed battles waged between Thian and Rothshire.

"Then I wish it were him here now. He would have left no stone unturned to punish the perpetrators of such an atrocity. Maybe that is why no one step foot in our shrine during his reign."

Horace turned away from his mother, not because her disappointment in him hurt him, but because such words from her sometimes made him doubt himself. It had taken years for him to accept that he didn't want to be the man his parents wanted him to be. He would be a much better man. And he had to hold on to that conviction, however much his mother lashed out.

"I am sorry to disappoint you, Mother. Wija is not an option, and it shouldn't be in any civilized society. If you have grown that herb without my permission, I must ask you to destroy it forthwith."

"Look at me when you speak to me."

He obliged.

"The scrolls that went missing . . . Zesta will never forgive you if you don't regain them."

"Is it the goddess or you who wouldn't forgive me?"

"Both."

Horace sighed, taking in her quivering lips. "We will regain the scrolls. I promise you that. Even I don't want the details of herbs like wija to fall into the wrong hands."

"Yet your prisoner knew about it. Isn't it proof enough that she stole the scrolls?"

"There was not enough time for her to study the contents of the scrolls after stealing them. I am not saying she didn't steal them, but her knowledge might be from another source."

"There are no other sources. The scrolls in my care were the only written record for all those perilous mixtures and concoctions, and they were entrusted to me. And the other scroll . . ." She ended feebly, clutching her choker and stumbling toward the seat.

Horace had never thought that he would witness his mother fall to pieces. Furious? Yes. Stubborn? Yes. But seeing her slumped in his chair, rubbing her forehead with shaking fingers, unsettled him.

He went to her and took her hands in his. "Mother, no one can use that knowledge without procuring the herbs first. We can find the thief and the scrolls before that."

"It is not just that." She looked at him with a watery gaze.

"What is worrying you?"

She opened her mouth to say something but then shook her head. "Nothing."

"You are hiding something."

"No one has ever accused me of lying." She thrust her prominent chin forward.

"That is not at all what I said. You have a tendency to keep important information from me. Like when you handed over the security of the shrine and greenhouse to Raya."

"I didn't think I needed your approval for that."

The defiance won, and her distress faded to the background. Horace was grateful for that, for he hated seeing her crumpled form, but it was not an argument he would concede just to appease his mother. What was she thinking, entrusting the security of important artifacts to a barely eighteen-year-old child?

"You put too much pressure on her. How many roles do you want her to play at one time?" he asked as gently as he could.

"It is nothing she can't handle."

"Where is she?"

"At the healers' residence, the last I heard."

"Was she injured?"

"No, she is seeing to the comforts of the injured soldiers."

"Let us go there, then."

She gripped his hands tighter. "Promise me you won't be harsh on her."

"On her? No, I will not be harsh on *her*, Mother."

"Oh, take your indignation out on me as much as you want. I don't mind."

"Don't I know that?"

He led her out of his chambers and to the vestibule that opened to a covered balcony. Plants were arranged on different levels here on wooden planks that took up most of the wall. The rest of the vertical area was taken over by creeping vines dotted with buds that would open only after sunset. Even their sweet fragrance was held within to be released only when the time was right. Roses, on the other hand, filled the enclosed space with colors and scents.

None of the plants in there were precious or dangerous, yet his mother gave them the same attention she extended to the rare herbs she cultivated in her conservatory. If given a free hand, she might convert the entire palace into a greenhouse.

He wouldn't mind that if all the signs of bloodshed left behind by his father were replaced by thriving plants. Maybe he should commission paintings of groves and gardens, and then his mother would finally agree to take down the gory paintings one was forced to look at while walking through his palace.

"You won't harass Raya with questions," his mother stated as they opened a door and descended the steep, well-worn stairs to the grounds.

"I promised I wouldn't be harsh, but she must answer for what happened under her command."

"But she is only a—"

"Child? You forget that more often than not. You want her to be a soldier and a healer and a princess rolled into one."

"Oh, don't be jealous now."

"Jealous? Me?" He extended a hand to his mother to get her down the final step that was steeper than the rest. She took it.

"You have always been jealous of my love for her and of the fact that she is special to me." She walked across the ground with rapid short steps.

A paved path led through a row of hibiscus bushes of variegated shades. Early birds chirped from between the branches as they went about their business. The cheeriness of the ground did not permeate his mood. He had no mean task in the upcoming days. Not only did he have to reclaim the stolen scrolls but he must also jump over the hurdles caused by his mother's interference.

"Why would I be? I have full assurance of your love for me." He smiled as expressions of pride and defeat struggled to take over her face. Pride won in the end. She had failed to put him on the defense, but she was proud of his answer.

"I will not distress Raya," he assured her. "But she is too young to be overburdened with so many immense responsibilities."

"She is capable, and whatever happened tonight was not her fault." She paused by the well outside the low wooden gate that led to the healers' residence.

"Why do you think I am trying to find fault with anybody here? I am only interested in finding the truth."

He pushed open the creaking gate, and the spicy aroma of thyme welcomed him. The healers' residence had three blocks—sleeping quarters, laboratory, and infirmary. The tiled roof extended over all three buildings, merging them into one, but at the ground level, pathways bordered with the purple and white blooms of creeping thyme separated the structures.

At this early hour of the day, the grounds in front of the healers' residence would normally be deserted. Only his mother and Raya had access to the laboratory, and the infirmary served only the residents of the palace. But today, Pari and the soldiers were present outside the buildings, along with the prisoner.

Raya came running out of the infirmary, wiping her nose on the sleeve of her tunic. Her eyes were red and her kohl had formed a streak down her cheek, merging with a slight cut. She looked otherwise unharmed.

Horace didn't plan on questioning her now, but he would see that she was properly trained to take up more responsibilities, if that was what she wanted. Just being considered *special* by his mother was not reason enough to burden her with charges beyond her skill.

"It doesn't look good," Raya said. "Both of them are still unconscious."

"Who were harmed?" Horace asked. He had just heard about the injuries suffered by the soldiers but hadn't had time to inquire more after them.

"Jianther and Cade." Raya named two lads who had recently been recruited to his private service.

"How many were patrolling the garden?"

"Just the two of them and Shauri. I was down for a round when the intruder appeared in the conservatory."

"I told her that would be enough," his mother said before Horace could comment on the inadequacy of the protection. "No one knew about the presence of anything valuable."

"Even if no one knew about the scrolls, it is widely known that you possess some of the most valuable herbs on the continent," Horace said quietly, casting a glance at Deena. "That's what she says she came for. To break your *iron grip* on the rare plants."

Lady Len scoffed. "I see to their free distribution. Nobody had any complaints about that. She is lying through her teeth. She somehow found out about the scrolls and stole them."

"Mother, please. Not so loud."

The presence of the scrolls in Thian had been a secret. There was no reason for it to be publicized now. If they could break the rogue healer, they could retrieve the scrolls and secure them within the palace, for which continued secrecy was highly desirable.

His mother's words, however, were not missed by anyone within a mile's radius. Pari pursed her lips as though her worst fears had come true. She did not react in any other way, the trained soldier she was. Or it could be because she had to immediately lunge forward to hold back Deena, who had advanced toward his mother.

4

"I stole nothing." Deena struggled to escape the grasp of the soldier whose fingers circled her arms, digging into her skin, but she failed to move even an inch toward Lady Len.

From the moment Lord Thian had apprehended her, it was clear that more severe crimes than trespassing were being laid on her doorstep. He had spoken of grievously injured soldiers, and now his mother was accusing her of stealing some scrolls she hadn't even heard of. If she didn't speak up now, it would be akin to accepting her and Kran's role in all that had passed.

"Who'd believe the words of a thief?" Lady Len whipped to her, her nose ring shivering as she breathed hard.

"What scrolls are you talking about?" It would be meaningless for her to steal some scrolls belonging to the lady. They must see that. Furthermore, they would find nothing in her bag or her hut—which would prove her innocence. Well, the innocence of whatever they were accusing her of. She would admit anywhere her real reason for entering the greenhouse.

"Don't feign ignorance," Lady Len said. "A healer like you who thinks she is beyond the laws of the universe would have much to gain from getting her hands on those secret techniques and preparations for herbs and medicines."

Deena swallowed a pang of guilt. So the scrolls contained medical and herbal secrets—something she would have been tempted to look into had she known of their existence, but she wouldn't admit that now.

"Do you mean the kind that you keep a secret from the common folk who suffer because of a lack of such treatments?" She did not bother to lower her voice.

Lady Len seemed to be the type of person who would hear someone only if they spoke louder than her, but she was still the mother of Lord Thian. Any moment, a sword could find its way to Deena's throat, or worse, she would lose her chance to plead her innocence. Yet, Lord Thian remained motionless except for a slight twitch of his mouth.

"How dare you talk to me like that?" Lady Len spat.

Deena took a deep breath to calm herself, but it just rattled in her chest. The clear sky and lush greenery around her did nothing to reduce the despondency into which she was sinking. "I did not do it. Steal the scrolls, that is, or injure the soldiers. I am a healer. It goes against my sacred oath to harm those whom I am sworn to heal."

"But you were in the garden," the girl who had just joined them said. Wisps of hair had escaped their knot and formed a halo around her head. That and the red eyes and the kohl spread under them were testimony of the rough night she had experienced. "The blisters behind your neck are proof. You were the one hiding among the pulitra leaves. Shauri, come here. Isn't she the one you saw?"

"I didn't deny—" Deena began.

Lord Thian raised a hand, and his eyes flashed a warning. "You won't speak unless asked to do so, and you will get a chance to speak." His strong jaw tightened, challenging her to disobey his command.

But she did not intend to, and she stiffly nodded. She knew from Kran that Lord Thian was a man of integrity. She would have to wait until he decided to hear her out, and try not to rile up his mother in the meantime.

A young soldier with floppy hair that fell over a blackened eye came up from behind her and stared at her.

"Yes, Raya. She is the one who ran out of the greenhouse, but this was not given by her." He touched his eye. "There was an accomplice."

"What time was it when you saw the accused outside the greenhouse?" Lord Thian asked.

"It was just past midnight, my lord. Our shift had just begun."

"So, it can be concluded that she entered during the change of guard," Lord Thian said.

"There are only two ways for you going forth," Lady Len said. "Tell us the name of your accomplice and the location of the scrolls, or count down the days to your death."

"I had no accomplice, my lady. I planned and executed the inspection of your greenhouse on my own. And that is all I did. Now, if you want to kill me for that, go ahead. You needn't hesitate. After all, I have no noble blood running in my veins, and that means my life is of no value to you."

Lady Len's eyes sparkled. "How dare you take that tone with me?"

Lord Thian stepped in front of his mother as though getting ready to throw another shield between her and Deena. If only he continued the questioning instead of letting his mother take the reins.

Deena returned Lady Len's stare, refusing to back off. She would answer nothing from that lady now. Maybe that would force Lord Thian to ask the questions—logical ones.

"When that man attacked us, she ran away," Raya said. "That would have given her ample time to get to the shrine and attack Jianther and Cade."

She must have been the female voice that Deena had heard last night outside the greenhouse. The cut on her cheek confirmed her involvement in the brawl with Kran.

"You saw me running to the gate, didn't you? I went out of the garden, not further within."

"You could have rounded back in once we chased that man out." The girl sounded flustered, as if she were groping in the darkness, and Deena did not feel the same anger at her accusation as she did at Lady Len's.

"I deny doing that," Deena said as politely as she could.

"How are Cade and Jianther?" Lord Thian asked. "Is there any chance of one of them regaining consciousness?"

"Cade occasionally stirs," Raya said.

"I am taking her to the infirmary," Lord Thian told his mother, indicating Deena with a bob of his head. "If Cade becomes conscious long enough to recognize her, one piece of the puzzle will be in place."

"We are coming with you." Lady Len pulled Raya along with her.

Lord Thian did not refuse. He directed Deena up the few steps and to the large porch with a marble floor that had four rooms leading from it. Deena had a sense of returning home as the scents of poultices and medicinal powders wafted out of one of the rooms. The pleasantly bitter smell of curcumin indicated wounds had been dressed up.

And sure enough, in the room lay the injured soldiers—ones she or Kran had supposedly attacked. Lord Thian had said that the soldiers would identify her. There was no chance of that, as she had been nowhere near the shrine. And she believed Kran when he said that he had inflicted only minor injuries. Kran's victims were probably Raya and Shauri, whom he had faced in front of the greenhouse.

But then someone had attacked these other soldiers and disabled them, probably to steal some scrolls that belonged to Lady Len. And that someone also had long black hair like Deena.

The soldiers, though, were in no condition to prove her innocence or guilt. One of them was covered in bandages as though he had no unbroken bone in his body, and he drifted in and out of wakefulness even as they watched. His head swiveled one way and the other on the soft pillow, staining it with the paste that was applied on his forehead.

The window by the bed was closed, probably with the hope that the darkness would help him fall to sleep, but a sleeping draught might be more helpful, given his condition. It would, however, be too presumptuous of her to mention it when two healers were already present in the room.

The soldier's mate seemed to be in an even worse condition. Black curtains separated the room in half, obscuring the bed of the latter, yet intermittent deep groans could be heard from behind it. The two healers carried on a low conversation in one corner as Deena waited patiently with Lord Thian and Lady Len.

One of the healers stepped toward them. He was young in years, but it was belied by his intelligent eyes and careworn face. "My lord, Cade talked a few words, but it made little sense. It was something about his mother."

"What about Jianther? What is his condition?" Lord Thian asked. "Is he—" A loud groan of pain and an even more intense silence interrupted him.

"He is unconscious but feeling pain. His skin is burned, but it is also scorching hot, like his insides are burning."

"We were mulling about immersing him in a cold tub," Raya said.

"Is it a magic spell?" Lord Thian moved toward the hidden bed and looked behind the curtain. "Or perhaps there is a poison that could have this effect on him."

"We thought of that possibility." The healer cast a glance at Lady Len before shifting his eyes to the embroidery of the burning leaf on his robe. "And so we gave him thendril, hoping it would stop the effect of any poison. So far, I don't think it has had any success."

"Thendril alone won't have much effect if the poison is veritria," Deena said.

She might incriminate herself by revealing her knowledge about the mix that could have such an effect on the soldier, but she couldn't stand by and watch the poor man suffer when she could do something to alleviate his suffering. "A combination of amaran leaves and mehua bark with some more ingredients has been known to be used in ancient times to torture enemies, and the effect has been described as something you see here—burns and an increase of internal body temperature. The poison can work through the skin."

"Ha," Lady Len exclaimed, making Raya wince. "This is a confession."

"I may never exonerate myself in your eyes, my lady," Deena said through gritted teeth, "but that soldier will immediately die if he is immersed in cold water. The temperature difference will constrict his blood vessels, and his organs will fail."

The healer opened his mouth to protest, but then he looked at Raya and sighed.

"I was telling Raya the same thing, my lord," he said. "It seems like we will just have to watch him suffer."

Lord Thian drew his mother aside and whispered, but Deena still heard it.

"Can I trust that veritria was not concocted here?"

"Do you think I am a fool to do that?" she asked aloud.

"Quietly, Mother. Anyway, the knowledge doesn't seem to be limited to the scrolls if she knows about it." Lord Thian glanced at Deena with a raised eyebrow.

"My lord," Deena said, "if the question is about me being aware of that poison, I read about it in some old parchments that my uncle possessed. He comes from a long line of healers and trained me in the art of healing. Knowledge has been passed down from generation to generation for centuries, including that of prohibited mixtures and vicious poisons. There were rare parchments that he had forbidden me to read—"

"And so you ensured you read them," Lord Thian remarked before she could say the same.

"What a convenient explanation!" Lady Len snorted. "You know about that concoction because you stole my scrolls that had that information."

"Mother," Lord Thian called with forced patience, "if she learned about it from your scrolls, then how come she prepared the mixture and brought it along with her to the shrine?"

Another groan came from the wounded soldier behind the curtain.

"Amaran leaves," Deena said. "It is responsible for his condition when mixed with other ingredients. But when used alone, the leaves have a cooling effect on the body. If his body is covered with them, it might ease his suffering without abruptly cooling the blood vessels."

"I know where to get them," Raya said. She wiped her eyes of the tears that she had been silently shedding until then. Maybe the soldier was her friend. His condition seemed to have upset her more than it affected the others in the room.

She ran out of the infirmary.

"Raya. Raya," Lady Len called, but she didn't stop. "I don't understand why we are giving importance to the word of a criminal."

"It is an excellent suggestion, my lady," the healer said. He was rewarded with a sharp glance, and his tall frame stooped. But he continued weakly. "It won't do any harm, even if it doesn't help him. We will undress him and prepare him to be covered with amaran leaves."

"We will wait outside," Lord Thian said.

The porch had a small seating area with stone benches attached to a low wall. Trellises covered two sides of the porch, through which wound the vines of thendril with their tiny bright-red leaves. The rare and powerful antidote that she had to scout hills to collect grew abundantly in Lord Thian's backyard. She had tried to propagate the herb several times, but it hadn't worked.

"Deena. Isn't that your name?" Lord Thian asked.

"Yes, my lord."

"What else do you know about this poison?"

"Only what I read. I don't have any practical experience with it," Deena said. She had been curious to gain as much knowledge as she could, but she had never dared experiment by brewing the said poison.

"And did you read anything about an antidote for it?"

"Not exactly, but antidotes are tailored according to the ingredients of the poison. Since I know the contents of veritria, I might be able to design an antidote."

"You seem to have knowledge beyond your age." He eyed her intently.

Deena fought against the warmth creeping up her neck.

"I am not dismissing the possibility of your hand in the crime," he continued quickly, either to stop her from feeling too pleased with herself or to prevent his mother from exploding with rage. "But I needn't tell you how dangerous it would be if scrolls containing similar knowledge fell into the wrong hands."

"I understand, my lord. My uncle never let me forget the danger of that forbidden knowledge once he learned I read the parchments without his permission."

"Yet you stole the scrolls that contained the same knowledge." Lady Len's voice dripped with sarcasm.

"If I already know the contents of those scrolls, there is no point in me taking them, is there?"

Deena gripped at this defense that had just then occurred to her. If the scrolls only contained ancient medicinal knowledge that she was already privy to, then she had no motive to steal them. She glanced from Lord Thian to Lady Len, willing them to accept the defense. The former appeared thoughtful, while the lady gave her a smirk.

"Even you can't know everything."

It was true. She did not know everything, but her uncle had trained her as though she were his own child. Kran had never shown any interest in botany or medicine, while Deena never hesitated to scout out wild leaves or brew potions. Kran's father had shown no hesitation in making her his heir. From the age of twelve, she used to visit patients with him and had committed all his words to heart.

Even when she had read the forbidden parchments, his warning had not been tinged with anger, but pride had laced his words as he'd emphasized why she should never pass on that knowledge.

No, she was not being arrogant by challenging Lady Len. She took a deep breath and released it.

"Not everything, my lady, but I think I would know a lot of what is contained in your scrolls. For instance, veritria is mentioned in no ancient texts, but I have read about it in my uncle's parchments, and I presume it was also mentioned in your scrolls. The source of both the parchments and the scrolls seems to be the same. Test my knowledge if you wish."

Lady Len looked at her speculatively and then asked in a soft voice that was primed to unsettle her. "What mixed with sereka leaves would clot blood?"

It was one of the least used techniques for stemming bleeding because of the associated risks.

"Brethlyn," Deena said. "Although more than two drops on an open wound can burn the site."

"The reason for using metal gloves while handling heliatin?"

"Its thorn can induce paralysis."

"A flower that disguises as a leaf . . ."

"Eela."

"I didn't finish my question. A flower that disguises as a leaf fools the pollinators. Why would eela do that?"

"Because eela is not at the mercy of pollinators. They spread under the ground and could sprout out miles away from the parent plant. The root is the valuable part of eela, but once you cut even a portion of the root, all trees from the family that spread from that root will die away. It contributes to the rarity of the tree, which is why we healers struggle to get a hold of them. Yet, I saw miniature eelas with individual roots growing in your greenhouse."

"So you don't know everything." Lady Len smiled derisively.

The parchments she had studied from had no information on propagating rare herbs. Maybe the scrolls contained them. Her defense was crumbling.

"No, my lady." Deena kept her voice steady. "I never claimed I did. My interest is only in making my knowledge accessible to the needy, unlike you."

"Are you trying to blame me for the knowledge I hold? For serving humankind by helping them get the rare herbs?"

"Hardly serving if said herbs don't reach the ones who need them. I had to jump through hoops to get heliatin for a little girl, and I know of several others suffering because their blood is not noble enough to gain easy access to the medicinal herbs they need."

"What is stopping you from foraging for those plants and propagating them if you have the same knowledge as the scrolls?"

Deena sighed. "I don't have the resources you have—men to dive under the Greylan Sea or to climb the tallest peak of Haiga. You have the means to help thousands, but you sit atop it, uncaring."

"Horace, are you going to stand there and tolerate her insulting me? Or would you hand me a weapon to give her the reward she deserves?"

"Neither," Lord Thian said.

The speculative manner in which he eyed her did not ease Deena's agitation. It looked like she was nowhere near proving her innocence in his eyes, and challenging his mother had not helped her.

"I have a proposition," Lord Thian said. "Healer Deena, if you want to prove your innocence, Jianther has to wake up and confirm it was not you who broke into the shrine. Here is the deal. Harness your knowledge and prepare an antidote for veritria. If you save Jianther's life and help us catch the culprit who broke into the shrine, assuming it isn't you, I will acquit you of trespassing in our conservatory."

5

"What?" His mother and the healer exclaimed together in a rare moment of united astonishment.

Horace did not trust the healer's protestations, and he had willed himself to ignore the innocent conviction in her eyes. For one, she was hiding her accomplice, and Jianther's words before he lost his consciousness were about a woman with long hair.

Yet Horace was against the use of a truth serum like wija that would torture the accused before proving their guilt. His one chance of getting the truth out of her was to make the healer let her guard down. To accomplish this, she had to believe that he was giving her a chance to escape punishment, that he believed in her skills.

Then he would have somebody study her. She would certainly make a mistake before long that would reveal the secrets that she was now holding close to her chest.

"She claims she can make an antidote to the poison. Why shouldn't we use her skill?" Horace asked his mother. He would explain his plan to her later, and she wouldn't stop him then, but right now, he could see her hackles rising.

"But I don't have the resources to—" Deena began.

"Everything you need will be provided to you, and Raya will monitor all your experiments. Mother, don't you trust Raya? Nothing she concocts will reach Jianther until Raya and Noaran approve. If she is innocent, nobody has higher stakes in Jianther's healing than her. Don't you agree?"

Raya returned clutching a sack, saving him from whatever damnation his mother had been aiming his way.

"Where did you find so many leaves so soon?" his mother asked, her attention diverted.

Raya murmured something and went into the nursing room.

"My lord," Deena said, "I will indeed help to form an antidote for veritria, but the other soldier, the one heavily bandaged, seems to be in a delirium."

"Doesn't take an expert to know that," Lady Len scoffed.

"If he gets undisturbed sleep for a few hours, he may regain his full consciousness. Then he can tell it wasn't me at the shrine. A sleeping draught might help him sleep, and also he could be moved to a different room. The sounds may be waking him up before his brain can rest."

"Our healers know what to do," his mother said before he could reply.

But Raya, who appeared outside the room, murmured, "I'll tell that to them," and went back in.

"Pari, would you step outside with me?" Horace asked, ignoring his mother's accusatory stare.

First things first, Deena must have an eagle-eyed observer, and there was no one present who could do that task as good as Pari. Her silent, calm demeanor inspired trust and, to an extent, hid her competency as a warrior.

Pari accompanied him to the ground, well away from the infirmary.

"What do you make of all this?" he asked.

He had earlier felt that she had something to tell him. If so, this would be a good time.

She thought for a moment before answering. "The roots of this issue are spread more widely than that of the eela tree. Even if the healer is guilty, I feel like it is part of a bigger conspiracy, something that has been brewing for some time now."

"Why do you say that?"

He had received no sign that something was afoot on his land, but he had been away for longer periods of time than usual.

Pari bit her cheek and shook her head. "No, I don't want to say anything now without getting a few more relevant details. Will you let me make inquiries before revealing my suspicions to you?"

"Certainly. Did you know anything about the scrolls that Mother spoke about?"

Only a few had known about the presence of the scrolls in the shrine. Other than his mother, sisters, and Raya, his chief counselor, Garim, was privy to the knowledge, as was Noaran, the healer. But the soldiers who guarded the premises, including Pari, had not known of their existence.

"Never heard about them before now," Pari said, "but I gather their disappearance could cause much trouble."

"Yes, trouble is the word. We need to retrieve the scrolls and smoke out her accomplice. Whoever inflicted that much damage on those lads cannot be someone ordinary. I tussled with him, but he did not exhibit any sentar powers."

"Do you suspect he is a mage?"

"There had been no signs of that either."

Pari's eyes narrowed in thought, wrinkling her smooth forehead as she pondered what he'd said. "But you would say he was well-trained? Not a common burglar, but possibly a soldier?"

"He was agile, but I did not get to see much of his skills, as he ran away, helped by her." He nodded his head toward Deena.

"That one is hiding something. I can sense it," Pari said.

"And I want you to find out what that is. She will be in your custody, still a prisoner, even though I am not throwing her in the dungeon. Get her cleaned up and lodge her in a room in the healers' residence. Give her the illusion she is being allowed a free hand in the development of the antidote, but run everything through Noaran first and don't let her out of the room. Provide her the ingredients she needs.

"You shouldn't have to wait for long for her to misuse the freedom I am granting her now. Even a small misstep from her could lead us to the scrolls or her accomplice. Remain vigilant and gain her trust."

"I was hoping never again to be a spy. The deception is abhorrent."

She had once been part of his father's vast spy network that had been essential in the days of strife with Rothshire. Peace with Rothshire had been Horace's primary goal when he'd succeeded his father, and as a result, the spy network had considerably shrunk.

"This is hardly a spy master's work. You merely have to observe her and ensure she doesn't do any further damage. It comes under your role as my trusted soldier and includes no deception or disguise."

Pari made a face to let him know his assurance did not fool her, but bowed all the same. "As you wish, my lord. I wish you equal success in convincing Lady Len."

His eyes went back to the porch, where his mother and Raya carried on a whispered conversation in the corner. The healer Deena stood where he'd left her, watching them warily like a mouse cornered by cats. If his plan worked, this mouse would lead them to the scrolls before the knowledge in them could be misused.

Two hours later, his man woke him up as instructed, with a tray of food and a message from his chief counselor. It was a request to summon the council to discuss the events of the previous night. The members of his council would demand all the details of the burglary, and he was not ready to give it to them yet.

At the same time, he did not wish to lie to his council. He needed time to gather all the facts before deciding what to divulge to them.

"Is Garim present in the palace now?" he asked Seagal, who was arranging a fresh robe for him.

The latter faced Horace and turned slightly to the left to get a good view through his functioning eye. "Yes, my lord, but he said he would see you after you are well-rested."

"Time for rest seems far away, Seagal."

The elder man gave a sympathetic smile, although he wouldn't be aware of what was worrying Horace. He had been an employee in the palace for only five years, but Seagal knew some of what troubled seif lords. He had served in the army of Thian under Horace's father for over two decades and had a glass eye to show for it. Despite being eligible for a pension from the seifland, he opted to continue working.

"Could I bring you anything else?" Seagal stood in attention, looking more like a soldier than a servant.

The solutions to my problems, thought Horace, but he said, "Nothing. Thank you, Seagal. Tell Garim that I will join him at the shrine in an hour."

"As you wish, my lord." He drew the curtains open, letting in the blinding light of the afternoon sun.

It reminded Horace of that bed in the infirmary hidden behind curtains and the groans emanating from there. He sat morosely as Seagal left the room after arranging all his clothes.

The alluring smell of the dishes on the tray gave Horace pause—the rice was steaming hot, but a wash was highly desirable.

He must be covered with all the dust and grime he'd collected on his way from the Western Frontier. Not to mention the mud that had clung to his trousers as he'd chased the healer. When the conditions of the healer's captivity had been settled, he'd had no energy left for a bath and had dragged himself to his room and slumped on his bed.

Mercifully, his mother had not protested further about giving Deena the option to save Jianther. She had not even waited to hear his explanation that he was ready to give. Instead, she hurried away with Raya to the palace without waiting to see where the healer was housed. He could only hope that she did not find out the full extent of facilities he had given Deena before he had time to detail his plan.

The warm water soaked his skin and untied the knots in his neck and back. Frequent ventures to the Western Frontier were taking their toll, and he must plan to stay in his seifland for longer periods.

Prince Coraen did not need his assistance much these days. After the defeat of the syrelins three months ago, peace mostly reigned in the Western Frontier. There had been instances of hauries and chirelas crossing over from Thisaur and creating trouble in the human villages, but better relations with the flechas had worked in their favor. The soldiers could now scout the hills without fearing the flechas. Also, the presence of Lady Leonara meant the prince had a capable sentar warrior in his army. Neither Horace nor Malion would be missed much.

Malion had long been focused on saving and rebuilding the seifland of Alayster. Now, Horace must do the same for his seifland.

Thian might not need much rescuing, but the burglars had waited for his absence before acting. That was troubling.

He vigorously scrubbed his damp skin until it was red. Healer Deena and her accomplices must have been planning this burglary for a long time. First of all, they had to learn about the value of the scrolls and their contents, and then they had to figure out that the scrolls were present at the shrine. They must have watched the palace and shrine closely before executing the break-in.

If the security of the shrine had been under an experienced soldier like Pari, such scouting and suspicious activities would have been spotted. That was who he had left in charge. Instead, his mother had handed over the responsibility to Raya without even consulting him.

The fragrant rice and chicken awaiting him did not tingle his taste buds, because his focus had shifted to the unpalatable task at hand. His mother would have all the counterarguments ready for when he would question her about Raya's involvement in the entire issue. Or she would again accuse him of being jealous. There was no rationale for him to feel jealous of a child.

He had been fourteen when his mother had first introduced the new baby in the nursery to him. He already had two younger sisters and had not been in the mood to gain one more. She had been a wee little thing, all crinkled, with a headful of curly black hair, not so different from everyone else in the family. Although his mother had claimed that she was the child of a friend who could no longer take care of the baby, he had later concluded that she was an illegitimate child of someone in his large family that extended all over Thian.

His mother loved Raya as her own, and even his sisters adored her. He had mostly ignored her, as he had focused more on his training. In those days, he had wanted nothing more than to be a worthy successor to his father. But that avoidance had not been based on animosity, and as the girl's current guardian, he had her best interest at heart. He was ready to provide more training for her, if being a soldier was her goal. Or he could arrange for lessons if she wanted to be a healer. But someone would have to convince his mother that she mustn't burden Raya with expectations to excel in every field.

Garim was the obvious choice. His mother would heed Garim's words, as he was a disinterested party and a proven trove of wisdom. Horace swallowed the rest of the meal, regretting his inability to enjoy it, and hurried to the shrine.

Under normal circumstances, the garden was accessible to the public, but today it was out of bounds, as the gates were locked. The conservatory's arched glass walls glittered in the rays of the sun, and armed soldiers stood alert all around it. Another attempt at a break-in couldn't be ruled out. The one who currently possessed the scrolls would need the plants growing in there in order to prepare the mixtures and concoctions listed in the scrolls.

The shrine, however, had only a single guard outside. Nothing of value was left in there, or nothing that was valuable to anyone else but for the family. Zesta's idol inside the sanctum had remained on these grounds for generations, and regular prayers and homage were offered to the goddess by members of the family. Just outside the walls of the palace, the goddess of life and justice had a grand and equally ancient temple dedicated to her, which invited in all and sundry. But this shrine was private.

Even the murals that adorned its walls represented this ownership. Images of his ancestors paying respect to Zesta were hand-painted with dyes derived from plants. These were often refreshed, but their origin would date back to at least a couple of centuries.

Garim stood by the hexagonal building, examining one of the murals that stretched over a side. The sleeves of his simple gray robe were rolled up, and his short figure fit just under the eave of the circular sloping roof. It shaded his bald head from the harsh afternoon sun, but he wiped sweat from his forehead as he sauntered to the back of the shrine.

"Garim," Horace called, "I'm sorry for the delay, but why didn't you wait inside the shrine?"

The solo guard looked startled, and his eyes darted from Horace to Garim and back.

"It is nothing to worry about," Garim said, more to the soldier than to Horace. "You were doing your duty, and you did it well."

Horace nodded his agreement. He had left specific instructions to not disturb the scene of the burglary until he could inspect it. The door had suffered little damage, but its iron bar appeared to be twisted. A padlock would no more fit through it, and so a chain had been used to secure the door. The sentry unlocked it for them.

The interior gave no indication that a crime had occurred on the premises. The freshness of the scents of seel oil and camphor showed prayers had been carried out the previous evening, as was the norm. Light filtered in through the cracks in the windowpanes that dotted the hexagonal wall.

Inside the sanctum at the far end, the black stone idol of the goddess stood in all its glory, surrounded by petals offered the evening before. One of her hands was raised in a benevolent gesture, and the other held the end of the silk draped around her, represented through intricate carvings in the stone. The sculptor had also adorned her body with jewelry, using similar carvings, leaving no requirement for the presence of gold or other precious metals. In short, there was no temptation present in the shrine for a potential thief, except for what had lain hidden beneath her feet.

A stone on the ground had been removed, and it lay beside an upturned cauldron. A hole was where the chest with the scrolls had been.

"They knew where it was and had gone straight for the chest," Horace observed. "It wouldn't have been too difficult to carry it away once they had it, given its handy size. Why didn't Mother just store it in the palace?"

"Considering only a few of us knew of its presence here, she would have thought it unnecessary. That also brings us to the source of the leak. You must not shy away from questioning everyone who knew about the scrolls."

Horace smiled. "Let's begin with you, then. In your thirty years of service at this palace, have you ever mentioned the scrolls to anyone?"

Garim returned the smile and shook his head. "No, my lord."

"That is the extent to which I will be able to question you or Raya or my mother or her trusted healer. At the moment, none of you is a suspect, and it would be unjust to treat you as one."

"If that is how you feel about it, then you are unqualified to do this investigation." Garim bent his head to enter the low arched doorway of the sanctum, stating the bland truth as was his wont.

Horace had to admit that he wouldn't be able to do a good job of viewing the people close to him with a suspicious eye. Unfortunately, he was the only one who had the authority to do it, especially to question his mother. He did not for one moment think that she was the source of the leak, but he would also have to question Raya and Noaran, which would eventually offend his mother.

"The arrested healer is a citizen of Alayster, isn't she?" Garim asked.

"Yes." Horace stooped low to enter the sanctum. The smell of cloves lingered in the air, probably from the previous day's offering.

"Would you be informing Lord Alayster about the incidents?"

That was another thing he had pushed to the back of his mind. His instinct was to inform Malion, but he did not want to do it until more was known.

"I was thinking about that." Horace replaced the stone to cover the hole and righted the cauldron. A weird sensation shot through the tip of his finger, and he hastily wiped his hand on his robe.

"What is the matter?"

"What was in that cauldron?" A burn throbbed on his finger.

"I presumed it was an offering from yesterday." Garim made to pick up the cauldron.

"No. Don't touch it."

"Don't touch what?" His mother stood outside the sanctum with a stricken-looking Raya. "Garim, I expected you to inform me before you came down here."

"I left a message, my lady," Garim said.

"I did not receive it, and my son does not believe in including me in any of the decisions pertaining to this incident, although what was lost belonged to me."

"What was in this cauldron, Raya?" Horace asked.

The speed with which his mother talked gave him the feeling she wanted to divert his and Garim's attention from the cauldron. And he might get a straight answer from Raya than from his mother.

Raya opened her mouth to reply, but his mother said quickly, "An offering for the goddess."

"Raya, do you have something to tell me?" he asked again, curling up his fist to stop the burning sensation. It did not work.

"It was me, my lord. It was all my fault. I made veritria."

6

"My lord," Raya said, "I must confess or I will die. Mother Len, you must forgive me for speaking, but he needs to know. It was a terrible mistake. I . . . I made that concoction. It was a mistake. I should never have done that. I didn't know it would . . . I thought . . . I thought I should know everything before I became worthy of . . ." Her voice broke, and she covered her face in her hands to hide her tears.

"What are you talking about?" Horace did not expect to get any reply over the sobs. She had changed out of the silver armor and soldier's attire, and her face had been cleaned of the streak of kohl and dried blood. With her floral dress and fresh face, she looked so much like a child that he regretted snapping at her.

"Lower your voice, Horace," his mother hissed. "Don't forget where you are standing."

"I am sure Zesta will forgive me. She also deserves the truth." He carefully controlled his tone.

"She knows. She saw everything." Raya kneeled before the idol, her voice breaking as though that thought was unbearable to her. "I was studying the scrolls . . . and I came across veritria. The preparation was complicated. I didn't think I would succeed. But I did."

"Mehua bark and amaran leaves aren't rare. How was the preparation complicated?" Horace prevented his voice from becoming overly critical. She looked guilty enough.

"But there were more ingredients. I don't remember the exact constitution. I just followed the instructions. And . . . and it also had to be instilled with my senria . . . in the right quantity to destroy without killing. That was the challenging part."

Horace jerked his head to his mother and back to Raya. He hadn't been aware that Raya had control over her senria. No trainer had been assigned to her. And he didn't know that senria could be used to destroy others without first being manifested into weapons.

"And how did you plan on testing if you were successful?" This time, he did not hide the bite from his words. She would have had to use it on a living creature—human or not—to find out the efficacy of the mixture.

"No. No. I would never have tested it," Raya said frantically. "I planned to show it to Mother Len this morning—the color and texture was as mentioned in the scroll. Then I would have thrown it away. I wouldn't have tried it on anyone. I hadn't even read through its various effects or else I would have recognized Jianther's symptoms."

"Why, Raya?" Len's shoulders drooped dejectedly, but her eyes were full of concern for the girl she had raised with a lot of hope.

Garim moved uncomfortably behind Horace, as though he'd rather be anywhere else. The truth must be struggling to get out of him—that Raya must be punished for the oversight. A young man was burning as if in Kalantra's fire because of Raya's recklessness. She hadn't even studied the effects of the poison she was crafting. That showed that she wasn't ready for that knowledge.

"Was the cauldron full when you left it here?" Horace asked, giving a hand to Raya to lift her up.

Raya nodded, unable to get the words out, but she took his hand and stood.

"And do you think most of it was used on Jianther?"

"I . . . I left an empty bottle near it, which is missing. They must have taken the remaining veritria with them." Her face settled into a stoic expression, as though she were preparing herself for any retribution that came her way.

"Do you have any more of the amaran leaves you collected?"

"Yes, my lord."

"Bring a couple of them to me. I touched the cauldron, and now my finger is affected."

His mother did a double take.

"Fortunately, only the exterior. It must have been just a trace. The heat is not bothering me much," he lied.

Raya slammed the door open and ran past the confused sentry, who dutifully closed the door behind her.

"Garim, will you arrange for the council to meet tomorrow? We will tell them about the break-in and about the stolen prized possessions without detailing what the possessions were. Most shrines have jewelry. Let that be the assumption."

"Yes, my lord." Garim, too, left the shrine.

"Now, Mother, it is time we both had a heart-to-heart."

"In here?" She backed up a couple of steps from the sanctum but did not exit it, her eyes now fixed on the idol and the balance of justice carved at its feet.

"Let us do this in the presence of Zesta so that both of us speak only the complete truth. The goddess of justice deserves the truth."

"Are you calling me a liar?"

He took in a breath of the camphor-scented air and said calmly, "No, I am not. You, however, hide things from me."

It was nothing new for his mother to hide her decisions from him, more often because she doubted his support—like the time she presented Raya as a prospective bride for the crown prince of Athora. But this was not the same. They shouldn't be in two minds about the dangers of their present situation. He pressed his finger down to numb the burning sensation.

"What was Raya speaking about when she said she wanted to prove her worth? Why do you require her to do such dangerous things to prove herself to you?"

"Not to me." Len sighed.

"You are the one she always tries to please."

"She wants to prove herself to her mother, not me."

"What? Didn't her mother give her away because she couldn't raise her? Isn't it the mother who must prove her worthiness in this situation?"

"Shush. Have a care of what you speak!"

"Why? What did I say wrong now? Mother, this won't do. I need to know everything if I am to solve this current issue. No more secrets from me, please."

"It is a secret that I am sworn not to speak about." His mother turned away from him and to the sanctum. "But now I see no other way. If there is another way, then show it to me."

Horace didn't know what to reply to that, but it appeared as though she didn't expect a reply from him.

"She entrusted them to me," she said, fiddling with the rings that adorned all her fingers. "Both the scroll and Raya—because she trusted me."

"Who?"

"Zesta."

"The goddess?"

"Yes."

"Zesta of Thisaur?"

"Yes."

"You are talking like Zesta was your childhood friend."

"Not childhood. We met in my youth, and for a while, we were . . . close."

Horace narrowed his eyes. Was his mother blushing? He would never have thought that was possible, but her face was suffused with a shade of russet, which implied she had known Zesta intimately.

"Did someone fool you, perchance?"

"What do you take me for? In the days I have known her, I have seen her animate a hill made of rocks. It was to impress me. Even so, she did it."

No mortal in living memory had even claimed to have seen the gods and goddesses of Thisaur. Mythologies often related stories about them descending to the human plane. And what he was hearing sounded very much like one of those myths.

"Oh, don't you dare ask me any further questions. It was before I met your father, but eighteen years ago, she came to me again with her baby and a chest full of scrolls. She said her child wouldn't be safe in Thisaur. Their law requires all half-bloods to be servants of Niferon, and Zesta procreated Raya with a human."

"She sounds like a romantic."

"Have a care, Horace. She is the goddess of life."

"Yet she needed one of us to create a new life."

"Be that as it may, from that day forth, I guarded both Raya and the scrolls with my life. The plan had always been to hide them in plain sight without revealing their importance to anyone. When Raya was of age, I told her everything and gave her the scrolls. That had been my instruction."

"And what did Raya have to do to prove herself to her mother?"

"We didn't know. Zesta left a message in one of the scrolls in an alien script. I couldn't read it, although at first, I thought it was an ancient script of Cele. She said that Raya would be able to read it when she became worthy, and then Zesta would ordain Raya as her successor. Seemingly, Niferon cannot enslave Raya once she becomes a successor to the goddess."

Horace stared into the earnest black eyes of his mother, feeling like a lost boy. It had been bad enough that they had lost scrolls that contained secret medicinal knowledge. Now it seemed that was not all. One of the scrolls was written by the goddess herself, and they did not even know what it contained.

"We are in dire straits, Mother. Can't you request Zesta to help us?" He looked at the idol, imagining the sculpted face animating with life, but the stone remained unmoving.

"How am I to reach her? It is not as though I have a direct line of communication with the land of the gods."

"Isn't she seeing all this even if she isn't here? Aren't they supposed to be omnipresent?"

Lady Len snorted. "They are capable of much less than we humans give them credit for, although they can do much more than we can. No, Horace. We are on our own. No gods will help us. We need to retrieve that scroll. If only you'd let me use wija, given the contingency we are in."

"No."

"I am sure of that healer's guilt."

"I am not, but we have other ways of finding the truth."

"Are you going to confirm her guilt by letting her have free access to my laboratory?"

"She does not get free access, only an illusion of freedom. She will slip up and do something wrong. Pari will watch her like a hawk, and Raya can also be there to limit her access. It is only fair that Raya work on the antidote."

"And how long do you think that will take?"

"I cannot predict anything now, but I won't stand by and let you torture her, Mother. We live in a civilized world."

"Do we?"

Raya returned, clutching amaran leaves and a bandage. She wrapped the leaves around Horace's finger and bandaged it. The shock of his mother's revelations had taken his mind away from the burn, but the application of amaran leaves immediately soothed it. He couldn't even imagine what Jianther had gone through.

"Did the leaves soothe Jianther's pain?" he asked Raya.

"He has slipped into a state of unconsciousness, but his body has cooled down."

So Deena's advice did help in relieving the poor lad. Maybe the healer was trying to win their trust by appearing to be helpful. He would let her play her game, whatever it was.

"My lord," Raya said, "I was only trying to see if I could accomplish the most complicated task in the scrolls, and I am ready to—"

"I understand, Raya. Mother has told me everything. The time for your penance will come."

"Certainly, my lord," Raya said.

"And remember, the only person you have to prove yourself to is Jianther. Save him."

Raya nodded solemnly while his mother maintained a sullen silence.

Horace looked back at the idol of Zesta. If the goddess wanted her child to prove her worth, she would have to do more than be an unmoving stone idol.

7

Deena looked from the stoic soldier at the door to the healer Noaran. Both did not have a response to her request.

"It wouldn't be ethical," Noaran said at last, "to draw his blood without his consent."

"But he is in no condition to give his consent." Deena touched the bandage that Noaran had placed around her neck. It was helping neither the itch nor the sting from the cut by Lady Len.

The pain from the poison had caused the young soldier's mind to go into oblivion, although the timely application of amaran leaves helped to cool down his body. It didn't look like he'd wake up again as long as the poison remained in his bloodstream. He was currently being kept nourished by an infusion of aziril. The only chance he had was if an antidote was administered before his body wasted away.

For that, an antidote must be designed. Whatever Lord Thian had been thinking while assigning this task to her, she couldn't afford to fail—not just because it would acquit her. A life was at stake here.

She had been given all the necessary instruments to carry out her experiments in a room in the healers' home. Her few essentials were brought from her hut. Even a hot wash, clean clothes, and a meal were granted to her under the strict scrutiny of Pari, the soldier who watched her.

The narrow cot given to her rendered more comfort than a prison cell would, and through the barred window beside the bed, she could look out at the maraya tree in full bloom, its flowers emitting the citrus scent that was characteristic of its fruit.

These comforts were an illusion, and her status was that of a prisoner—a status that was affirmed by the bars on the windows that were affixed after she moved into the room. Pari and an equally unfriendly red-haired male soldier named Bentir took turns keeping watch throughout the previous day and night.

She had tried to strike up a conversation with Pari but had failed. The woman had kept her wide hazel eyes studiously averted from Deena the entire time. She sat by the door, exhibiting no interest in the conversation between Noaran and Deena. A single bronze bangle adorned her wrist, and her silver armor shone in the bright light of the sun, giving life to the lightning bolt and bow that were engraved on it—the insignia of Thian.

"We can't test our antidotes without examining his blood," Deena said.

Noaran fidgeted on the chair he had pulled up from the small table in the corner. He had come at Deena's request to discuss the further steps that she wished to take, but till now he had spoken more about restrictions than about possibilities. She wouldn't be allowed to use the laboratory, and instead, the things she needed would be brought to her room. If she did not have everything she needed at the reach of her hand, it would only slow her down. But it was only what she expected. After all, she wouldn't be allowed into the very place where she could find details about all the herbs that Lady Len controlled.

It was, however, illogical to argue that a patient's consent was required to draw their blood when they were in no position to give that consent, even though this code was followed by most healers.

"Mother Len would never agree to such a method," Noaran said, like that was the ultimate answer.

Deena paced between Pari and Noaran, for that was all the space the tiny room afforded.

"Ask Lord Thian," Pari said.

Even then she did not turn her face to look at Deena, and if Noaran hadn't been in the room, Deena would have thought that she had imagined it.

"If Lord Thian insists—" Noaran began.

The door opened and the man himself walked in, looking quite different from how he had appeared the previous day. A scarlet robe worn over a black tunic and trousers had replaced his riding costume. His hair was swept back, and a stud earring glinted in his left earlobe. One of his fingers was in a bandage.

"What should I insist on?" he asked.

Pari and Noaran jumped up from their respective seats. He raised his hand to show it wasn't necessary, but they remained standing.

"I would like to draw blood from Jianther, my lord," Deena said. "And I need your permission for that."

Lord Thian looked at her for a heartbeat and moved to Noaran. "How is Jianther today?"

"Not much difference, my lord."

"And Cade?"

"He has been moved to a separate room. His sleep has been peaceful while it lasts, but we had to administer the draught thrice already. He keeps waking up even when there are no other external disturbances."

"So the advice to give him a sleeping draught did not actually help." Lord Thian stared down at Deena.

"Er . . ." Noaran looked from Lord Thian to her.

"Maybe something else is disturbing him, which I can tell only if I am allowed to examine him," Deena said. It was unjust to expect her to solve everything remotely.

"You mean there is something that Noaran here was unable to spot that you think you could?"

"You cannot pit one healer against another, my lord." She did not wish Noaran's enmity, but his mortified look indicated embarrassment rather than anger. "That is why we often work as a team for intricate cases. One healer might spot that which another does not."

Noaran cast an appreciative glance toward her and visibly relaxed.

"Examine Cade," Lord Thian said. "If you afford him any comfort, I will heed your judgment and let Noaran draw Jianther's blood for you."

"I will gladly examine him."

Noaran took them to the infirmary and to the private room where Cade lay. The soldiers outside the room threw the doors open, and a thick scent of poultices wafted out—curcumin, jaira, ginger, ajinthya—nothing was spared in ensuring that the inflammations subsided.

Sunlight was kept out of the room with thick curtains on the windows, but the young soldier was not in a deep sleep. He grunted as they stepped into the room.

Casts held the soldier's bones in place along his thigh, forearms, and rib cage. The swelling was particularly worse around the rib cage, and that might be causing the distress. The sound of his strenuous breathing indicated the same.

"We are giving him enough ajinthya to soothe his pains," Noaran said.

"What about the swelling?" Lord Thian asked.

"That won't disappear so fast."

Deena kneeled by the bedside and ran a finger over the rough, bumpy outer layer of the bandage. Something was not right. The painkiller and the sleeping draught should allow him to rest peacefully for hours at a time. Yet he was under some distress.

"The cast," she said. "It must be loosened."

"Won't that impair the repair of the bones?" Noaran asked with genuine concern. He was not saying that for the sake of argument.

"Not if we rebind frequently after monitoring the progress."

Noaran looked thoughtful. He stepped up to the bed, examining the bandages himself. "Do you mean the cast is causing the swelling?"

"No, I fear it is pressing the ribs into the lungs. Check his breathing. If you loosen the cast, it should relieve the trauma and he can sleep more peacefully."

Noaran did. "That seems to be correct. I will redo the cast as soon as my assistant is back."

"I can help you," Deena said, "if Lord Thian agrees."

"Go ahead," Lord Thian said. "Noaran accepts your suggestion, and so I will allow it."

He did not move from his position, his stance promising her that he would be watching each of her actions minutely. If he thought she would harm this poor soldier further, he must indeed stay and observe her.

Noaran went out of the room and returned with knives, a fresh cast, and an orange salve smelling like cedar oil. Deena held the delirious soldier as Noaran removed the old cast around his rib cage and reapplied the balm to the swellings. As he set the new cast, Deena molded it with gentle pressure, being extra careful not to traumatize the lungs. The soldier's breathing became smoother as they laid him back on the bed.

Deena couldn't help but hold her head high as she got back on her legs and turned to Lord Thian. "We trust his sleep will be undisturbed now, my lord."

His eyes flickered to Noaran and back to her. "So it would seem."

He stepped out of the room where Pari waited for them.

"Noaran, do you have anything against drawing Jianther's blood?" Lord Thian asked once the door to Cade's room was closed by the guards.

Noaran sighed. "Mother Len might not like it."

"What about you?"

"As the lord of this seifland, you have the authority to command us to test his blood, my lord." Noaran's voice was pleading. It was clear he did not want to be the one to challenge Lady Len's authority.

"Then do it. You have my consent as long as his safety is not compromised. The council is meeting tomorrow. I will be back after that to check the progress."

"Please do not expect miracles, my lord," Deena said.

Even with access to Jianther's blood, she was venturing into territory she was unfamiliar with. She had designed antidotes after examining poisons. It had been a skill her uncle thought she should acquire, as similar techniques came in handy while preparing medicines for newly discovered illnesses. But the process usually took days, if not months. If Lord Thian wanted a cure in a day, he would be disappointed.

"It is you who must expect the miracle. Also, Raya will join you to assist so that Noaran can monitor the patients' needs adequately." Lord Thian ushered Pari to the grounds, and the two spoke in whispers.

After that, the soldier took Deena to her room to wait for Jianther's blood and other equipment she had requested of Noaran.

Horace hated to admit it to himself, but the deft manner in which the healer relieved Cade's discomfort impressed him. It was a minute alteration, but even Noaran had not spotted what was troubling Cade. With this attention to detail and her vast knowledge of herbs and medicines, she should be able to prepare an antidote for veritria. The question was, would she do it if Jianther could implicate her?

He meant to ask the leader of the healers' guild if he or anyone else in the guild had knowledge of veritria and its antidote. He couldn't depend on Deena, not when she was hiding her accomplice.

If only Pari could act more friendly toward Deena and win her trust, he might get his hands on some vital information that would help in apprehending the accomplice. But Pari seemed reluctant to fall back on the lessons she'd learned as a spy. She spoke of duplicity.

It was something he, too, abhorred. Playing mind games had been his father's area of expertise, not Horace's. That had been how his father had collected allies and destroyed enemies in his longstanding feud with the seifland of Rothshire. Once upon a time, Horace had considered his father a hero who annihilated the wicked and preserved the innocent. But then he had learned that all the battles and skirmishes with Rothshire had only been to gain land and other resources.

When he had succeeded as the lord of Thian, he had resolved to put an end to all the scheming, spying, and rivalry that benefitted none other than the egos of the lords concerned. He had successfully built peaceful relationships with Rothshire—a peace based on trade and economy rather than military prowess. He had also vowed to himself that his integrity would be beyond reproach and that he would extend to others the same good faith that he expected from them. Yet, now he would have to use subterfuge like his father.

"My lord." Garim brought his attention back to the assembly hall, where he was meeting his council members.

The six members had slowly trickled in while he was immersed in his thoughts, and they now sat on their respective seats lined on two sides of the massive hall. Each seat coincided with a towering pillar of white marble that together held up the elaborately painted high-vaulted ceiling. His mother was the last to arrive, and she took her assigned seat beside him at the end of the hall. Garim sat on his other side.

"Thank you for coming, respected members." Horace forcefully cleared the scowl from his face.

He was not obliged to give the council all the details, as the scrolls and the shrine were the private property of his family. They were merely his advisory body, and they needed to know only as much as what the public must know. Yet, as they were the leaders of the six guilds, they could help him prevent wild rumors from flying around among the people, now that he was conducting a widespread search all over the seifland and beyond.

"Two nights ago, the shrine on our premises was broken into and pilfered. Two of our soldiers suffered injuries while trying to prevent it."

"What has been taken, my lord, if I may ask?" Eriana from the guild of the priests said. The light filtering in through the stained-glass window behind her cast an ethereal halo around her golden hair.

"A chest with some valuables belonging to my mother." He stuck to the truth as much as possible. As a priestess of Zesta, she might have heard about the scrolls that once belonged to the goddess, but even if such stories existed in the myths, there was no reason for her to suspect that Zesta would have given those scrolls to Lady Len. Even he had not wrapped his head around that idea.

Farhaz and Sharin, from the guilds of healers and scribes, respectively, leaned toward each other and talked in low voices.

"We are all interested to hear what you have to say," Horace said.

Farhaz adjusted his turban and turned to Horace. He had been in the council since the previous Lord Thian's time and rarely approved of Horace's actions. That did not bother him much. He believed that no ruler should function without allowing room for criticism, but he preferred that criticism to be made to his face rather than behind his back.

"It is nothing, my lord," Farhaz said. "We were just wondering if the valuables that Lady Len possessed had anything to do with the herbal knowledge that she jealously guards."

Beside him, his mother sat as still as the stone idol of Zesta. She was of the firm opinion that the dangerous knowledge in those scrolls was not for all eyes, nor were the rare herbs that she had painstakingly procured and grown. Still, the healers could get what they required through a special request made to Lady Len, which not many healers appreciated. They wanted the freedom to grow what they needed to carry out treatments. Farhaz might prove to be an ally to Deena if he ever got to know why she entered the greenhouse.

"As you correctly understand, she jealously guards her possessions," Horace said. "Since it does not belong to the seifland and is a private person's property, I am not at liberty to disclose the details. But I wanted to ask you whether you have come across the poison veritria."

"Veritria?" Farhaz crinkled his brow. "Never heard of it."

"Can you make inquiries in your guild if anyone has heard of it or of its antidote?"

"Yes, my lord."

"And the arrest that was made?" Sharin asked.

"The suspect's details will be disclosed after their crime has been confirmed. The investigation is going on, but neither it nor the search for the lost property need unsettle our citizens. That is the assurance I want to give you.

"Also, I want to assure the farmers that the river water dispute with Rothshire will be settled before the summer travails reach their peak. Garim is traveling to Rothshire today for that purpose."

Jevis from the guild of farmers bowed his head. "The southern villages will be glad to learn that, my lord."

A few more matters had to be dealt with, like agreeing about using the trade surplus for the betterment of artisans. The presence of the heads of both guilds was an ideal opportunity to hash out any differences that might arise among the guild members, and for the next two hours, no one questioned about the burglary or the missing possessions.

Once Garim led the members of the council outside the assembly hall and the guards closed the door firmly behind them, his mother rose from her seat.

"It was foolish of you to disclose the name of the poison to the entire council."

"They are not our enemy, Mother." An overwhelming sense of exhaustion swamped Horace. She was never going to approve any of his actions, and in the coming days, he had to take several pertinent ones.

He had to prepare the water-sharing treaty with Garim and also attend to the reports sent back by the search parties that rode toward Feryar and beyond. Whoever they had been chasing seemed to have fled into Alayster. It was also time to involve Malion in the matter. He could do that without revealing details about the scrolls or Raya's parentage. Another task was to write to his emissaries to keep an eye open for unusual activities on the continent. If the poison cropped up somewhere, the culprit could be traced back to that location.

"No, they are not our enemy," his mother said while walking to the door, "but they will remember you mentioned veritria. Now that the poison is out in the open, it can be used anywhere, and they will connect it to you." And she left him.

8

Deena scrubbed her hands vigorously in the basin of warm water that lay on the table. Raya had given her gloves to work with, and it was unlikely that the poison from the blood could affect her now. But even a small contamination could hinder the dexterity of her fingers when there was much work to be done.

The tiny room was cluttered with all the devices that she had requested to test Jianther's blood. Despite spending long hours bent over the work desk that now lay parallel to the bed, she did not get a complete assurance of her success. After wiping her hand, she removed the bandage from her neck and wiped the sweat. She then began clearing the table.

Raya had gone to the icehouse in the city to arrange for a cool box in which they'd store the vials in the sweltering room. This would be necessary until the final antidote was stabilized.

Only Pari was present with Deena. She had remained silent throughout the day as usual, but now the soldier moved toward the desk and looked at the different vials with interest.

"All of these look the same to me," she said. "Is the antidote ready?"

"Far from it," Deena said. "All of those contain the same ingredients in different proportions. It will take a while before knowing which is effective."

"Lord Thian will not be pleased to hear that."

"Well, who is aiming to please him?"

The soldier laughed. It was odd to hear the tinkling laugh, not the least because Pari had not even smiled in her presence before, but the laugh lit up her grim face, making her almost unthreatening.

"Why do you look so taken aback?" Pari rounded the desk, averting her eyes back to the vials in which Deena had separated the different herbs that she had chosen for her experiments. A fresh bunch of thendril leaves lay scattered on the desk, along with a bowl of the same leaves crushed, accounting for the garlicky smell in the room.

"Nothing. I didn't know you were interested in what I was doing."

"I am very much interested in Jianther's recovery. And if by doing it, you can prove your innocence, then I have nothing against it. I would not wish the dungeons on an innocent."

"But even if the soldiers say it was not me, everyone can conclude it was an accomplice of mine."

"An accomplice with equally long hair?" The gold within Pari's eyes deepened. She touched her own curls rolled up at her neck. "If you weren't a suspect, I would have been even now requesting you to share the recipe of your hair elixir."

"I promise to do that once we get to the other end of this."

Pari opened her mouth like she wanted to say something more, but she decided against it and returned to her seat.

"Are you a sentar warrior?" Deena quickly asked. She did not want the conversation to end. It was like a breath of fresh air in the stifling room.

"Yes."

"At some stage I might need to instill the mixtures with senria. Ideally, we would need the senria of the person who brewed the poison. That is what gives veritria its notoriety. Oftentimes, it is only the poisoner who can be the savior, but in this case, as in all others, the poisoner wouldn't want to save the victim."

"Just tell me when you need it."

"Thank you." Deena smiled with genuine gratitude.

Pari tucked a rogue strand of black hair behind her ear and turned away as though the smile discomfited her. She reverted to being the morose prison guard.

Deena returned to the table, clearing away the random leaves and barks that did not make it to the different solutions she had prepared. It was not her intention to put the soldier in a tough spot, and she hoped the request had not put a pause to the friendliness exhibited by Pari.

Shortly Raya and Bentir arrived with her lunch, relieving Pari, who might return in the night if they followed the same routine as the previous day. While Raya moved the vials to the cool box, Deena tackled the plate of rice and fish given to her.

No one could criticize the delicious dishes that she was allowed to enjoy. The fragrant rice and spicy fish stew couldn't be the normal fare given to prisoners. She washed the lunch down with chilled maraya juice—its bittersweet flavor an apt companion for the spice.

By that time, Raya had wheeled in a cart to take the cool box and the remaining ingredients to the laboratory. She was followed by Lord Thian, who must have come to assess the progress. There was nothing much to report to him. She informed him about the vials she had prepared and the time it would take for a result to be known.

"My lord, if none of the antidotes I prepared works, would I be allowed to use some of the rarer plants in Her Ladyship's garden?"

"After the way you insulted her, it may be a hard ask."

"It is for Jianther's sake."

Lord Thian shrugged. "She would still argue that it is your tactic to learn about her secret collections, which is your confessed motive for entering the garden."

"It is really hard that none can challenge Lady Len." She did not hide the bite in her voice.

"Are you aware it is my mother you speak of in that disrespectful tone?"

"Very much aware, my lord." She turned to help Raya, who was pretending to be invisible, and placed the basket of discarded leaves on the cart. "I also request permission to use Pari's senria while testing the antidotes tomorrow." She didn't want the soldier to run into trouble with Lord Thian for doing so.

"Why Pari's?"

"Because she is available here most of the time, and since she is a sentar warrior, her senria is more powerful than mine."

Lord Thian looked thoughtful. "You can if she consents."

"Thank you, my lord." She hoped he would leave.

He did not budge, however, and continued staring at her with his shrewd eyes, as if he were trying to decipher what was going on in her head. Once Raya had cleared away the vials, Lord Thian instructed the soldier to wait outside.

"Have you thought any more about revealing who your accomplice was?"

She was not expecting the question, and the confusion must have shown on her face.

"I needn't tell you how harmful it would be if the scrolls fell into the wrong hands." He held her gaze. "I know you care about the lives of others. How can you not act when the lives and welfare of thousands are at stake?"

His tone was warm, and for a moment, Deena wished she had something to offer him, some information to give, so that she could be in his good books. Then she shook herself. It was just a tactical step by Lord Thian to win her trust. He had no warmth for her.

"I stand by what I said. No one was with me when I broke in, and I did not steal the scrolls."

A veil of icy blankness fell over his emerald-flecked eyes, and he turned to leave. "I will be back tomorrow to check your progress."

Then he exited the room and spoke to the soldier who was waiting outside. A sharp pain in her back made her swirl around.

Something had struck her. A parchment wrapped around a stone lay at her feet. In a flash, she took hold of it and stuck it under the sheaf of parchments already on the desk. It was not a moment too soon. Lord Thian looked at her one last time before leaving. By the narrowing of his eyes, it was clear that he had noted the shade of guilt on her face. She stared back at him defiantly until he was out of sight.

Bentir sat by the door, looking as morose as Pari had. Deena took the parchment to the bed along with the others under the guise of perusing them. She unrolled it unobtrusively and read.

Be ready tonight. I will come to fetch you.

It was unsigned, but the illegible handwriting was undoubtedly Kran's—the number of times she had struggled to read his messages. She lay down, looking out of the window at the maraya tree that shaded her from the early summer sun. There were still many hours left for the night, but there was no way she could tell him not to come. And how did he hope to get her out when she was so closely guarded?

The truth was she did not want to escape like that. She shoved the message into her blouse. It was now her personal challenge to save Jianther and help find the real culprits who stole the scrolls. If she succeeded at that, she could hope for some leniency from Lord Thian and his mother, on whose mercy the welfare of her other patients depended.

She clutched the sheets in frustration. There was nothing she could do now but keep her senses alert for the night, and for that purpose, she forced herself to give in to her drowsiness.

It was not the brightest of decisions, however. A severe case of grogginess took over her when she woke up at dusk. She tried to jot down more ideas for the antidote, but the combinations she wrote made little sense. Noaran would easily understand that, but he never came into the room that evening, so she kept up the pretense.

Pari returned as expected at night to guard her. If Kran arrived to rescue her, he would have to face off with Pari. Deena sighed at the unsavory prospect because not only would Kran not know he was going to fight a sentar warrior but also she did not want Pari attacked.

The soldier sat beside her and not at the door as Deena ate her dinner of flat bread and curry. Even the exotic herbs in the dish did not distract her from what was coming.

Pari was interested in the new combinations that Deena had written, but fortunately did not know enough to understand that they were improbable.

"Didn't you say your uncle taught you all about herbs?" she asked, replacing the parchments on the desk.

"Yes. He was also my foster father."

"And your parents?"

"Died when I was an infant. What about you?"

"My mother is a dressmaker. She and my sister live near the Haiga range. Do you have siblings?"

"No." Deena wondered if her reply was a tad too abrupt, but technically, she did not have a sibling. Kran was her cousin.

Once she finished eating, she forced a yawn.

"I would like to go to bed now."

"I heard you were asleep for the better part of the afternoon and evening." Pari arched one of her perfectly shaped eyebrows.

"My brain is dead tired after all the thinking," Deena mumbled.

In a few more hours, Pari might regret treating her in a friendly manner. She willed Kran to use some distraction technique to get Pari away from the room instead of attacking her. Then she knew what she would do. She would send him away before further harm was done.

She curled up on the bed, facing the window, as Pari moved back to the door. A small lantern on the wall threw a dim light in the room. It had been alit throughout last night, with Pari periodically refreshing the oil. The chirping of crickets took over the silence of the night.

Was that the crack of a twig? Deena tensed and held her breath. A shuffling sound floated into the room like the careful shift of tiles on the rooftop. Boots scraped the floor behind her as Pari got up to investigate. Deena sensed Pari bending low to inspect whether she was asleep, and she tried to regulate her breathing to a steady rhythm. Then a pungent smell floated into the room—of burning oaflin leaves.

This time Deena held her breath in earnest, but behind her, Pari coughed and, with a grunt, fell to the floor. Deena stood up, holding her blanket over her nose. The soldier lay face down, senseless. A tile moved over her head, then another, revealing the brilliant moon and a face covered with a mask.

"Go. Get out of here," Deena said in a loud whisper, her voice muffled by the blanket.

"Give me your hand." The upper half of Kran's body lowered into the room, and he extended both his arms.

"No. I am not coming." She batted away the hand. "It won't help."

"All the guards who could stand in our way are sleeping now. What are you afraid of?"

"I am trying to save someone's life, and by doing it, I can prove my innocence."

Kran made an irritated sound. "I can't leave you here. Just come. And we will prove your innocence some other way."

"No. Please, Kran. Listen to me—"

A whip of light extended through the air and bound around Kran's wrist, pulling him. He tumbled down in a rain of shattering tiles and fell on the cot, breaking it with a resounding crack. Pari was on her feet, a glowing mask of senria covering her nose. It must have protected her from the ill-effects of oaflin smoke, which had dissipated by now.

Deena could only stare like a halfwit as Pari manifested a sword in her free hand. "Get to your feet and stand down."

Kran got to all fours and slowly rose, rubbing his hip with a hand. He must have hurt himself and was struggling to stand straight. Deena made a frantic movement toward him but was held back by Pari's stern glance.

The soldier shouldn't have taken her eyes off Kran, for then he pulled the whip with all his might, throwing Pari across the room.

He shook his head in disappointment at Deena and hurried to the door. Before Pari was back on her feet, he disappeared into the night.

9

Horace hadn't been able to sleep. He had to write a difficult letter to Malion, informing him about the actions of the healer from his seifland, while also politely preempting any request to transfer the prisoner. He hoped the letter wouldn't cause a dent in the good relations he shared with Malion. As individuals, they were friends, but as lords of their respective seiflands, they would sometimes have to make decisions that would displease the other.

He sent the letter out by a courier but sleep still eluded him. Taking a walk in the brisk night air might help. Also, it might aid in making sense of the different threads of these events that did not yet make a full-fledged tapestry.

The night-blooming cereus had permeated the garden with its heady perfume. Horace paused a moment to enjoy it when a distant shout alerted him.

It came from the direction of the healers' residence, and the voice belonged to Pari. He sprinted over the grass, leaving the roundabout path. The appearance of someone running toward him slowed him at first, but then the figure took a sharp right turn and headed toward the gate. Horace took off after him. In another moment, Pari was by his side.

"Soldiers, alert," she shouted, and lashed her whip at the runner, who had now reached the closed gate. No one responded, and the whip missed him by a few inches. He started clambering up the iron bars of the gate.

She lashed again, and this time, the whip wrapped around his ankle, dragging him down. His sword was out from its sheath in a flash, and it cut through the whip, Pari's senria sizzling in protest.

Horace's sentar sword extended from his hand, and the blade arced toward the fallen man. The latter parried the attack and jumped to his feet in a fluid motion, his metal sword and dark eyes gleaming in the moonlight. It was the same man who had fought him in the canal—the same build and the same technique in which he held his non-sword hand, ready to punch.

Pari's sword came whistling through the air and slashed the man's arm. He did not even let out a cry as he returned the strike, which Pari blocked with a shield.

Two against one might not be considered just odds, but Horace did not plan any leniency toward the intruder. He lunged forward, his sword aimed at his opponent's flank. A devastated cry paused his blade.

"No. No! Please don't." It was Deena.

The man took advantage of the pause and kicked Horace's sword hand, but he hadn't accounted for the latter's grip, which did not let the sword go. Before Horace could aim another blow, though, Pari had manifested a rope of senria to bind the man's hands and arms to his torso. He fell to his knees. Pari whipped off his mask.

"Kran," Deena cried, and ran to the man. "You shouldn't have come." She kneeled beside him, cupping his face.

There was no doubt. This was her accomplice—the one she had lied through her teeth to protect.

Kran. That name was familiar, and the face too. Horace had seen him on several occasions with Malion, both at the Western Frontier and in Athora. He was a soldier of Alayster and Malion's loyal friend. He was also the father of the child who'd needed heliatin, for whom Deena had come to Thian, she being the healer who had treated the child. After all that, the duo showed their gratitude by breaking into his family's shrine.

Kran stared defiantly at Horace and Pari and tried to shake away Deena and the rope that bound him.

"Is this how you repay us?" Horace asked the kneeling man, struggling to keep his roiling fury in check.

Kran's defiant eyes lowered to the ground.

This complicated matters more. It was too late to intercept the letter to Malion, which he would have worded differently had he known about the involvement of a soldier of Alayster in the break-in.

Horace ignored the bitter tang in his mouth and turned to Pari. "Where is the night guard? Why hasn't anyone come after all this ruckus?"

"Oaflin leaves," Pari stated coolly. "Everyone on the grounds must have been put to sleep. I escaped only because I shielded myself in time."

"It can't be discounted that he has harmed them like before. Take him back to the palace and send out the sentries. Ask them to spread over the ground and ensure everyone is safe and alive."

Kran emitted a hoarse protest, but Horace signaled Pari to take him away from the scene, and she did it with her sword held to his neck. There was no further protest.

Horace turned to Deena, who was still on her knees. "You. All your lies have unraveled. The number of times you protested that no one helped you break in, and it turned out to be the very man whose daughter you were treating with herbs procured from my mother. I gave you a chance to redeem yourself, and this is the gratitude I receive."

Her silence unnerved him. He half expected her to get back on her feet and argue her case—that she had not stolen the scrolls, or that Kran had forced her to do it. Instead, she stayed on the ground, her shoulders gently shaking from the shock or the sobs she was suppressing. He couldn't house her in the healers' residence now after this blatant attempt at escape. She and Kran would have to be removed to the dungeon after questioning, and new ways must be devised to make them confess.

"Get up. You are also going back to the palace to be held until morning." His voice was harsher than he had intended, but he did not regret it. He had always prided himself in keeping his anger in check, but whenever his trust was betrayed, that resolution was a difficult one to keep. And she had broken his trust—the trust he had unwillingly bestowed on her.

Even when he'd been unsure of her guilt, he had thought she showed admirable spirit in things she believed in—especially in her duties as a healer. A part of him had even hoped that she could design an antidote for veritria.

They walked toward the silhouette of the palace that sprawled against the moonlit sky, Horace with his sword at the ready, although he did not expect her to make a run for it now. She seemed to have given up all hope, and somehow, he found that disappointing.

A few windows in the palace lit up like portals opening in the air, but the wing occupied by his mother and Raya was still shrouded in darkness. It wouldn't be easy to explain to his mother that his experiment with the healer had failed. She would even argue that the intrusion by a soldier of Alayster was an act of war and expect him to send his army to Alayster like his father would have done. He would definitely not follow that path. He trusted Malion enough to know that this was not an act of war by that seifland and was perpetrated by individuals without the consent or knowledge of Lord Alayster.

The unwelcome memory of Malion stealing the heliatin herb intruded into his thoughts. He shook it off. That was also a betrayal of trust, but it did not fall in the same league as stealing the scrolls and harming soldiers of Thian.

Before they reached the palace, sentries had streamed out with handheld torches and unsheathed swords. They fanned out over the grounds, searching for the night guards. Horace wanted to join them, but he had to ensure that the healer was properly confined.

He entered the palace through the door that led to the atrium and proceeded up the stairs to his official quarters. That was where Pari had taken Kran, for in there was a room that his father had once used to converse with his spies. It had no windows and only a small ventilation that could not be accessed from any balcony. Even though Horace did not use the room for the same purpose now, it came in handy when he had to hold someone before sending them off to the dungeons. That was where the healer and her helper would stay for the time being.

Past the assembly hall, the court of justice, his private study, and the library was the spy cell. Two guards besides Pari were present in the room. Handcuffs and ankle restraints replaced the rope of senria binding Kran. It was a good decision. Given a chance, he would try to break free, even if that meant he had to attack the soldiers. When Deena went toward Kran, Horace stopped her.

"No, you may not conspire with each other." He turned to his soldiers. "Keep them separate. At sunbreak, they will be shifted to the dungeon. Pari, come with me."

He walked out without a glance at the prisoners. Once the soundproof doors were closed, he flopped down onto a chair in the middle of the room, rubbing his forehead with his hand. The surrounding shelves loomed threateningly, with the spines of the books forming a uniform gray mass in the unlit library.

Pari paused on her way out to his study. "I take it you know the man?"

"Yes, he is from Alayster and is close to Malion. The betrayals come from directions I least expect."

"We mustn't jump to conclusions." She manifested blobs of lights and placed them on the two peacock-shaped lamps on either side of the door.

"What do you mean?"

"We know for a fact that he was here tonight to get Deena out, but nothing else is proved."

"What other proof do we need? He was the person I saw with her that night—the one who escaped into Feryar."

"I don't disagree, but when I feigned that the smoke from the oaflin leaves affected me, I heard them talking. She refused to go with him because she wanted to stay and prove her innocence and also help Jianther. That is not how the guilty behave."

"Maybe she was bluffing, knowing you were conscious."

Pari eyed him challengingly. "You are questioning my skills now. From the time she mentioned she had used oaflin leaves to disable the guards outside the garden that night, I have been alert for its usage. As soon as I felt the pungent smell, I shielded my nose. She was on the bed facing away from me, so she couldn't have seen it. I pretended to fall on the floor with my face down because I wanted to catch her in the act, but when Kran appeared on the roof, she refused to go with him. I think Deena is saying the truth. She had nothing to do with the break-in at the shrine or the attack on Jianther and Cade."

Horace swallowed hard as he tried to make sense of this information. He trusted Pari's judgment, but that would mean the real culprits were still out there, with he being no closer to finding them.

"But what about Kran?" he asked. "Although I don't want to believe it, we cannot discard the possibility that he was the one who broke into the shrine."

"I have no argument against that, but I made those inquiries I promised."

She hesitated.

"Whatever it is, tell me. Do you suspect anyone?"

Her boots clapped toward him, and she dragged a chair from between two shelves and placed it opposite him. "Whoever carried out the burglary would have staked out the scene before."

"Yes, that is a valid deduction. Did you see someone near the shrine under suspicious circumstances?"

"It was not suspicious at the time because I hadn't known there was anything valuable in the shrine, but since the burglary, it has been pricking me that I did nothing about it." She shifted in her chair. "It was almost three months ago, when you were at the Western Frontier. Mother Len had held a feast here in honor of Raya."

He knew of the feast. His mother had been planning to present Raya as a bride for Prince Aethan—a scheme he had opposed, but Raya was his mother's ward, and so he couldn't do much about it other than try to convince his mother that it was a bad decision.

Now he could see his mother's logic, even though he still couldn't agree with it. She must have thought that a goddess's daughter must at least be the queen of a land. That might even have been good training for Raya if Zesta ever made her a successor. But she was too young to marry the crown prince, and also someday, if she were to sit on Zesta's throne, she would have outlived her husband and children and everyone she knew.

"Did she let visitors into the shrine during the feast?"

Many noble families must have visited the palace that day. In fact, if someone had to get to the scrolls, it would have been a good night to act. It was the night that Malion had stolen the heliatin herb.

"Not visitors. Just one. The valiant warrior Tandon, nephew of Lord Rothshire. He had shown great interest in the ancient history of the shrine, which Mother Len had found flattering."

"But you found it suspicious?"

"Not when he expressed those sentiments, but later that night, he drew quite a lot of attention to himself."

"Some of that reached me."

He had been at the Western Frontier, and Thili, the enchantress, had brought the news to him. Val Tandon had misbehaved with their guest Gaelia and later also with a maid out on the streets.

"The thing is," Pari continued, "throughout that night, he did certain things purportedly under the influence of alcohol, but he never took a sip. I recently made some inquiries, and someone even saw him empty a glass in a potted plant. I bet Lady Len would have been furious had she seen it. Then he used his inebriation as an excuse to step out of the feast, but I followed him. He sauntered into the garden and the shrine. I had no reason to stop him, but when I made my presence known, he slipped away."

"Was there any reason you were watching him this closely? You said you didn't find his admiration of the shrine suspicious."

"No, but . . . but there was something else he admired—someone else. Earlier that day, I saw him being over friendly with Raya. It caught my attention because I thought Raya was trying to shake him off."

"He has been known for showing unwelcome interest in women, but I never thought he would target someone of Raya's age."

"I remained in their presence to offer Raya help if she needed it, but his interest was mostly again on the shrine, even though Lady Len had already told him all that she could."

"Was there any mention of the scrolls?"

"No, I would have remembered if there was. The first I heard of those scrolls was when Mother Len accused Deena of stealing them. Do they contain anything more harmful than secret knowledge about herbs?"

"Isn't that harmful enough? I am glad you told me about Tandon. He has given some trouble to Malion, Lord Alayster, and he was also spotted at the Western Frontier, helping the syrelins, presumably mind-controlled by them. I am not so sure about that now."

10

Deena's head pounded as she sat opposite Kran on the floor, trying to catch his eyes. He kept them averted, but when they accidentally met, she did not see accusation in them, just defeat. It was the greatest ignominy for him—a soldier of Alayster—to be bound up like this in a foreign seifland, a land that had helped his child. If she could, she would have shouted at him, asking him why he'd come to save her when he could have been safely back with his wife and child now. If he could hoodwink half the soldiers in the palace to gain entry, he could easily have made it across the border to Alayster.

She also fervently hoped he had used only oaflin leaves to disable the guards around the palace. Any more injured soldiers and their case would become extremely feeble, not that it had any strength now. She had avoided looking at Lord Thian, but she had felt the fury radiating from him. Any chance of getting into his good graces had vanished by no fault of hers, and more devastating was the fact that she could no longer develop a cure for Jianther.

Clutching her knees close to her body, she lowered her head onto them, attempting to tune out the walls closing in and the oppressive silence that seemed to amplify Kran's labored breathing. There was not even a window to let them see a bit of the sky. The ventilation on top of the wall opposite her was covered with a black screen.

She had almost dozed off when the door opened again.

"Come with me." It was Lord Thian. His rage seemed to have simmered down, but she couldn't be too sure, as his face was like a mask.

With a fleeting look at Kran, she followed him out of the confined space, involuntarily filling her lungs with air tinged with the scents of parchment and ink as she stepped outside to the massive library.

"You can continue with your experiments," Lord Thian said without betraying any emotion. "It seems I owe you an apology for accusing you of trying to escape."

"Why?" She did not understand why he was apologizing when Kran did try to break her out. Lord Thian's expression still gave her no clue, but his eyes darkened as he gazed deeply into hers.

"Because Pari believes you had no intention of escaping, and I trust her words. She was the only one among the night guard who was not tricked by the oaflin smoke, and she heard your conversation with Kran. I am sorry for my harsh words earlier. You did not deserve that," he ended warmly.

The pounding in her head slowed down and was transferred to her chest as she realized she was standing too close to him and also that she had not responded to his apology.

"I . . . my lord, I . . ."

He slightly smiled at her confusion.

Someone cleared their throat behind her. Deena swiveled around to find Pari standing in the shadows. The latter gave her a reassuring nod.

Deena turned back to Lord Thian. "Kran was only trying to save me because he didn't know you had given me a chance to prove my innocence. He really shouldn't have. Can he be . . .?"

"No, not yet. He has done no lasting harm tonight, but we are still not sure of the role he played in the first break-in," Lord Thian said.

"My lord, now that I do not have to hide his identity, I can tell you what his role exactly was. He is the one who attacked Shauri and Raya."

"I see."

"He promised me he didn't harm anyone, and true to his word, both of them had only minor injuries. He followed me that night, presumably to stop me, but when I was almost caught, he had to intervene. He has this protective streak and always tries to keep me from harm's way."

"He did not succeed very much, did he?" There was a hint of humor in his words, but she might have imagined it, for his next words were spoken in all seriousness. "He will have to remain in custody till the investigation is concluded, but I assure you we will look into the possibility of his innocence and at other angles. You can use that time wisely to secure that cure."

With a grateful nod of her head, she agreed. It was much more than Deena had hoped for, and a faint ray of hope brightened her heart. She hadn't realized how much she had valued being in Lord Thian's good graces.

"Can I have a word with Kran? Not in private."

"Yes, you may." Lord Thian led her back to the cell, and he and Pari stood on her either side.

"Kran," she called softly. "Why did you come?"

"Because Mother would have killed me if she learned I abandoned you."

His mother would have been indeed heartbroken had she learned of Deena's predicament, but her own action brought that fate upon her head. Mother Sheila wouldn't have blamed Kran for it.

"All right," Kran conceded. "I felt guilty after running away and leaving you like that to be captured by . . . by Lord Thian. So I returned and scouted the palace grounds in a borrowed armor of Thian." He rubbed his bound wrists on his chin and darted a glance at Lord Thian.

"Thian's armor, huh?" Pari said, possibly wondering how to cover up that loophole in their security.

"Can you promise me not to do any other stupid thing as I try to prove our innocence?" Deena said.

Kran's nose flared. "You are one to talk of stupid acts. All this wouldn't have happened if you hadn't decided to forage the greenhouse." Then he sighed. "Yes. I promise. My hands are tied." He raised the cuffed wrists again. "Literally."

"You will be unbound and moved to a larger cell within the palace for the time being," Lord Thian said. His demeanor was no longer accusatory, but his voice did not give away the extent of his leniency.

"Will you . . . will you be telling Lord Alayster of my captivity?" Kran's voice shook uncharacteristically.

"I must." Lord Thian, too, did not sound happy about it.

"Well, that is that." Kran's lips pinched together.

There was nothing she could say to take that heaviness from him, so Deena bade him farewell and accompanied Pari to the healers' residence. They were lodged in a different room for the rest of the night, as the roof in the previous room was damaged. It had a bigger bed and did not have any signs that it was a makeshift prison. The windows were free of bars, and the bed was more comfortable, but she had no intention of sleeping.

Her work desk and parchments had been shifted to the new room, and she sat down to rework the combinations she had written the previous day. She might feel the need to rest later, but this second chance had made her brain more alert, and she wanted to make the most of it.

Pari sat quietly by the door, not questioning the strange behavior. Pari's words had given her this second chance, yet Deena did not have the courage to talk to her or thank her after the way Kran had attacked her. She scribbled more ingredients, extending her mind to herbs that were not normally in usage. There was a high chance that Lady Len had them in her greenhouse or would know how to procure them. That mighty lady wouldn't stand in her way when it could save a soldier of Thian.

By the time the golden glow of dawn arrived and the chirps of the earliest of birds flitted into the room, she had exhausted all the knowledge in her head. She had a sheaf of parchment ready to show Raya when she'd come with the soldier who would relieve Pari.

On an impulse, she got up. "I am sorry for the way my cousin acted."

Pari turned to her, a smile dancing in her eyes. "He was harmed more than I was." She sighed. "I could imagine he acted in defense, although that is not a commentary on his role in the events before last night."

Deena did not argue. There was no use arguing with no proof. "If you hadn't spoken up for me, whatever you said, I would still be in that cell with no opportunity to do this." She waved a hand at the desk.

"It was my duty to report back the truth to Lord Thian. I only told him what I heard you speak."

Deena couldn't remember what exactly she had said, other than she had refused to go with Kran, but whatever it was, it had given her a temporary reprieve. When her replacement arrived in the morning, Pari bid Deena farewell, something she had never done before, and told her she would return by noon.

It was with a cheerful frame of mind that she greeted Raya that morning, waving her sheaf of parchment. The girl was left open-mouthed, seeing the sheer quantity of herbal concoctions Deena had planned to prepare. Raya flipped the pages with growing interest, and her brows furrowed in focus as she read.

"I am glad you didn't run away last night." She smiled as she handed the parchments back to Deena and lowered her voice conspiratorially. "Although Mother Len was fuming when Lord Thian told her he thought you weren't guilty."

"My cousin is responsible for that scar, you know." Deena looked at Raya furtively. "We are not entirely guiltless."

The girl ran a finger over her cheek. "Who is?" She bit her lips and focused on clearing the table.

Noaran, too, arrived to check on Deena and was amazed by the number of parchments she had filled. "I wouldn't have thought up half of this. Mixing eela with mehua? That is risky, but it might work, as they are from the opposite ends of the toxicity spectrum."

"That is the idea." Deena paused. "Was anyone harmed last night?"

"Not that I heard of. There was a platoon of sleepy soldiers in the palace this morning asking for a cure for their languor. I told them it shall pass if they drink lots of water. Was I correct?"

"You know you are. It was just oaflin."

"Just oaflin! And the things that leaf can do."

Before long, Noaran left to inspect his patients, and Raya and Deena carried on with the experiments. The smoky smell of the burner filled the room, and the pestle ground relentlessly on the mortar as leaves, barks, petals, and roots were crushed to release their juices. Vials were soon filled with murky brown, clear green, brilliant red, or translucent blue solutions, all of which had to be tested with a drop of Jianther's blood to see if the veritria was diluted.

Raised voices outside the door made both Raya and Deena look up from their work. The rumbling in Deena's stomach hoped it was her morning meal. Lord Thian wouldn't deprive her of food, yet her meal had been delayed, and the sun was already halfway up the sky.

But what waited for her was not the comfort of warm food, but the chilling sharpness of Lady Len's tongue.

"How dare you continue using my facilities? Who let you in here?"

"Mother Len—" Raya began.

"Raya, why are you still helping her after what she did last night?"

"But Lord Thian said she could continue working," Raya said feebly.

"Lord Thian," Lady Len muttered, clenching her teeth.

"Greetings to you too, Mother." Lord Thian appeared behind his mother with a cheerful expression, which Deena was sure he had forced onto his face just at that moment, because the strain had not completely left his features.

Lady Len swiveled to him. "I agreed with your little experiment, but now that her companion has been caught, this is ridiculous. I don't, for a moment, believe she is innocent."

"Raya, Deena," Noaran yelled from outside the building.

"What now?" Lady Len shouted back.

Noaran lost all his exuberance as he arrived at the door and replied in a meek voice, "Cade is awake, my lady."

11

No one stopped Deena from following everyone to the infirmary where Cade was housed, but only Noaran entered the room. A silent look from Lord Thian was enough to stop even his mother, and since they were outside the patient's room, Lady Len couldn't continue shouting. Deena savored the respite as she sent a fervent prayer of gratitude to the heavens.

The recovery of any patient was always an opportunity to rejoice, but this particular one could be the eyewitness who could exonerate her and Kran. A few minutes later, Noaran made an appearance.

"My lord. Cade is conscious and alert at last. He can speak to you now."

"Come with me," Lord Thian told Deena. "But don't speak unless I instruct you."

The room differed from the last time she'd been there. The curtains were drawn open to let in the healing rays of the sun. A mild incense powder burned in a pot in one corner, dissipating the overwhelming smell of poultices. It was clever of Noaran to think of these factors that would give Cade some sense of return to normalcy.

Cade's eyes were wide open, his mouth set in a grim line. Bluish-purple bruises marred the parts of his torso not covered by bandages or salves. He lowered his chin instead of a bow on seeing Lord Thian, but then grunted.

"No, don't move." Lord Thian stepped closer to him so that Deena would be in Cade's vision. The young soldier did not show any signs of recognition.

"Do you remember anything of the night you were attacked?" Lord Thian asked. "Don't strain too much if you don't."

Cade blinked rapidly as though trying to ferret out the memory from the foggy depths of his brain, lulled by the potion that suppressed pain.

"Nothing, my lord."

"That is all right. It will come back in time."

"No. There is nothing to come back. One moment I was standing under the mehua tree, and the next I was pushed to its trunk with a force like a gale."

"You mean no one struck you?"

"No, whatever attacked me was invisible. I slammed into the tree multiple times and lost consciousness."

A moment of silence reigned in the room as the listeners took in this information until an impatient clucking sound broke it.

"Maybe he is confused," Lady Len said. "He must be feverish after suffering so much. What invisible force can throw him against a tree?"

Deena was wondering the same, but there had been no fever when she'd last checked him, and it would be out of place to examine him now.

"There are such forces," Lord Thian said. "Mages."

"On our land? Never."

Even Lady Len couldn't be so arrogant as to think she could control the movement of mages. They mostly lived outside the borders of seiflands because they submitted to no one, but if one of them decided to travel into Thian, no one could stop them or even know they were a mage unless they publicly exhibited their power.

She had heard of a mage who currently lived in the palace of Alayster—Byuton—and even Kran was acquainted with him. It would be foolish, however, to mention that now, as it would only further incriminate them.

"Do you remember seeing her somewhere?" Lady Len pulled Deena further in front of Cade.

Cade's forehead wrinkled, but it cleared soon enough. "Yes, my lady. I remember."

"Ha!"

"I took my nephew to her last month for an elixir for his stomachache." He gave her a feeble smile.

She did not remember Cade's face, but a child had come to her the previous month with stomach pain. The patient had had her complete attention, while the bystander had merely been a figure accompanying him.

Lady Len let go of her and scrunched up her fist. She opened and closed her mouth with no words coming out. Then, with effort, she turned to Deena. "Don't think this absolves you." She cast another glance at Cade and Lord Thian and swept out of the room.

Cade's recovery did not clear her of anything, but it also did not implicate her further in the crime. Deena was determined to see this as a positive development. No mage could be linked to her, although Byuton could be linked to Kran, but Kran should know better than to reveal it.

Mages were not the most trusted group of people on the continent, for good reason. Their name had been linked to many deaths and disappearances, including those of Lord and Lady Easther, yet no one could bring them to justice. It was now up to Lord Thian to find out who attacked Cade, and her full focus could go to curing Jianther.

Cade recognizing her as a healer and not as an intruder had some wonderful outcomes. Lady Len left her alone for the time being, and Lord Thian opened up the laboratory for her.

When she stepped into the laboratory for the first time behind Raya, Deena had a sense of being in a dream-like state. It would be any healer's dream to work under the fragrant canopy of dried lavender, mint, and thyme that hung from the ceiling. The air was rich with the spicy scent of herbal brews and the earthy aroma of dried leaves. Every available surface was lined with arrays of shelves glittering with bottles, cylinders, and tubes marked in a meticulous, tiny script. They contained all the necessary constituents known to her.

This meant she could prepare the antidote at the same time as writing its formula, instead of waiting for Raya to bring her the ingredients. Pari and Raya moved her parchments to the writing desk on which quills and ink pots were neatly arranged. By the desk was a hearth on which stood a giant cauldron. Several bronze and copper pots for brewing potions hung to its side.

Pari and other soldiers still stood guard in the laboratory and in her room, but the doors of both were no longer closed. She had the freedom to move between them, but she spent most of the days bent over the stained wooden workstation that stretched across the center of the laboratory.

She was able to prepare the antidotes quicker than she had anticipated, and they rested in the cool box to give the ingredients time to amalgamate. On the third day, she instilled them with Pari's senria and stabilized them.

"Should I use my senria too?" Raya asked.

"It won't be necessary," Deena said kindly. The girl was no sentar warrior. Even if she had an earnest wish to help, a weak senria would not be of much use.

The antidotes she had prepared, however, had no effect on the veritria present in the blood samples. Deena, Pari, and Raya sat in silence for a few moments to digest their disappointment.

"I have yet to test the recipes containing eela root," Deena said. "I was hoping it wouldn't be needed, as Lady Len closely guards that plant. There are no samples here in the laboratory. Anyway, it must be freshly crushed."

"I will ask His Lordship's permission," Raya said.

Raya went to the palace to seek Lord Thian, and Deena continued working with the materials available in the laboratory. Half of the work was mechanical—separating seeds from pods or grinding barks until they were a smooth paste.

Pari helped her crush leaves and juice petals, even though those were not tasks anyone expected her to do, and she stayed on for a few hours even after her replacement arrived that day, returning to her quarters only when it was time for lunch.

By sundown, Deena had prepared over twenty vials with the available ingredients and had set everything in the cool box in the storage room next to the laboratory.

She yawned and stretched.

"It must have been a long day for you," Lord Thian said from the door, and extended a small casket. "Here is what you asked for."

Deena received the casket, her hands shivering slightly as she opened the lid. These were the roots she had been desperate for to treat her young patient who suffered from seizures. All that time, it had been so easy for some people to obtain it.

"What is wrong?" Lord Thian asked. "Is it not fresh enough?"

"It is, my lord," Deena replied. "I am surprised you managed to convince her."

She clamped her mouth shut as soon as she'd said it.

"I will convince her later."

"Yes, my lord." Deena fiddled with the casket and spoke quickly to hide her embarrassment. "It was the unavailability of this root that made me get into your greenhouse. A patient of mine needed it with some urgency, but I had not intended to steal it, only to find if the rumor was true and it was available here."

"You only had to apply for its usage through the proper channel."

"No channel of mine led to this palace. Even the head of your healers' guild failed to help me."

What the head of the healers' guild had said was that Lady Len had denied successfully cultivating the eela plant.

"And you thought by exposing its availability in our greenhouse, you could twist my mother's arm to get the root."

"Not anything so uncivilized, my lord, but yes, I was desperate to save a life."

Lord Thian seemed lost in thought for a moment.

"Prepare the medicine for your patient and give me their address. I will see that it is delivered. Ask for more root if you need it."

"You would do that?"

Lord Thian's eyes softened. "It is the bare minimum I could do for my citizens."

"And what of citizens of other seiflands who also need these herbs?"

He sighed heavily. "It is not a simple issue. The toxicity of ingredients like heliatin and eela stipulate a check on their supply. You of all people should know that. Proper regulations must be in place before we decide about freer distribution."

"There. You have successfully silenced me."

"That is an impressive achievement indeed." His face lit up with a smile she had not witnessed before.

Deena wetted her lips before continuing. "Sometimes I wonder if this is a fool's pursuit. We will always miss a key ingredient for this antidote—the senria of the person who made the poison. Pari's senria had little effect, and I presume the same could be said of any other sentar warrior."

"Is that so? You mean the senria of the person who made the poison would be most effective in the antidote?"

She nodded. "Without doubt. But what a predicament! We can't find the poisoner if Jianther is not cured."

Lord Thian went into another of his deep thoughts. His face tautened and then relaxed, only for his eyes to crinkle up again.

She did not realize that she had been shamelessly studying his face until the green sparks from his eyes fell on hers. She swallowed and looked away.

"I will be back tomorrow," he said. "And I might be able to bring something useful to you."

12

Horace recognized the difficulty of the task, but that did not reduce its necessity. He had to reveal Raya's role in the production of veritria to Deena. But she had no allegiance to Thian and could easily let the world know about Raya's action.

On the other hand, she already knew a lot about the scrolls and about the plants cultivated by his mother. If she was ever to leave her captivity, he would have to swear her to secrecy. And his instincts told him that if she gave him such a promise, he would believe her. In that case, he might as well not hide Raya's action. The priority was to save Jianther and find the real intruder.

With that conviction, he set out to find his mother first thing in the morning, instructing Seagal to cancel his breakfast. He couldn't eat without settling this matter.

At this hour, he would normally expect to find her on one of the balconies, tending to her plants, but Seagal had informed him that she had not yet left her chambers. That did not bode well. For one, something was troubling her or she would never stay cooped up indoors. For another, when she was among her plants, she was more amenable. And her amenability was a crucial requirement if he was to convince her to let him reveal Raya's action to Deena.

He let himself into her suite of rooms, as no maids were in sight. The sitting lounge was empty. An untouched tray of bread and fruits lay on the high table in the center of the room, along with a closed jug of maraya juice. She hadn't even eaten her breakfast. Apart from the food tray, the fresh flowers in the enormous vase by the window and the drawn red velvet curtains indicated that the maids had been in and out of the room, but at present, none of them were there. Was his mother still in bed?

She hadn't talked to him much since the day Cade woke up, but he'd thought that was because she had no argument left in her. He hadn't thought that she was indisposed, by any means. He knocked on her study door. There was no reply. That room, too, was empty. Her tomes and papers were meticulously arranged on the desk and the low shelf beside it, but the candle on the desk had burned out and had not yet been cleared. So, she had been at her desk during the night.

The door leading to her bedroom from the study was closed.

"Mother," he called.

There was no answer, just a rustle.

"Mother." He considered opening the door without her permission.

"What do you want?" came the disgruntled response.

"I want to speak to you."

"Come in."

Len sat at her dressing table in a pleated black skirt that engulfed the whole chair. Her hair was carefully put up in a bun and a rose adorned it, but her eyes, though expertly lined with kohl, proclaimed that she hadn't slept.

"What do you want?" she asked again in the same tone, without turning to him.

Her hand lay over a closed book bound with green leather. A quill stuck out of it.

"I wanted to consult about something."

"Or tell me what you have decided."

"Didn't you sleep well? And why is no one here to attend to you?"

"I sent them away. Stop questioning me and tell whatever you came in to tell." She looked at him through the mirror, keeping her stiff back to him.

"Can we move to the sitting lounge? Your food is getting cold."

"Then go and eat it, considering you skipped your breakfast."

"How do you know that?"

"Am I not your mother?" She finally turned to him.

"Then let us both have food. Please come with me."

She sighed and followed him, still carrying her book. Pausing in her study, she placed it on her desk and continued to the sitting lounge.

Horace picked up a plate of fruits and cheese-filled bread before sitting down to make the conversation as casual as possible.

Len, however, did not touch the food and waited for him to speak.

"Mother, the antidotes cannot be complete without a key ingredient."

"You mean the eela root you took without my permission didn't work?"

He knew he would have to pay for that. "I meant to tell you about that but didn't want to trouble you before its result was known."

"I see."

She saw right through him.

"All right," he said. "I wanted to avoid a confrontation."

"Yet here you are, poised to tell me something else that you think will displease me."

"It is Raya," he blurted out. "We need to use her senria for any antidote to work against the veritria she made."

Her eyes hardened before she wearily sat on the chair farthest from him.

"Is that what your healer claims?"

"Yes, although she doesn't know it is Raya."

"And you are going to tell her?"

"If only you allow, Mother, but think of what is at stake. I won't let on anything about Raya's parentage, only that she experimented with the recipe in the scroll and ended up with veritria."

"And you don't think the healer will use that information against us?"

"She is in our custody now, but I believe even if she is freed, we can be assured of her discretion."

"So you trust her that much, do you?" She tilted her head and eyed him in a way that made him feel she saw right through him. As far as he knew, she did. That was why every time she doubted him, he doubted himself.

"She has aided in Cade's revival and is dedicated to the patients she serves." He knew it wasn't a direct reply, but there was no logic to him trusting Deena, and there was nothing he could say to convince his mother to do so, except impress on her the necessity of the action. "It is a gamble I am ready to take."

She did not break eye contact, but her voice was strained when she spoke. "It is not as if you consult me before your every decision."

"But Raya is your ward."

"She is your family." Len got back to her feet with a restless shake of her head. Then, with an enormous sigh, she said, "Make the decision on your own and be responsible for its consequences. Don't disturb me with it again."

She returned to her study without another word, closing the door and bolting it from inside. A clear signal for him to leave.

When Horace arrived at the healers' residence, Raya and Deena had already started working in the laboratory, with Pari, of all people, cleaning after them.

The most capable sentar warrior in his seifland was brushing up littered leaves and twigs from under the table, laughing at something Deena had said. It was evident that Deena had her complete trust.

Raya was scraping a vibrant green paste from the mortar, the crushing of which must account for the smell of mint permeating the room.

He cleared his throat, and the three of them turned toward him.

Pari clumsily put the broom away and shrugged. "I can't stand the untidiness."

"If only all swords could be replaced by brooms," Deena said, returning to her work.

Raya sniggered.

"You lot look more cheerful than ever. Has there been a breakthrough?"

"Not really," Deena said, tightening the cap on a small bottle. "But we are very hopeful. There was a marginal dilution of the poison in one of the samples after we used a mixture of eela root and mehua bark."

"That is indeed hopeful. I wish to have a word with Deena alone. Raya, if you could wait outside with Pari, I'd be grateful," Horace said. "It will only take a few minutes."

Pari reverted to being the cool, collected soldier and led Raya out of the room, closing the door after her.

Deena looked at him with wide, apprehensive eyes, the brown in them deepening to a darker shade.

"It is nothing to worry about," he said immediately. If anything, it was he who must be fearful of revealing this vital information, but he quelled the uneasiness that crept up his throat and sat on the bench opposite her that Raya had vacated. "I want to share something with you, something you must promise not to reveal to anyone else. No one."

"Oh."

He had her full attention.

"Do I have your word?"

"Yes, my lord."

"The veritria—it was brewed on our premises by one of our own—Raya. She was experimenting with a recipe in the scrolls without completely understanding the implications. I touched a bit of it too." He raised a finger, the tip of which looked seared.

Deena was not sure for how long she remained silent. Time made no sense any longer. So the veritria had been cooked up by someone in Lord Thian's family, using the scrolls owned by his mother, and yet she and Kran were being held for the attack on Jianther.

"Deena?"

The softness in his voice did not melt her heart. "You are telling me you have known this all along?"

"She confessed straightaway."

"And what is her punishment, my lord?" Deena curled up her toes under the table in an attempt to maintain a steady voice.

"Punishment?"

"Are you letting her go free because she is one of you? Of noble birth? Kran is being held captive for a much lesser sin." Her voice rose despite her resolution.

The friendliness disappeared from Lord Thian's face, and she felt a sense of loss. No, he had never been her friend. He was the lord of the seifland who would hide and protect his noble family members and not afford the same courtesy to ordinary mortals.

"I would hardly say that is captivity." He looked around them. "He is lodged in the palace, even though he broke into our premises twice and attacked our soldiers. Maybe not Cade and Jianther, but he attacked others, and being a soldier of Alayster, he should have known the consequences."

The logic of his argument did not take away from the fact that he had let Raya go unpunished. And if he hadn't hidden the fact that Raya was the poison maker, their quest for the antidote would have had much more success. He watched her sullen silence for a while before releasing a heavy breath.

"Look, I did not come here to argue. Yesterday you said the antidote needs the senria of the one who made the poison. I am giving that to you."

Although she felt the need to reiterate the unfairness of the situation, she couldn't deny the value of the information he was providing her with.

She said in a carefully controlled tone, "Does Raya know you are revealing this to me now?"

The girl had given no sign, either of guilt or apprehension, when she had been working alongside Deena earlier. Although, now that she thought about it, Raya had been distressed to witness Jianther's condition, and her assistance in the laboratory had been stoically and earnestly rendered.

"No, I did not tell her. She made a mistake and can't refuse to rectify it. I will inform her now. All I ask of you is to keep this information to yourself. To everyone else, she will just be assisting you as usual—even Pari or Noaran cannot know the truth. Can I trust you with that?"

"I already gave my word." He couldn't expect her to be gracious now, yet she might as well express her gratitude. She was very much still dependent on his goodwill, not just to prove her innocence, but also to help her young patient in the city. "I'll be glad to have such a straightforward solution to our key problem."

His lips clenched, showing he recognized the ungraciousness in her gratitude.

Lord Thian left the room to talk to Raya, and Pari returned. She did not ask Deena anything, although curiosity was writ on her face. It was a good time as any to give her the half-explanation that would make it easier to use Raya's senria.

"Lord Thian suggested I use Raya's senria in the antidotes, as he is hoping to train her as a healer."

"The poor girl is burdened with too much expectation," Pari commented in a low voice.

"How is Raya related to Lord Thian?" Deena knew she wasn't his sister, as she had addressed his mother as "Mother Len" rather than "Mother."

"She is not related to Lord Thian," Pari answered quietly, keeping her eyes on the grounds. Lord Thian frequently waved his hand at the laboratory, and Raya sent nervous glances in their direction. "I believe the family has fostered her since she was a newborn."

"Ah!" Much like Kran's family fostered her, although she had detected no sibling bond between Lord Thian and Raya.

"But she is treated like royalty by Mother Len," Pari said. "Raya is coming."

Deena focused back on the task at hand. She had been mixing powdered eela root with secanut oil to prepare the concoction that Lord Thian had promised to deliver to her little patient. She would keep it ready, although it wouldn't be surprising if he had forgotten all about it.

Sure enough, he left without mentioning anything about that. Raya sat opposite her, absentmindedly sweeping the dried leaves on the table with her finger. Her lips shivered, and she bit them. For some inexplicable reason, Deena felt sorry for the ward of Mother Len.

"We will start instilling the antidotes with your senria in the evening, once the current batch has amalgamated," Deena said.

Raya gave a grateful nod, her eyes shining, and she continued brushing the leaves off the table into a dustpan.

"Oh no, I forgot something." Raya raised her head. "Lord Thian said that you must hand over the medicine you have prepared for your patient and their address to Pari, and when her shift ends, she will arrange for it to be delivered." She turned to Pari.

"I will do that," Pari said.

"Thank you." Deena couldn't help but smile. Lord Thian had not forgotten after all.

13

Once Pari's shift ended, Deena could not stop herself from asking Raya the question that had been troubling her. "It is not my place to ask this, but why did you do it?"

Raya licked her lips. "I was . . . I was trying to prove something . . . to myself. That I am not completely useless."

"No one is completely useless," Deena protested, despite her resolution to direct some of her rightful anger at Raya.

"I sometimes feel I am. Mother Len showers me with so much praise that I do not deserve."

Deena couldn't imagine what that was like. Kran's mother loved her like her own, yet never failed to admonish her when the need arose. Different people had different ways of showing their love.

"It might be because she loves you a lot," Deena said, although she had no wish to defend Lady Len.

Raya looked at her knee as she spoke, her beautiful curls falling on her cheeks and hiding her flush. "If only Jianther is saved, I will never complain about anything again. It seems so stupid that I would even complain after everything Mother Len and Lord Thian have given me."

Deena did not reveal that she was thinking along the same lines. It was not stupid, but it seemed rather ungrateful. Not many orphan children would get the privilege to be fostered by the lord of the seifland and be showered with praises by the lady of the land. Even Deena had been extremely lucky to have been fostered by her aunt and uncle, and to gain a brother in Kran.

"My hopes for Jianther have increased with the use of your senria." The girl seemed in need of encouragement, which Deena could freely give.

Raya returned a grateful smile through teary eyes.

Over the next two days, the antidotes they had prepared had varying effects on Jianther's blood sample. The combination of eela roots and mehua bark with Raya's senria instilled in it was their best find. Even though the poison was not entirely neutralized, its intensity was reduced.

"For the time being, let us pretend we have succeeded in finding an antidote," Noaran said at the end of another grueling session of calculations.

Deena had also arrived at the same decision, and the next step would be to test the antidote for any potential dangers.

"We will have to test it for any harmful reactions," Deena said.

"Naturally," Noaran agreed. He left to tend to Cade, who was being prepared to be shifted out to a larger healers' establishment in the city.

By the next morning, Deena had successfully completed most of the tests she could do in the laboratory. The only thing remaining was to test it on a living creature.

"We will need a mouse to do the next part of the test." Deena turned to Raya, who had been silent since the previous evening.

Raya swallowed. "Do we have to do that?"

"It is only a mouse," Pari said. "I can get one for you."

"It is the only way to know for sure." Deena observed Raya's disturbed face. She hadn't known the girl had a love for mice. "Although I have eliminated the presence of most toxins," she reassured her. "The chances of the creature being harmed are extremely low."

"I mean, we needn't experiment on anything else. I can vouch for its safety."

"How?"

"I administered some of it yesterday to myself."

"What?" Pari exclaimed, while Deena fought to produce any sound.

When the sound came out, it was garbled. "How stupid! What?"

"I had to do it. It was the only way . . ."

Deena understood what was left unsaid. It was not the only way to test the antidote, but it was the only way Raya could make amends for harming Jianther.

It was too late to scold the girl, or to impress upon her that one thoughtless act could not be rectified by another.

"Are you feeling well?" Deena asked. "Was there any pain or nausea after you took it?"

Raya shook her head.

Behind her, Pari rolled her eyes and shook her head in an exasperated manner.

"I must warn you, Raya, there could be long-term side effects. For Jianther, I was not planning to consider them, as we have little time to save him. But for you, to put your health at risk in such a way . . ." Deena sighed. "We must inform Lord Thian, and the antidote can now be given to Jianther."

That evening, in Lord Thian's presence, the antidote was administered to Jianther. It was the first time Deena had seen Lord Thian after their row about Raya. He did not talk to her in the infirmary, but that could be because the atmosphere of the room demanded silence.

There were no curtains to screen Jianther's bed now, although all attempts had been made to lower the temperature of the room. Noaran had ensured that Jianther was housed in the part of the infirmary that had the most shade, and he had also covered the roof and the floor with amaran leaves that helped in cooling the room.

His body had long since cooled down, but amaran leaves were also being used to render comfort to his parched skin. Even though he was in a coma, the infusion of aziril kept his vitals going. That and the fact that he hadn't come across a large quantity of the poison.

"I will sit by him overnight to see if there is any change in his condition," Noaran said after administering the antidote. "I am feeling hopeful."

The solemn group nodded and exited the room.

"May I talk to you, my lord?" Deena quickly asked before Lord Thian could get away.

"Is it to shout at me?"

Raya let out a short giggle before stifling it.

"I would never dare shout at you," Deena said.

"I could count the number of times you have done it."

"Let's go back to the laboratory while they decide whether or not to shout at each other." Pari led Raya from the porch.

"What is it you wanted to speak to me about?"

"Is the burn on your finger troubling you?"

"Not as much as other things," he said sardonically before his voice turned earnest. "Not much. It is a minor irritation."

"Nevertheless, if the antidote works on Jianther, I will give it to you too."

He nodded.

Deena looked around them to ensure they were alone. No soldiers were present to guard any part of the healers' residence as they had done in the initial days she had been there. She hadn't noticed when they had stopped the regular guards. Pari and her replacements had continued as before.

"Raya has been really helpful, even at great personal risk to herself."

"I heard something about that." His voice hardened disapprovingly.

"I don't condone that action, but now I can see why you didn't punish her."

"And why is that?"

"Because she is punishing herself with her guilt that is burning her from the inside."

"You are wrong. I did not punish her because the intention to harm was not there when Raya made that poison. Punishment must be in proportion to the crime, and hers is to atone for her carelessness."

"Is this a principle you apply equally to everyone?"

"I may occasionally slip up. As in this instance when I took your intrusion into the greenhouse too lightly and gave you a lot of freedom. So much so that even my mother is refusing to talk to me these days."

"I am not complaining about myself, but Kran had no intention of harming at all. He does not deserve to be locked up."

"Doesn't he? He is securely lodged in a room in the palace, not in the dungeon, which is where anyone who attacked my soldiers would have been sent to."

"Can I see him?"

"No."

She had not hoped for a positive reply, but the abrupt answer unsettled her.

"And one more thing. Lord Alayster wrote to say that he was sending an envoy to argue your and Kran's case."

"But you are determined not to be swayed by any such envoy."

"I will extend all courtesy to Lord Alayster's envoy, but as you well know, I am not easily swayed."

"I will be on my way, my lord." She made it to the steps leading off the porch.

"I thought you wanted to know how your patient was doing."

"Oh yes, I do." She stopped. Pari had informed her that the concoction had been delivered to the child's family and another healer assigned to tend to him. He was no longer her patient, as she wouldn't be able to see him or assess his condition.

"Farhaz wrote to me. He is a member of my council, but I am sure you know him—the leader of the healers' guild."

"Yes, I had applied for his help when things became hopeless."

"The child, whose condition is rapidly improving, was assigned to him. He is coming tomorrow to thank my mother for sharing the herb, but I assume he wants to negotiate for more such sharing."

"Is that not a good thing?"

"Only if the healers handling these herbs know the risks of using them."

"Then isn't it better to ensure that such healers have the requisite knowledge to handle those plants than to prevent any healer from having them?"

"Isn't that what we do? That is why heliatin, with its paralysis-inducing thorns, is distributed only through healers in its consumable form. The reason is not widely known because we do not want anyone to use heliatin thorns as a weapon, like the flechas do. The only reason you had trouble finding it in Alayster was due to the trade restriction. The moment we realized that was the case, you were allowed to set up your practice here.

"As for the root of eela, procuring it isn't that easy, and even in this garden, it is scarce. Distribution has to be based on priority."

He paused to take a breath, but his eyes never left her.

"I don't deny anything you said, my lord, but only want to add that if there was someone the healers could approach for such priority cases, the herbs will reach the patients."

"And you don't think my mother is that someone?"

"I am already a prisoner here, and I don't want to worsen my situation."

"Never took you as one to mince words."

"I am sure you would know what is best to do, my lord. I only wanted to present the case in front of someone who could act, and it seems my intrusion into the greenhouse served its purpose."

"That is not the lesson from this, but as I promised, when this is resolved, we can discuss more about the just distribution of herbs."

With those words, he walked away.

When she returned to the laboratory, Pari and Raya seemed to be waiting expectantly.

"How did it go?" Raya asked.

"How did what go?"

"We didn't hear any shouting," Pari said, "and you are smiling so wide as if the antidote worked and Jianther is on his feet."

Deena touched her cheek. She hadn't realized she was smiling, but Lord Thian's final words had made her feel lighter inside. He wanted to discuss the future of the herb distribution with her. The lord of a seifland had taken her words seriously and promised to act on it. Yes, she was happy, but not as happy as she would be if Jianther would get up from his bed or if Kran was freed.

"The child for whom we sent the medicine is improving." That was another news that had made her happy. "If only I could get Kran out of prison. I am the only reason he broke the law."

"I don't see a chance of that happening." Pari's words were as firm as Lord Thian's. To both of them, he was just an intruder who attacked their soldiers.

"I understand he is your brother?" Raya was more sympathetic even though she was one of the soldiers Kran had attacked.

"Yes, much like Lord Thian is for you. I was raised by his family."

"Lord Thian is kind to me, but . . ."—Raya looked confused, as if wondering whether she should complete the sentence—"but he never talks to me. I think a brother would, wouldn't he?"

"Yes, he would," Deena said. "He would also irritate you and prank you and make you cry."

"Sisters, too, do that," Pari chimed in. "I have one."

"But they would also stand between you and all the dangers of the world," Deena said.

Raya sighed. "I would love to have a brother or sister."

As far as Deena knew, Lady Len had two daughters, but maybe they no longer lived in the palace, or they were not close to Raya. It was not her place to pry, but Raya's face made it clear that being fostered in the palace of the seif lord was no guarantee of happiness.

14

Horace decided to be present when Farhaz met his mother, and so the meeting was to be in his library. Something told him that a moderator might be necessary when the leader of the healers' guild talked to Lady Len, even though the stated purpose of the visit was to express gratitude. If Garim were present, Horace would have gladly handed over the role of the moderator to him, but he was not expected back from Rothshire yet.

A few moments ago, a messenger had brought a letter from Rothshire, which lay on the desk beside him, waiting to be opened. He needed to clear his head before reading about the water-sharing treaty, which he hoped could soon be signed. It was time he received some good news, and the scorching heat outside, even when dusk was fast approaching, was a reminder about the importance of that treaty to his farmers in the plain land.

He also had to visit the healers' residence. Word had reached him that there was no improvement in Jianther's condition overnight, but Noaran reported he'd heard something like a grunt, although he couldn't confirm it. Noaran must have imagined it. The intense wish to see Jianther awaken was not limited to Noaran. By this time, it appeared they were chasing a rainbow that moved further and further away. He must keep their morale up as long as they kept trying. But first, he had to deal with his mother and Farhaz.

They arrived at the same moment, ensuring that he did not have to talk to either of them alone. Once again, his mother had shut him out for four days, evidently staying in her room the entire time. To prepare for her visit, he had ordered all the windows of the library to be opened so that fresh air and sounds from the garden could waft in. The golden hue of the sky, the rhythmic digging of the gardeners' shovels, the sprinkling of water, and the smell of freshly turned earth might tempt her to get out of her room more often.

"Lady Len," Farhaz greeted her with a bow, his orange turban going slightly askew over his forehead. "I am here to deliver a message from the family of the child you helped."

"Child?" His mother did not exhibit the full extent of her puzzlement.

He had not informed her about Deena preparing the medicine with eela root for someone outside the palace walls.

"Yes, my lady. He was suffering from seizures, but the mixture that came from the palace worked its magic. He had an episode last night, but he recovered from it before it worsened. The parents wanted to inform you they were forever indebted to you."

His mother turned to Horace but only gave him a knowing look before speaking to Farhaz. "As I have always maintained, my son is a just lord of the land. And will this child need more medication?"

"Not for now. The given supply will suffice. The parents were miserable and desperate for help after his old healer left with no notice. She was the one who came from Alayster."

"She did not leave," his mother said. "She is working for Horace now, and she is the one who prepared the medicine."

Horace did a double take. Lady Len was crediting Deena with preparing the medicine, even though it was done without her permission.

"Any credit for its success," she continued, "and any responsibility for endangering the child's life belongs entirely to her."

That made more sense.

"Ah!" Farhaz exclaimed. "So, she succeeded in gaining your permission. She had come to me for that, but I was, as you know, helpless. I hope we can expect more such graciousness from you in the future, my lady."

His mother's smile took on a dangerous quality, and Horace decided it was time that he separated them, but the leader of the healers' guild didn't seem to have noticed the wintry smile and continued talking.

"The connection between the healers' guild and the palace must be strengthened in the light of the current events."

"What events?" his mother asked before Horace could put forth the same question in a more controlled manner. "It was just an act of burglary of my personal possessions."

Farhaz straightened his turban and blinked. "The burglary? No, that is not what I meant. The incident in Rothshire. Didn't you hear about it? Both sons of Lord Rothshire were found dead in their beds."

Horace swiped up the letter and broke the seal. He hadn't noticed that it was the seal of the seifland of Rothshire, with the shape of a mountain embossed on it and not his own. The hand was also not Garim's, and the signature at the end belonged to Lord Rothshire.

For the eyes of Lord Thian,

Today I send you no good wishes, for I have none left with me. My sons died what could only have been gruesome deaths, as evidenced by the piteous condition of their bodies. Their skin burned from the inside out, and the absence of any fire points to the use of some unknown poison.

As it happens, your envoy was in our palace at that time, and considering our long history of feuds since the time of your father, I am arresting him. The only way you can free him is to declare war against us.

When I find even a shred of evidence that Thian, the land of secret herbs and poisons, had anything to do with the deaths of my sons, you can expect that war to reach your doorstep.

Signed and sealed,

The lord of Rothshire

"Yes, Farhaz, you are correct." Horace tried to fold the letter, abysmally failing in this simple task, as his fingers did not obey his command. The tip of his finger that had touched the trace of veritria stung. He had been ignoring the pain until now. "The coming days will be challenging." He had to pause to let the dryness in his mouth pass. "If that is all, we will have to meet another time. The news from Rothshire is serious and needs my full attention."

"I understand, my lord. Was there a mention of a poison?" Farhaz looked shrewdly from Horace to Lady Len. "That was what the traveling tradesmen said."

His mother's face took on a strained expression. It was nothing to what she would feel when she learned the contents of the letter. The poison was clearly veritria, and its source was Raya. It would be too coincidental to have the same poison pop up in the neighboring seifland within a couple of weeks of its disappearance from Thian. Worse of all, he had requested Farhaz to ask around about veritria. His mother's reprimand rang in his ears.

"No particulars," Horace answered.

Farhaz seemed to expect more, but he would have to depend on the word of mouth that would trickle in from Rothshire, if it already hadn't.

"I will take my leave, then, my lord." He bowed and left the room.

Before the door was properly closed behind him, Lady Len clutched Horace's hand with a cold palm. "What is it? Tell me it wasn't veritria."

"It is as you fear." He handed her the letter.

"No, it can't be." Her hands shook. "What will happen now? And you already told the healer about Raya's role in all this."

"I have her word. I trust her."

"Why?" Her voice was pleading for a change, sounding as though she needed a reason to trust Deena too. But he had none to give her. Even if he had, his mind had hit a total blank.

"I don't know. Mother, I must ask you also to leave now. I need to think about the next action."

Horace went to his desk, not checking if his mother had left the room. He wished he had reassured her more, comforted her, and encouraged her to get out of her room, but he didn't have any words of comfort or encouragement to offer. The swish of her skirt announced her departure, and he was filled with a humming in his head and the monotonous digging from the grounds below.

So, whoever had stolen the veritria had acted, and the news had reached him even before any message came from his emissaries. There was only one explanation. The messengers were stopped at the border and may also have been arrested. He had been a fool to dismantle the network of spies set up by his father. At least that was what his mother would say, and there was truth in it. How could he have believed that he could fend off a war between the seiflands just by focusing on diplomacy?

The goal of the perpetrator could indeed be strife between Thian and Rothshire. Or were they trying to take control of the seifland of Rothshire? If so, Lord Rothshire's life was in danger, and the person who would benefit the most by his death was the one who was first in line to inherit—his oldest nephew, Tandon.

Pari's suspicions were not out of place. He would have to go after Tandon if he was to find the truth, and that would be no easy task, as Tandon was a valiant warrior in King Monrae's army. Any action against Tandon would alienate Monrae and his army.

He didn't know for quite how long he sat in the library, looking around at the ornate shelves, hoping that a solution would jump out of the leather-bound books and yellowing pages. The sun had set outside, and the sound of the gardeners had moved further away.

His inertia was quite unfitting for the lord of a seifland who was facing the possibility of war. He would need all the support he could garner.

Malion would stand by him and support him from the east, but Alayster was recovering from a decade's worth of financial setback, and their army had undergone some depletion. If Rothshire had Athora's help, Thian's chances would be severely compromised. Attack could come not just from the porous border with Rothshire but also from Easther, which was under King Monrae's control.

He felt an urgent need to talk to someone about the use of veritria. Deena. Yes, he wanted to talk to her.

So to the healers' residence he went. The gardeners had moved to this location, drawing water from the well outside the gate and watering the dry ground, eliciting the calming scent of petrichor.

Nothing much had changed in the infirmary. Jianther's state was the same as the previous day, although Deena had administered another dose of the same antidote to him.

"I don't want to increase the concentration of the ingredients," she explained when he visited her in the laboratory.

The worktable was still cluttered with leaves, roots, barks, dishes, and tubes that were remnants of her experiments. The guard Bentir paced by the unlit furnace. He didn't seem to be interested or involved in the proceedings as Pari had been.

"Why is that?" Horace asked distractedly.

"It might affect the toxicity of the antidote. So, another dose seemed logical."

Most words slipped through the thoughts that were fighting for his attention. Deena gazed up at him with concern in her eyes.

"Is anything the matter, my lord?"

Raya looked up from the workbench.

"Nothing," he said abruptly, fixing his eyes on Deena. "Can I talk to you outside?" Then he turned to Raya. "It is nothing to worry you, Raya. I want to discuss something about Kran."

Raya nodded and returned to the parchments she was studying.

Horace stepped outside under the darkening sky.

"What is it? What is wrong with Kran?"

"Nothing. It was just an excuse to get you away from Raya's hearing. Veritria has surfaced in another land," he said grimly. "Heirs of Lord Rothshire were murdered using that poison."

Deena gasped and sent a frightened look to the laboratory where Raya sat. "What does that mean for us?"

Even in his foggy brain, he noted her use of the word "us." It was not her headache. It was his, and probably Raya's too, who would face severe repercussions if her role in it ever came out.

"Can I trust you to keep the secret?"

"Certainly, my lord. I don't want any harm to fall on Raya, and this, at least, was not her fault. Whoever stole the poison is responsible."

"But it will mean war for us... for Thian, I mean."

"That must be a heavy burden on your shoulders. Will catching the real culprit help now? Maybe you can present the truth to Lord Rothshire and avoid a war."

He smiled lightly. It was an ingenuous suggestion, even though Lord Rothshire would not believe anything he claimed. The innocent hope in her eyes, however, lightened some of the burden he was carrying.

Deena stumbled where she stood. "Fires of Kalantra. What is that? Do you feel it?"

Yes, he felt it too. The earth rumbled as though its core had shaken. He caught hold of her arm to steady her, struggling to maintain his balance as the ground moved beneath his feet. The rumbling stopped as soon as it had begun, but it was only a moment's respite. The ground in front of the laboratory burst open in a flurry of stones and dirt, revealing two tall, furry brown creatures among the dust.

15

Horace encased Deena within a shimmering shield before manifesting a sword and a spear. The sentar shield, sword, and spear would have limited effect if these creatures unleashed their full power. The only way was to kill them before they had a chance to do it.

Hauries. Their thin, wiry human torsos were topped by comically disproportionate rat-like heads with wide gaping mouths and overlong teeth. The heads turned to him, and both gave identical sneers, their narrow lips curling up to expose jagged teeth.

He threw a spear at one of them. The haurie flicked it away with a spindly, hairy hand and rushed into the laboratory.

Raya's scream froze Horace's blood, but the hauries had not reached her. Bentir had thrown himself between her and the creatures. He had no sentar shield to protect him. A haurie's hand blazed with fire and extended like a vine—a vine made up of fire—and wound itself around his neck. He kicked his legs as the fiery limb raised him up to the ceiling.

Horace leaped over the awning gap on the ground left behind by the hauries, but it was too late. The smell of burned flesh and the limp body of Bentir on the floor welcomed him in the laboratory.

With a yell of fury, he barged into the haurie. This time, he did not miss. He thrust the sword into the haurie's chest and turned the blade with a crunch. The creature let out a strangled cry and fell on top of the lifeless soldier.

Horace manifested another sword and a whip and turned toward the remaining haurie that was bent over the worktable. Raya cowered on the other side of the table, her shivering hand clutching an iron tool used to squeeze seeds.

"Come," the haurie said hoarsely to her.

Horace lashed his whip around the haurie's neck and pulled it back, toppling the low shelves in its path. Glass bottles and vials crashed to the ground, spraying liquids everywhere.

"Get out," he yelled at Raya. "Get help."

She scrambled to the door. The haurie's hand clasped her skirt, preventing her from escaping. The hand was not fiery, but the haurie's neck had turned into a bright scarlet cluster of flames. The fire cut through Horace's sentar whip, sending him reeling backward onto the broken shards of glass. This was what he was afraid of. Weapons, sentar or not, could hurt the hauries only as long as their bodies were made of flesh and bones.

Raya used the iron tool to repeatedly punch the furry hand that held her skirt until, with a squelching sound of crushed flesh, the hand let go of her. She ran to the door, and the haurie lunged after her. It was as if it wanted to capture her alive. If it wanted to kill, it would have used the power of fire like it had with Bentir. Whatever its intention, it had to be killed before it turned on its fiery limbs again.

Horace jumped on top of the bench and stepped on the table, scattering the leaves and pastes. Dishes used in the experiment clattered to the floor. With another leaping jump, he landed between Raya and the haurie, giving her time to get away.

The haurie evaded his slashing sword by getting onto all fours. His next strike landed on its shoulder to the left of the flames that still danced where its neck should have been. The cut drew blood, but not for long, as the fire spread from its neck to its shoulders and down its left arm. Its arm circled Horace's sword in several loops and reached his wrist, twisting around it and squeezing.

The scorching heat burned his hand, and a yelp escaped him. Horace stopped focusing his senria onto the sword. It fizzled out while another sword manifested in his left hand. He pommeled its hilt on the haurie's face, realizing too late that he should have used the blade to pierce it. With a squeal of pain, the haurie let go of his hand, but before he could slash its chest, the fire had spread to its torso.

This was not good. It not only left him with no space on the creature's body to attack, but also raised the possibility of the haurie exploding. That was what they were most feared for—heating up their bodies to make it into a dangerous incendiary device. But it was too late to stop it now.

The fire had spread to its other limbs, and now, instead of a furry creature, what stood in front of him was a blazing form that could have been molded in Kalantra's never-dying fire pit. Weapons were useless against it now, unless he could reach it close enough to pierce its face, which was still rat-like and not touched by fire.

The haurie stood between him and the door out of the laboratory, closing off his only route of escaping into the open as the room itself turned blisteringly hot. A fiery hand, tipped by a claw of four digits, extended toward him, aiming for his neck, condemning him to Bentir's fate. Horace leaped out of its way and crouched on the floor. It wouldn't be long before the creature lost control of its rising temperature and became a ball of fire.

Splash. Sizzle.

The haurie's beady black eyes widened with confusion.

Splash.

It was being showered with buckets of water. The limb that had been aiming for Horace stopped and retreated as it turned to whoever was attacking it from behind with its worst enemy—water. It advanced out of the door, leaving Horace to scramble to his feet. Squeals and screams erupted, but water splashed on it again.

The fire on its neck, torso, and legs was quenched until only a few embers burned in the region of its stomach, but its hands that escaped the water by splaying away from its body were still on fire and extended to whoever was attacking it.

"That is all the water we have, my lord." It was Deena's voice. "Do something."

Horace didn't have to be told twice. He dashed to the door and, with a pirouette, sliced through the neck of the haurie. Its head landed in the pit that it had dug in front of the laboratory.

Deena and two men stood on the veranda in different states of petrification. The men—the gardeners—gaped as though their jaws would never close again. Deena hugged herself to stop from shivering. But the empty pails by their feet made it clear that they had saved his life.

"Thank you," he told them. His eyes went to Deena and then to the shield she had left behind to get to him. He withdrew it.

Raya and a group of soldiers ran to the laboratory, Pari in front of them.

"Bentir," Horace told them, commanding his mind not to go blank from the pain of his scalded hand. "He didn't make it, but he fought bravely. Make sure it is widely known. He will be cremated with the highest honors in Thian. And there is a whole lot of mess to be cleaned up in there."

He turned reluctant eyes to the scene of destruction that looked like a tornado had swept through it. Broken glass and clay were interspersed with scattered powders and pastes. Among them lay the lifeless figures.

Pari and the soldiers stepped into the laboratory to do what was needed. Raya stayed outside, struggling to breathe, probably too traumatized to step in there ever again.

"Are you feeling all right?" he asked her. "Better go to Noaran and have him give you something to calm down. I am going to Mother to tell her about this."

A warm, soft hand clasped his left wrist. "No," Deena said sternly. "You are going to the infirmary and getting that hand dressed."

She pointed to the scalded skin on his right hand. "Don't make me drag you there."

A smile escaped him at the improbability of that, but he followed her and Raya to the infirmary. He did need something for the burn that had taken over the pain lingering in his finger from the veritria.

Noaran gave Raya a concoction made from eela flowers to calm her nerves and advised her to lie down for some time.

Deena took Horace to the room recently vacated by Cade. The smell of the poultices that were used to treat him still lingered in the room, but it was overwhelmed by the scent that wafted in from the laboratory of all the potions and elixirs that had evaporated in the heat.

"I will never look at rats the same way." Deena held his hand tenderly while applying a paste made of dried amaran leaves. "Are they related to the rodents? What were those?"

"Creatures of Thisaur. Hauries. Their intrusion into our continent has been rare, so we don't know the story behind their unfortunate head, other than they can speedily travel far and wide by burrowing underground."

Horace gazed at the head bent low over his hand, tendrils of hair that had escaped from their thick plait playing around her face. She looked up at him, and then her long lashes shadowed the soft contours of her cheeks.

"Thanks again," he breathed. "What you used was the only weapon that would have worked against them. I didn't even have the sense to think about that."

"You wouldn't have any water inside the laboratory, would you? You did all you could."

"It was not enough. I was not quick enough to save Bentir. Or to foresee any of this happening."

"How could you have foreseen that creatures from Thisaur, of all places, would pop up here?"

"Perhaps not. But I also didn't anticipate veritria being used in gruesome political murders."

"Your rush to find the real culprit was to prevent such an eventuality, was it not? Be kinder to yourself. You have been doing your best . . . my lord," she added as an afterthought.

He watched her dress his hand with a soft gauze. "You can do away with that."

"It is better to dress the wound," she said.

"I meant the address. It will please me if you call me Horace."

Her lips parted, and then she moistened them.

"Will that lighten the load you are carrying?"

"Maybe not. But knowing that I have more friends than enemies will give me strength to carry the burden."

She smiled, and truly enough, it was like a cool breeze caressing his soul, more relieving than the amaran paste.

"Horace," she said, as if testing its sound and feel on her tongue. "I suggest a full night's rest with the help of a sleeping draught."

"I need to be alert," he protested.

"Yes, you do, for which you need rest."

He couldn't deny the truth of her words. The drain on his energy meant if a couple of hauries erupted from the ground just now, he would end up fried.

"Send the draught to the palace," he said, and then added wryly. "You will have to restock the laboratory after the destruction it just saw."

And now he would have to recount the attack to his mother. A crippling exhaustion swamped him, and he pondered taking the draught and curling up in the infirmary bed, the pristine white sheets of which felt so cool and welcoming, but he called upon the reserves of his strength and got up.

"I must leave now."

"I hope tomorrow brings you hope."

Hope was one thing he did not dare to have. But he gave her a stiff smile, not wanting her to see his weakness.

The soldiers had moved the bodies from the laboratory, and the palace servants were sweeping the shards of glass from the floor. He noticed little else as he walked straight to his mother's wing. It was a useless journey, as Lady Len had posted guards outside her door with strict instructions not to disturb her. She might not even have heard about the attack. At least that would be one less worry for her that night.

Seagal had everything ready for him to change and collapse right into bed, even the sleeping draught sent over by Deena. And that was what he did.

Horace took most of the next day tightening up security around his palace. The appearance of hauries, even in the Western Frontier, had been erratic. An attack on a seifland was unheard of, and they had not wandered in aimlessly. Both the creatures had targeted Raya, and so he sent word to Pari to keep a special eye on her.

He couldn't ignore the fact that Raya was the child of a goddess. If creatures from Thisaur were targeting her, it could be because of her parentage. His mother had told him how Niferon enslaved the half-blood children of other gods and goddesses. What if it was Niferon who had sent the hauries? Horace would be completely out of his league if he was pitted against the god of war. The threat from Rothshire was child's play in comparison.

Yet, the impending war with Rothshire was the challenge he was preparing to face currently as he studied the map of his seifland spread on his desk in the library. Later in the evening, he would meet his commander-in-chief, but before that he wanted to strategize the movement of his army without depleting them in the city, as threats were coming even from underground.

"My lord." A soldier stood in the doorway. "You have guests."

"Who is it?" Horace did not take his eyes away from the map.

"They are envoys from Alayster, but one of them identified herself as Lady Kendrek."

"Lady Ilyria? Bring them to the assembly hall. Is Mother out of her room yet?" He had checked on her in the morning but was again refused entry.

"No, my lord."

He let the soldier leave and rolled up the map. The envoys from Alayster might have wasted a trip. He no longer considered Deena or Kran his prisoners. Deena's actions had remedied her crime of trespassing, and even if Jianther never woke up, he planned on absolving her.

As for Kran, along with writing to Malion, he had also written to Prince Coraen and to several commanders in the Western Frontier, inquiring about him without giving them any specific details. All the replies he'd received painted the picture of an upright soldier whom everyone trusted to have on their team.

He would just have to send the envoys on their way, probably with a message to Malion, requesting his help in the oncoming struggles that Thian would face. Lady Ilyria was a welcome visitor. He had fought alongside her and knew he could depend on her judgment and abilities.

The envoys of Alayster, however, were not who he had expected them to be. Gaelia and a young man accompanied Lady Ilyria into the hall.

"Gaelia? I wasn't expecting to see you here."

Gaelia curtsied, a bang of hair falling over her eye. She swept it back, looking much younger and carefree than when he had last seen her. Her sharp features relaxed into a smile. "Malion would have come himself, but he is currently hosting a trading group from Izakura. This is Byuton Tantas, counselor to Lord Alayster." She indicated the man who was standing on tiptoe behind her to get a better view of the paintings of erstwhile lords of Thian above the doorway.

Counselor? He seemed too young to fit that role, but Malion's judgment was never poor. Undoubtedly, the seifland of Alayster had been severely depleted in recent years because of the trade restrictions, and that seifland might not be able to afford advisors of Garim's caliber.

"Welcome, Byuton. Come, please find a seat." Horace also chose a chair attached to a marble pillar, not wanting to take his normal seat at the end of the hall, as these were not the kind of envoys he'd been expecting. "Mother Ilyria, it is a pleasure to see you again after the conflicts of the Western Frontier. To what do I owe this pleasure?"

Lady Ilyria gave him a gentle smile. The sunlight streaming in through the stained glass reflected off the golden strands on her red head. "I was on my way back to Kendrek from the Western Frontier and had a few days' stop at Alayster when I learned . . ." She looked to Gaelia as though searching for the right word.

"When we learned of the incidents here." Gaelia completed the sentence for her.

"Ah! That needn't be a concern any longer," Horace said. "Deena and Kran are free to leave. I have no evidence to link them to whatever happened."

Although he hoped Deena would choose to stay on.

For Jianther's sake, he told himself.

His guests looked at each other, and it was young Byuton who spoke with a tone of maturity that Horace hadn't been expecting, especially from a lad who looked lost in the massive chair he was sitting on. "My lord, we heard about the break-in to a shrine of Zesta. But did the culprits steal anything?"

"Yes, something belonging to my mother."

"Was it a scroll, perchance?" Byuton sat up straighter, as though the expression on Horace's face was answer enough.

"I am not free to tell you." Horace recognized his voice was stilted, but he had not been prepared for this direct questioning.

"This is of the utmost importance, my lord," Byuton asserted. "You needn't break any promises, but if the missing scroll belonged to the goddess Zesta, then we are all in big trouble."

And here he was, thinking that no one knew about the existence of the scrolls, let alone the fact that one of them was written by Zesta herself.

His face might have gone stiff, because Lady Ilyria's eyes crinkled up in response, and the pervasive calm left her face to be replaced with a troubled look. "Horace, we did not know the scroll was in your shrine, only that it would exist somewhere on the continent. And we know of someone who has been after it."

"Who is it?" Horace gripped the armrests of the chair.

Boots stamping in the corridor outside interrupted them. The soldier who had brought him the news about the guests appeared at the door again. "My lord, you are urgently needed at the healers' residence."

What now?

Horace blinked hard to dispel the haze in his head. He had a hundred questions bursting out of him, but he couldn't ignore the call from the healers' residence after what happened there the previous day. "Can you excuse me for a moment?" he asked the hall in general.

"Certainly," Lady Ilyria replied.

"Provide them with refreshments," he told the soldier before leaving his official quarters.

He jogged all the way to the healers' residence, expecting more hauries to have appeared from underground. That fear made little sense, as the increased patrol meant that alert would be sounded all around the palace. Yet his heart raced on, causing discomfort in his chest.

The sensation could also be due to the revelations made by his guests. Malion's counselor knew of Zesta's scroll, something Lady Len had hidden so close to her chest. Also, Lady Ilyria had been about to reveal the name of whoever was after the scroll. He needed to get back to them as soon as possible.

As he entered the gate to the healers' residence, Deena came running out, the wide smile on her face announcing that whatever waited for him was not bad.

She stopped short of crashing into him and panted. "He spoke. Jianther spoke."

16

Deena had wanted to be the one to break the news to him, and thus the message they had sent to the palace had been cryptic. But now she doubted whether she should have startled him so with the information. He looked stricken, and his face was drawn as though instead of a pleasant surprise, he had received a shock.

Now that she thought about it, he'd had that look about him even before she'd spoken. Maybe he did not comprehend what she'd said.

"I added a dose of thendril to the antidote we were giving him," she said more slowly. "It worked. Last night Noaran said he showed signs of returning to consciousness, but now he actually spoke. Won't you come and see him?"

"Of course." His brow cleared.

Yes, he was relieved to hear the news, and his steps gained pace as he proceeded to the infirmary. Raya and Pari waited outside Jianther's room, the door of which was fiercely guarded by Noaran. He wouldn't let anyone in before Lord Thian arrived. She didn't blame him, but she considered Jianther her patient now. She deserved to see him.

"He still needs some peace, my lord," Noaran said, "but he can talk."

Raya, Pari, and Deena sidled in behind Horace, ignoring the glances of rebuke that Noaran was shooting in their direction.

The curtains around Jianther's bed and those at the window were open this time around, and he lay with his head averted to the window and his eyes open. He turned to them upon realizing their presence, his eyes sunken from the vagaries his body had undergone. The dark-brown patches and crinkles on his exposed torso—the effects of the poison—was starkly visible in the sunlight.

"My lord." His sound was guttural.

"How are you feeling now, Jianther?"

"As if I don't have a body anymore. Am I even alive?"

"Yes, you are very much alive, although you have been through a lot."

"Are you experiencing any pain now?" Deena couldn't help but ask. Her priority was to know the welfare of her patient, even though Horace might be impatient to hear what he had to say about the night of the attack.

Jianther looked at her, screwing up his eyes as though trying to remember something. "Do I know you?"

"Do you?" Deena's heart thumped faster. What was she going to do if the soldier misidentified her as the intruder?

"No, but the way you asked made me think you knew me."

"Oh, I know you. Along with Noaran, I have been treating you."

Jianther grunted, and the puzzlement left his face.

"Do you remember who attacked you?" Raya asked, moving to the bed.

"How is Cade?" Jianther tried to sit up abruptly, as though some memory had flooded into his mind, but he groaned and flopped down on the bed before Horace could catch him.

"Stay put, Jian," Raya said. "Cade is recovering in an infirmary in the city, but we need to know who attacked you. You said something about it being a woman before you lost consciousness."

"Yes, the most enchanting woman I have ever seen." Jianther sighed.

Deena couldn't help but smile. That description would never fit her, and she required no more exoneration.

"Can you describe her more?" Pari asked.

"She had long black hair."

"Like this healer here?" Pari nuzzled Deena to the front again.

"Not really. She was taller than me, and her hair extended to her feet, yet it somehow stayed adrift over the ground, sometimes blowing into the door of light she came out of."

"Door of what?" Raya asked.

"Light. I hear it now. Is it possible I dreamed all of it?"

"Tell us further," Horace said. "Only if you can."

"I will try. Cade . . . he flew through the air . . . hit a tree. I thought he died. Then I saw this woman . . . standing in front of . . . I don't know . . . I thought of it as a door of light. She went to the shrine. I followed her in . . . hesitating for a moment . . . I am sorry I hesitated."

Raya squeezed his hand as he continued with similar broken sentences that grated out of his throat. "I had never felt such fear and thrill. She was as frightening as she was beautiful . . . I went to her with my sword. Next, I knew something was sprinkled on me, and then . . . then there was pain."

"Will you recognize her if you see her again?" Horace gave Deena an indecipherable look.

"Yes."

Leaving Jianther to Noaran's care, the rest of them exited the residence.

Deena's first task was to administer a small dose of the successful antidote to Horace. Although it didn't bother him much, Deena did not want any remnants of the poison in his body.

"The three of you might as well return to the palace," Horace said once the antidote was administered. "There is something I want you to hear."

"Including me?" Deena asked.

He stopped and affixed her with one of his pensive stares. "Especially you. I am obliged to you for saving Jianther's life and mine, and you more than anyone deserve to hear what I am about to learn."

The sudden giddiness she felt at his words did not account for the tears that welled up in her eyes. She looked away so that he wouldn't see how she was making a fool out of herself.

"And I will make arrangements to release Kran," he added softly before turning away.

She clutched her skirt to prevent herself from breaking into sobs of relief. Pari laid a hand at her waist and led her on. It was too late for expressions of gratitude, as Horace was hurrying toward the palace, but she hoped he had read the relief and gratitude on her face.

In the palace, Horace took them through the court of justice to the massive assembly hall. She hadn't taken in its grandeur during her previous visit, considering her state of mind back then. The white marble pillars, the stained-glass windows, and the paintings of noblemen and women that covered the walls at both ends would need hours to be properly appreciated. She could barely scan the hall before she spotted a familiar face—Gaelia.

She came forth, her floral dress swishing around her ankles. "Deena, I didn't expect to see you so soon."

Deena took her offered hands. She didn't know whether Gaelia did it consciously, but a wave of refreshing energy hit Deena.

Deena looked at her questioningly.

"You looked tired," Gaelia said.

"But don't give away your energy so freely."

"I have been practicing to nourish without depleting myself." She winked.

Horace introduced Pari and Raya to Gaelia and the others present. They seemed to know who Raya was, but Pari was introduced as the chief of security of Thian.

"This is Lady Ilyria of Kendrek and Byuton from Alayster," Horace said.

Byuton the mage?

"And they have something important to tell us."

After everyone found seats in the hall, Lord Thian did not waste time with any more introductions. He did not explain the presence of Lady Kendrek or the absence of Lady Len, but Deena presumed that Gaelia and Byuton were the envoys promised by Lord Alayster.

"Lady Ilyria had been about to reveal something important when I was called away to the healers' residence. I don't know if this is relevant to what you were going to say, but our soldier, who saw the intruder, has finally recovered enough to describe her to us. To quote him—she was the most enchanting woman he had ever seen, and she appeared from a door of light. Also, she could somehow send one of the soldiers flying into a tree."

Horace chewed his cheeks, probably wondering whether his guests would take his words seriously.

"I suspect the hand of mages," he said.

"That is a portal," Byuton said. "The door of light that your soldier saw. And mages cannot create portals."

"Are you sure?" Pari asked. "There is a lot we don't know about mages. Who knows what all they can achieve with their fell magic?"

"I can tell you with some authority, soldier, because I am a mage." Byuton jutted out his rounded chin.

It was evident that none of the Thian folks were aware of this. Horace opened his mouth to speak but closed it as if deciding to be careful with his words. Raya's eyes widened, and Pari's scrunched up. It might not have been prudent for Byuton to reveal that he was a mage without being sure whether a mage was welcome in Lord Thian's palace. Nevertheless, he continued to talk. He might not have yet reached the age where one thought before one spoke.

"I am aware that I might not be welcome here because of who I am, and I would have chosen to stay away if the matter at hand was not this critical. I was happy limiting my activities to Bewar and Alayster."

"I grew up quite near the Bewar forest," Pari said, "and have witnessed fell magic being used."

"Not all mages use fell magic. It is like saying all kranis are criminals."

"Kranis?" Raya whispered to Pari.

"Us. Non-mages," the latter replied through pursed lips.

"And Malion trusts a mage enough to . . . um . . . listen to his council?" Horace's raised brow indicated he did not consider it prudent.

"Yes." It was Gaelia who replied. "Byuton has time and again proven to us that our fear of mages is unfounded, and he has been a true friend to Malion and me."

"Yet there are the likes of Segura who serves King Monrae," Horace said.

Deena had never heard of a mage serving the king, who was well-known for his prejudices against the mages.

"Yes, my lord," Byuton said. "There are the likes of Segura who step into the forbidden realms of magic. He is under our scrutiny, but portals are beyond the reach of even the likes of him. It is not of our world."

"It is of this that we want to apprise you of, Horace," Lady Ilyria said. "The time for secrecy is over, as the threat is more imminent now, but I believe you trust everyone you brought into this meeting."

"I do." Horace did not hesitate to reply, and Deena felt a wave of gratitude wash over her.

Lady Ilyria left her seat and got to the center of the hall, walking a few paces up and down before speaking again. "Our continent is unknowingly hosting an enchantress from Thisaur—"

"Thili?" Horace asked.

"No. Everyone knows who she is. There is one more enchantress in our midst. Most of what I am going to say was told to me by Thili. Not just to me. Gaelia and Leonara also know about this, as well as Byuton. The name of the enchantress is Heera, but in our land, she is known as Mentra."

"Are you speaking of Queen Mentra? Prince Coraen's mother?" Horace leaned forward.

That was the second queen of King Monrae, but Deena had never heard of her described as an enchanting beauty. Wasn't that how the enchantresses of Thisaur were universally pictured? She had also heard of Thili from Kran, but even that enchantress did not fit the expectation. Kran had described her as an irritating little bird.

"The very same," Lady Ilyria said. "The description by your soldier of an enchanting beauty also points to her—although it must be her real form he saw and not the form we are used to.

"She is on a mission here, for which she has waited too long, and a crucial part of her plan is to steal the scrolls of the gods, which contain the key to their powers. We have to assume that she has at least two with her now—Varys's and Zesta's. That gives her immense powers when one considers how powerful she was to begin with."

Lady Ilyria paused, probably to give them time to digest the information. Deena needed that moment of silence. But what was she to make of Lady Kendrek's words? Gods? Enchantress on a mission? She couldn't grasp the meaning or import of what was being related.

"She was behind the attack of the syrelins both in Alayster and the Western Frontier," Lady Ilyria continued, "but those were child's play compared to what is coming. If all she plans comes to fruition, we will lose our continent as we know it. Thili warned us of this, but we were hoping Mentra would step back and not act. We were wrong. If she now has stolen the scroll of Zesta from you, it won't be long before she goes after the others or uses the scrolls for her selfish goals."

"Do you mean to say that the scrolls stolen from here belonged to the goddess herself?" Pari laughed at the absurdity of it, but one look at Horace made the laughter die.

Horace gave a solemn nod. Deena realized she was gaping at the revelation and closed her mouth. It had been bad enough when they had thought that someone had stolen dangerous medical knowledge, but the stakes seemed to be much higher than that. She looked at Pari and Raya to share her surprise. While the former gave her a look that screamed that the whole idea was preposterous, the latter was expressionless.

"Yes. Zesta entrusted it to my mother, as unlikely as it might sound," Horace said.

"Not so unlikely," Byuton said, "if her heir, for whom the scroll was intended, was also handed to Lady Len at the same moment."

Horace did not speak, but there was only one person who was handed over to Lady Len as a child. Deena sent a surreptitious glance toward Raya, and her doubts were confirmed by the girl's withdrawn expression and clenched lips.

"The identity of the heir is not important," Byuton continued, although Deena was sure most present in the hall had drawn their own conclusions, as they were pretending not to look at Raya.

"The attack by the hauries," Horace said. "Could that have been orchestrated by Mentra?"

"Hauries? Here?" Lady Ilyria asked.

Horace related the events of the previous evening.

"I had concluded that their target was . . . Raya," Horace said.

Deena had not realized that, but it was true that the hauries had gone straight for Raya instead of attacking Horace or herself, when they had been standing much closer to where those creatures had erupted from the ground.

The hall fell silent until Byuton cleared his throat. "It would seem the identity of the heir is important. I presume Raya is the intended heir."

"I am her daughter," Raya said softly, too softly.

"I guessed as much," Byuton said, as though he found nothing unusual in learning that the girl he'd just met was the child of a goddess.

A whispered conversation broke out between Gaelia and Lady Ilyria, and Pari turned in her chair to shamelessly stare at Raya.

What was it like to be the child of a goddess? Was that why Lady Len doled out special treatment to Raya? The girl would never know if she was loved for herself or because of her origin. No wonder she hadn't been happy about the attention showered on her.

"I wouldn't be surprised if Mentra is the one who sent hauries after her, though I can't fathom why," Byuton said.

"I almost thought all this was done to instigate a war between Rothshire and Thian," Horace said. "After what happened to the heirs of Rothshire."

"That could also be a part of her plan." Lady Ilyria retook her seat. "She wants to gain control over our seiflands, and one way to do it is through the threat of a major war. I am sure Rothshire, at least, would seek the help of Athora. She already has control over many valiant warriors in Athora's army."

"How coincidental," Pari said. "We were talking the other day about a valiant warrior who acted suspiciously."

"Val Tandon," Horace said. "We had even concluded he might be at the center of all this, and he is the new heir of Lord Rothshire."

"You are not wrong," Gaelia said. "Tandon is an integral part of her plan. He is her staunch supporter."

"She is an enchantress after all," Raya said.

That was what Deena was thinking. Besides their beauty, enchantresses were also known for seducing mortals to do their bidding.

"In this case, the enticement might be different," Lady Ilyria said. "As far as I know, Mentra practically brought up Tandon and his brother. It created a huge ruckus years ago when the queen took the boys away from the palace of Rothshire, but the word had been that they were being ill-treated there after the deaths of their parents. That kind of loyalty is stronger than seduction."

"Tandon is a bad apple nevertheless," Gaelia said.

"But we don't know whether he is involved in the burglary at your palace," Lady Ilyria said.

"The poison that killed the heirs of Rothshire is veritria." Horace's eyes flashed past Raya. "It was also present at the shrine when the scrolls were taken."

"Ah! So the two incidents are indeed connected," Lady Ilyria said. "Is there any way of knowing whether Tandon is in Rothshire?"

"I have not received any word from my envoys, which is suspicious," Horace said. "And my counselor has been placed under arrest in Rothshire."

"Garim is under arrest?" Pari asked.

"Unfortunately, yes. I curse myself for weakening our spy network."

"Our focus shouldn't be Rothshire now," Byuton said. "It should be Mentra's next probable target—the scroll of Edri—which would empower her with the abilities of the goddess of air and weather."

"Why did all these gods leave their scrolls lying around on our continent?" Deena spoke for the first time. It seemed to be a very foolish thing to do. Why couldn't they have kept it wherever they were residing in Thisaur? Then the threat of power-seeking enchantresses wouldn't loom over human land.

"It is not random," Byuton said. "The gods left their scrolls where their successors could eventually find them. Edri, for instance, is the child of a Thisaurian and a mage from our land. She ascended centuries ago, and if she ever has a child whom she wants to hand over the power to, she would leave that child with our community."

Even the gods do not want to let their powers shift away from their bloodline, Deena thought.

"Why do these gods need successors?" Gaelia asked. "I thought they were immortals."

"Do you think the Edri who sits on the throne in Thisaur now has been there from the beginning of time?" Byuton scoffed, but Gaelia did not seem to mind his tone.

"How would I know?" she said. "But you would, I am sure. So enlighten us."

Byuton cleared his throat. "I know you are being sarcastic."

"Not at all," Gaelia protested. "I hold you in very high esteem."

"Then get ready to be swamped by some information. The seven gods of Thisaur, whom we pay obeisance to, are powerful beings who can control different aspects of our world. For instance, Edri is the goddess of air and weather, revered by us mages because spells can work only with the aid of that element. But none of these gods are immortal or omniscient. That credit belongs only to the ancient god—the creator of our world, the one who gifted magic to humans and gods, the one who is present in each spark of senria, the one whom we have all forgotten.

"The origin of the gods of Thisaur has been lost to us, but since Greylan is cursed or blessed to be in close proximity to Thisaur, our connection to them is much deeper than the rest of the world. Most of the current gods are half-bloods who can claim their origin from this continent. When their time ends, they will have to leave this world like the rest of us, but for them, it might take a thousand years compared to the few decades we have."

"It is their scrolls that are being targeted," Pari said. "If you ask me, the gods must step up and stop Mentra."

"It is difficult to get word to them," Lady Ilyria said. "Only Thili can cross the lock to Thisaur, and she is not on good terms with the gods. The truth is, she and Mentra have been hiding in our land. Even when Thili crosses over to Thisaur, she stays hidden from them. I could almost feel sorry for Mentra, if she were not trying to use us as pawns in her game. You know who enchantresses are, don't you, and what they have to do?"

Deena had some idea. Myths were filled with stories of the king of gods using enchantresses to lure his enemies, although it was difficult to imagine any of his enemies being an actual threat. After all, Niferon was the god of warfare and was more than capable of making his enemies quiver with fear.

"They entertain in the court of Niferon, don't they?" Raya asked. "I have heard Thili sing. Her voice is otherworldly."

"That is one of their duties—to entertain." Lady Ilyria looked uncertain, probably wondering whether she had to elaborate that enchantresses were expected to be willing lovers to Niferon.

"Not just entertain," Byuton said. "If Niferon feels that someone is getting a tad too powerful, he will use the service of an enchantress to steal that power from his enemy and transfer it to him, as enchantresses can leech out and transfer power during a sexual union." He got up and went to the table by the door, where a pitcher of water and a glass stood amid empty plates.

"Mentra and Thili are sisters who served Niferon," Lady Ilyria continued as Byuton drank water. "But they decided it was not a life they wanted. Mentra wanted a family, while Thili desired freedom. They ran away from Niferon, but he was able to track down Mentra, as she had not given up her original form like Thili had. He killed her husband and child, and she escaped to Greylan, where she started plotting against Niferon. Whatever she is doing now is to avenge her family."

17

There was a prolonged silence as the audience digested what was said. Horace did not doubt that most of them were wondering how they had landed in a story that was often labeled as mythological—tales of gods and enchantresses in which Niferon used the seduction games of the beautiful ladies in his court to defeat the demon princes who challenged him. It had never occurred to Horace that those tales were real, or that the said ladies would have performed their duties with reluctance.

He spared a glance at Raya. It was no wonder Zesta did not want her daughter anywhere near Niferon. Above the seat that he normally occupied at one end of the hall hung a portrait of his father, the man resplendent in an emerald-green robe and a drawn sword. In all the war camps that his father had set up, there was a small shrine dedicated to Niferon—a god who abused women and destroyed families.

"Yet we bow to him." Horace broke the silence when the others seemed too unsettled to speak.

"We bow to many who do not deserve our respect," Byuton said.

"But how are we to stop Mentra?" Pari asked. "I have to say, she has my sympathies, but we can't let her destroy our land and people to wreak vengeance on the gods. What kind of powers does she have?"

"She has a little from here and a little from there, which adds up to a combination that none of us possess." Byuton circled the silver bracelet around his wrist, from which various tiny amulets hung. "We have to put together everything we have learned from our collective experiences and from what Thili informed us. What happened to your soldier Cade, Lord Thian, is a clear example of the tarshish spell. So, she has the powers of a combat mage. Lady Leonara told us that the queen used a sentar weapon. So there is that." He returned to his chair but stood leaning on the pillar attached to it and continued.

"Now, getting to what Thili has told us—as far as she knows, Mentra has shifted between only two forms—the one we all have seen as the queen of Monrae and her original one, which your soldier saw. That does not mean she couldn't shift her form again. Thili was unaware of how she did it, because it is unlike Thili's shifting powers, which she got from true shifters. For instance, Thili can shift to a different species, whereas Mentra has chosen to remain a human woman. This brings a degree of difficulty for us, for we cannot be sure if Mentra is in this room with us in the form of someone we know."

An eerie silence filled the hall as Byuton fixed his gaze on each of those present, like he expected one of them to jump up and admit they were the queen in disguise.

"Isn't that a little far-fetched?" Lady Ilyria asked. "Now you are ascribing to her the powers of a pishara."

"Not quite." Byuton got up from his seat and rummaged for something in the pocket of his vest. "She is not a blood-drinker, and she is much more dangerous than those pisharas whose only claim to horror is that they can trick children."

He went to Gaelia. "Can I have your hand, Gaelia?"

"Not again." Gaelia groaned. "Can't we work on a secret word?"

"No." Byuton took her hand and pricked her finger with something—a silver needle.

Gaelia winced.

"You are a farmer, Gaelia," Byuton said. "You must be used to getting pricked by thorns."

"I don't do that deliberately."

"I need permission to do the same with the rest of you." Byuton looked expectantly at Lady Ilyria.

"But why?" Raya murmured, not looking thrilled at the prospect.

"Silver forces a shifter back into their actual form," Horace said, although he wouldn't have thought of roaming around with a silver needle.

"It won't hurt," Byuton assured her.

"It will," Gaelia said.

"Go ahead, Byuton, if you must." Lady Ilyria offered her finger. "We must get on with the task at hand."

She did not flinch when Byuton pricked her. It was Horace's turn next, and then Deena's and Pari's.

Raya blinked and pouted and crossed her arms. "I will not do it."

"As you wish, Your Majesty, Queen Mentra." Byuton gave an exaggerated bow.

"I am not her." Raya snorted.

Byuton shrugged. "Don't be scared that this needle will pass on any infection to you. It has magical properties."

Raya still looked reluctant.

"The scar on your cheek proves you are no stranger to blades," Byuton said, "yet you are afraid of a needle piercing your skin."

Horace caught Deena's eye. Raya had tested the antidote on herself. That had been a braver act than they had realized.

Byuton used the needle on his own skin with more force than necessary, causing scarlet droplets to trickle down his finger.

Raya marched to him, grabbed the needle from his hand, and pricked herself. "So there." She returned to her seat, looking slightly clammy.

"Since we have established that none of us is Mentra—"

"Are you going to do that every time you meet us?" Raya asked. "If so, I'd rather not see you again."

"We will just have to ensure none of us is left alone until I finish speaking about her strengths and weaknesses. Let me state at the very onset that we are currently unaware of any weakness.

"The attack by the hauries proves again that she will not hesitate to use creatures from Thisaur to serve her purpose—like she used the syrelins. But her real strength is her senria. Mentra's senria does not dissipate at the same rate as a normal sentar warrior's.

She has had decades to practice the art of self-replenishment and always had an excess of senria. Previously, she had also embedded her energy in inanimate objects to access it if she ever needed an extra recharge. This could be a certain difficulty if you ever have to face her. A lone sentar warrior could not accomplish much against her. Our best bet would be a team of sentar warriors and mages."

Byuton retook his seat. "She uses her senria to create portals too. In that strength, at least, she cannot ace Thili. Mentra can portal herself only to places where a sliver of her senria is present. For instance, Lord Thian, I believe in one of her previous visits, she might have left something in your garden that allowed her to travel there through a portal."

"Or Tandon could have done that for her," Pari said.

"Very much possible," Horace said. That thought had passed through his mind too. It could have been Tandon's motive in scouting the garden and shrine.

"It is a little solace to us," Byuton continued, "to think Mentra can't just pop up anywhere before setting up something to give her that entry. Now, coming to the powers of a combat mage—the tarshish spell that can push the opponent away and the kadintian spell that can immobilize the opponent can be blocked with a normal sentar shield. Being a mage, I shouldn't be announcing this, but that is just the truth, and you may as well know it. Use a double shield in her case, since her magic might be more powerful than what you'd expect from an average mage.

"The greatest challenge, however, is whatever powers she has amassed from the scrolls of Varys and Zesta. Thili has already witnessed the element of water obeying her command. Imagine how devastating it would be if the Greylan Sea or the Eastern Sea changed their boundaries. Or what would happen if she used the power of Zesta and animated the dead to serve as her army?"

"Couldn't we appeal to the prince, her son?" Deena shifted uneasily in her seat. "Wouldn't he be able to put a stop to her?"

Had he known the nature of the revelations that were to be made, Horace wouldn't have invited Deena to attend the meeting. He trusted her, but everything they'd learned was overwhelming. They were going to fight an entity that gave even an experienced sentar warrior like him the creeps. It was no place for a healer.

Pari listened with intense focus, but Raya's clamminess seemed to have gotten worse. She wiped her forehead with the sleeve of her tunic.

"Until recently, we were able to use his name as a shield against her harming our families," Lady Ilyria said. "She hadn't wanted him to know her truth, but now, she has gone too far. I think it is time we tell him everything, disregarding what she might do to us."

"Shouldn't we consult with Thili first?" Gaelia asked.

"It had been her explicit instruction to let go of the secrecy if Mentra went after any of the scrolls," Lady Ilyria said. "We hadn't known you had one, Horace, or we would have warned you."

"Even I hadn't known about it until it was taken." Such a powerful artifact had been on his land, and he hadn't given it any protection.

"Whoever guarded it had been scrupulous." Pari gave him a knowing smile.

One could say that of his mother, but even she might not have guessed the dangers of guarding the scroll of a goddess or what it meant. Or else she wouldn't have given the responsibility to Raya.

"Scrupulous, yes," Byuton said. "But some added security might have helped."

Horace agreed.

"You mean the magical kind?" Pari did not sound too convinced.

"Yes," Byuton said proudly. "The kind that is currently ensuring that Edri's and Prithi's scrolls don't fall into her hands."

"My mother and Raya had seen this scroll, but it was in a script they did not understand."

"The same with Edri's scroll," Byuton said. "It was certainly not in Cele. It could be a script of some language of Thisaur that the true heir will have to learn. But Mentra might already know it since she has already used Varys's scroll."

"What about the other gods?" Horace asked.

The scroll of Niferon himself would be the most valuable for the queen, but Avar's and Kalantra's, too, remained. What destruction could Mentra unleash if she had the power of fire and death?

"Thili is currently looking for Avar's and Kalantra's scrolls," Byuton said. "Once she finds them, our people will protect them. But she believes Niferon has not prepared a scroll. According to Thili, he is haughty enough to believe his time will never come to an end."

"I agree that Prince Coraen must be informed." Horace turned to Gaelia. "Does Malion know any of this?"

She squirmed in the gigantic seat and shot a guilty glance toward Lady Ilyria. "He guessed half of it, and after he returned from the Western Frontier and told me of the queen's presence there during the syrelin attack, I thought it fit to tell him about her true nature. So, when Thili informed me about the scrolls, Malion was with me."

"I should send word to Lord Kendrek too," Lady Ilyria said. "Or I should go myself. The seiflands must be prepared for whatever is coming. Horace, is there any way we could get word to Lord Rothshire? He ought to be on his guard if he is Tandon's next target."

"He will not believe a word from me," Horace said. "But we need eyes and ears in Rothshire."

"I will go," Pari offered. "I know what to look out for. Val Tandon is no sentar warrior. He will be no threat to me."

"But there are sentar warriors who serve him," Lady Ilyria said. "Leo came across some at the Western Frontier, and they all went unpunished, claiming they were all mind-controlled by the syrelins."

"I will discuss it with Raiker when I meet him this evening," Horace told Pari. Yes, it was time he reconstituted the defunct spy network of his father's time. It was a necessary evil with whatever was going on. "But even if you go, you must lie low. Don't take any action on your own. I will set up a chain of communication through the trading guild. At least for the time being, Lord Rothshire has not suspended trade."

A strange buzzing filled the hall, like dozens of bees were rushing out of their hive. Horace jumped from his seat, a sentar sword extending from his hand at the same time. Pari was already on her feet, her whip glistening in her hand.

"Fires of Kalantra," Deena exclaimed. "What is that?"

Byuton held up a hand. "I am sorry for startling you. It is just a message." He took out a bee-shaped crystal from his pocket and stared into it, his eyes moving as if he were reading something. His face scrunched up, and he bit the insides of his cheeks.

"Is something wrong?" Gaelia went to him, fishing out a similar crystal from her purse. It looked like a star. "Was the message from Malion? I got nothing." She replaced the crystal, mirroring Byuton's worried expression.

"No, it is from my father. There has been an attack in my village. Someone tried to enter the vaults attached to our prison, where our scriptures are stored."

"Oh, did they get the scroll?" Lady Ilyria asked.

"We had moved the scroll to another location, but some of the prison guards were attacked. They were sprayed with something, and their condition is severe."

"What is their condition?" Deena asked before Horace could put forth the same question. He had some idea.

"He did not specify." The young mage no longer looked smug but had gone deathly pale.

"Ask him if it looks like burns," Deena urged. "Or if their body is heating up. If so, ask them to be immediately covered with amaran leaves. It could be veritria."

"Lord Thian, can I have a parchment and quill?"

"Yes, come into the library."

Deena accompanied them.

Byuton scribbled a barely legible message onto the parchment and held his crystal above it.

"Don't be scared by what you see now," he told them. "I informed my father that it is safe to communicate with me through a projection."

The air sizzled and whirled behind them, taking on the appearance of fog, and the outline of a human form materialized in the air.

18

Deena stepped back as Pari and the other ladies appeared at the door leading from the assembly hall. Horace raised a hand to stop them. The form became translucent, smoke spreading and solidifying to form hands, legs, and a head. It was a man with a bald head, stooping form, and flowing robe. Through his smoky figure, the ladies were still visible in the doorway.

"Where is Father?" Byuton moved to the figure.

"He is with Tisila. I am the one who sent you the message."

"Is she . . . ?"

"She is alive but not in a good condition."

Deena approached them. "Are their bodies turning hot?"

"Yes." The figure turned to her. "We are trying to cool them."

"Nothing too drastic must be used," Deena said. "Nothing that causes a sudden change in temperature."

"Who are you?"

"She knows what she is talking about and has already treated one who was similarly afflicted." Horace stood by her. "You will help yourself by answering her question."

"Wait." The figure flickered and disappeared for a moment before materializing again. "I told them to hold the cooling spell. If you know how to help them, then tell us."

He cast concerned sidelong glances at the tall bookshelf by his side, but he was seeing something invisible to them.

"Cover them with amaran leaves," Deena said. "Do you have the plant in your area? It is a water plant. And then—"

"Yes, we can procure them." Smoke swirled within the figure before everything cleared away, leaving only still air.

"Grandfather," Byuton shouted into the air. "Stay and listen to the whole thing before you go."

The young mage's eyebrows were pinched together in a pained expression, which was in stark contrast to his demeanor a few moments ago in the assembly hall.

"Who is Tisila?" Deena asked softly.

"My mother."

"We know the antidote works. I will go to them myself if permitted and administer it." She looked at Horace.

He gave her a grim nod.

"The mages would never let a krani into their midst." Pari got to them while scanning the air for any reappearance of the smoky mage.

"My mother is a krani," Byuton said. "She is a sentar warrior, but not a mage."

"Oh! I didn't know that was possible," Pari said.

"She did not give birth to me," Byuton said. "But she is the only mother I know."

Pari's body shimmered as Byuton's grandfather reappeared exactly where she stood. She jumped away.

"It has been arranged. We have summoned amaran leaves, and now the affected are being covered. Oh, if only it will give them some comfort."

"It will," Deena said with conviction. "And if some slip into a state of unconsciousness, your healers should keep giving them an infusion of aziril."

"Er . . . we have no healers in our midst," Byuton said. "Our spells take care of most ailments."

That sounded both tempting and dangerous. Deena did not doubt that spells might act faster than the concoctions or salves she prepared, but those spells would not be tailored to the individual needs of the patients.

"We are aware of aziril," Byuton's grandfather said. "Tell me how to prepare the infusion and it will be done."

"She can send you written instructions through the crystal, Grandfather," Byuton said. "But we will need her expertise to prepare and administer the antidote."

"How soon can I get there?" Deena turned to Byuton.

"Five days with good, sturdy horses to pull your carriage. Four if you don't stop."

"I can carry the antidote I have already prepared, but I will also bring the ingredients to prepare more of it, now that we know the queen is actively using veritria, but . . ."

It wouldn't do just for her and the ingredients to travel to the mages. They would need Raya too.

"Raya would have to accompany me," Deena told Horace, almost reading the protest shaping up in his mind. "The antidote will not work without her senria."

"Why her senria?" Byuton asked.

A veil of reticence fell over Horace's eyes. He had wanted no one to know that Raya was the one to prepare the veritria, and that wish had only strengthened after the fate of the Rothshire heirs and the mages. Those seeking revenge could hunt the poor girl down.

"I . . ." Raya stepped up.

"Her senria had more healing powers than the others I tried," Deena said quickly. "Every person's senria is different—like Gaelia's has its nourishing quality. Maybe it's because of who she is."

Horace gave her a surprised look and an imperceptible nod of his head that could have signaled either gratitude or approval.

"But now that we know *she* is there, how safe is it for Deena and Raya to go to the Bewar forest?" Gaelia asked.

"As far as we know," Byuton said, "Mentra is targeting the scrolls and not attacking random people."

"Except when she sent the hauries to Thian after Raya," Horace said. "Her safety cannot be compromised." He paused and glanced at the map spread over his desk. "I will go with them. That route lies along the border between Thian and Rothshire. It will give me a chance to check on our border troops and boost their morale."

Byuton's grandfather disappeared after Deena gave him written instructions on how to prepare the infusion of aziril. The group headed back to the assembly hall, but none of them took their seats.

"I think this is a good chance that we shouldn't waste," Lady Ilyria said.

"What do you mean?" Byuton asked.

"Now that we know for sure that her next target is Edri's scroll, couldn't we set up a trap for her?" Lady Ilyria said.

"What sort of trap?" Byuton asked dubiously. "She has the combined powers of mages and sentar warriors. And she can escape quickly using a portal."

"Isn't it odd that she didn't portal directly inside our shrine?" Pari asked. "Tandon could easily have left something in there, and it would have prevented so much hassle for her. She could have quietly slipped in and taken the scroll with no one knowing about it."

"Leo had the same doubt after she appeared in the flecha cave," Lady Ilyria said. "We asked Thili about it and she said—"

"That magic does not work near the scrolls," Byuton interrupted. "That might be true for portals as well."

"Is that why she used the poison to attack the guards?" Deena asked. Even Jianther had not been attacked by magic when he was in the shrine.

"It would seem so," Lady Ilyria said. "Although the mage's vault hadn't contained the scroll. She could have wielded magic."

"She wouldn't have known that until it was too late," Byuton said.

"If she is vulnerable near the divine scrolls, it makes more sense to lure her to one and set a trap," Raya said.

She had been quite subdued until now, but maybe the prospect of traveling to Bewar to save the mages had perked her up. It had made even Deena believe she could be useful in some way in this battle that was not her own. The thought of the inevitable loss of life that would follow a battle sickened her, but at least she wasn't a warrior who would be forced to take lives. She could heal where healing was needed.

"What sort of trap?" Byuton asked. "Magical spells won't work, or there would be many we could use."

"What if the trap is not magical?" Deena asked. The enchantress herself had given her the idea. Mentra had used veritria when she thought the use of magic was not possible, hadn't she? Why couldn't they do the same?

"What do you mean?" Gaelia asked.

"What if she is immobilized once she touches the scroll?" Deena knew exactly what to use to accomplish that.

"How is that possible?" Byuton asked. "As we just found out, the kadintian spell won't work near the scroll."

"But poisons do," Deena said. "As the queen well knows. Why can't we do what she did?"

"You mean use veritria on her?" Horace asked, looking at her quizzically, and then gave a crooked smile. "I thought healers didn't hurt anyone."

"I stand by that conviction, but not all poisons kill. Some can just disable—the one found in the thorn of heliatin, for instance. A single prick can paralyze the victim until the antidote is given."

Raya shuddered. "I hate being pricked."

"The flechas use this thorn in their arrows," Lady Ilyria said. "Leo has some experience with it."

"But who is going to stay in wait and shoot this arrow at Mentra?" Byuton asked.

"That won't be necessary," Deena said. "The thorn can be embedded either in the scroll or near it so that she is pricked when she touches it. Her senses will be alive, and she will be able to see and hear everything, but the poison will not let her react."

"Brilliant," Horace said.

Deena struggled against the warmth that crept up her neck at the exuberance with which he'd said it, but he did not notice and continued speaking. "We could set up the trap, if the mages are willing. But this time it will have to be the real scroll of Edri, as she will be aware of how you tried to dupe her."

"Do you have enough heliatin thorns with you?" Byuton asked.

Deena looked at Horace and nodded. Lady Len's greenhouse had a sufficient supply of the plant.

Byuton paced the hall for a moment before he asked, "And also the antidote?"

"Yes," Deena said. "The crushed seeds of heliatin serve that purpose."

"It is an ingenuous plan that might work if we are careful enough," Byuton said. "I will write to Grandfather to increase security around Edri's scroll. Mentra shouldn't get to it under any circumstance before we arrive." Byuton returned to the library to find a parchment and quill.

Horace moved to Pari, and they talked about Pari's proposed travel to Rothshire. She was to join him in a meeting he was going to have with his commander-in-chief and the head of the merchants' guild. Lord Thian assured her that the latter would help her across the border as long as she didn't create any trouble for him.

Raya joined them, but Deena returned to her seat. Her role in Thian was over. After she rendered whatever help she could to the mages, she would return to her home in Alayster and keep her fingers crossed that all the sentar warriors and mages of Greylan could successfully stop that enchantress from destroying their land.

Gaelia and Lady Ilyria came up to her.

"It is a brilliant plan," Gaelia said. "I can't believe I was planning to grow heliatin without learning anything about it. How foolish of me! Good that Malion destroyed the plants even before Horace informed us of its danger."

"You did what you had to do for Sheila," Deena said kindly.

Gaelia returned the smile. "We are thinking about accompanying you to Bewar. Once your business with the mages is over, we can go to Alayster together, and Mother Ilyria will travel further to Easther and get on a ship from there to Kendrek. It would be quicker than going by land."

"That is very kind of you," Deena said, "but won't the mages mind so many of us intruding on their territory?"

"Byuton already invited me to visit his parents, so that shouldn't be a problem. And they would be foolish not to accept any help Mother Ilyria might provide in the fight against the enchantress. She is not a sentar warrior to be taken lightly."

Lady Ilyria smiled. "I wonder what a sentar warrior, however powerful, would be able to do against Mentra."

19

Horace let Byuton, Gaelia, and Lady Ilyria be led to different rooms in the palace to rest before their journey the next day. There was no point in delaying the trip. Byuton had extracted a promise from the group that the plan would not be discussed once they exited the hall—not even with each other. He made them take a solemn oath bound by his magic, which he assured them wouldn't turn them into toads if they broke it, but if they spoke about the plan to anyone, he would know about it. Given the risk they were taking and the capabilities of their enemy, it was a good call.

Deena and Raya went to the healers' residence to check on Jianther and pack the materials required for the antidote. Horace took Pari to the leader of the merchants' guild. Kerish hesitated initially to let Pari ride with the next caravan that headed toward Rothshire, but when he was told how the right information from Rothshire could help prevent a war, he relented. Easther's fall and Alayster's weakened economy had made Rothshire their major trading partner, and the merchants had no desire to lose the trading channels.

The meeting with the commander-in-chief of Thian also went well. Raiker was to oversee the movement of the troops to the outskirts of the southern villages, while Horace himself would scrutinize his soldiers along the Haiga range, which lay enroute to Bewar.

Thian at least had a geographical advantage. The hills of Haiga and the great lake of Semere would afford them a strategic view of any attempts at ingress by the Rothshire army.

Last on his agenda was a conversation with his mother. He hesitated before entering her quarters. The guards at the door had been removed, but she still had not presented herself outside her chambers. When she came out of her bedroom, his concern for her increased multifold.

Her eyes were red from exhaustion or the shedding of tears. She would never admit that it was the latter, but some great sadness was etched on her face as she stood by her writing desk.

A feeble attempt at a smile failed, and she asked in a shaky voice, "How are things progressing?"

"Jianther is awake, and he exonerated Deena."

"Good." Her eyes stared into the void.

Unlike during his previous visit, the rooms had an unkempt look. The windows were shut and the flowers in the vases had begun to wilt. There was a musty scent in the room, as though it hadn't been aired in a long time. An ink pot lay upturned on her desk, and no one had cleaned up the spilled ink.

Horace studied her. Streaks from her kohl lined her cheeks. She had definitely been crying. "Are you feeling well, Mother?"

"Yes, yes. I am." She blinked out of her trance but did not look into his eyes. "So, what is your next step?"

"I am riding to the southeast tomorrow to rally the troops at the base of Haiga. Raiker is taking care of the southern villages. I am taking Raya with me."

"Why?" She jerked her head to him.

He told her about the visitors, the attack on the mages, and Raya's decision to help with the antidote. She listened calmly, betraying no emotion. The haunting look in her eyes was replaced by something else—a calculating one.

"I will not let her go anywhere without me," she said calmly.

Horace sighed. "It will be a long, hard travel with little comfort. No maids or servants will be accompanying us."

"I don't care."

He had been hoping that his mother would administer the seifland in his and Garim's absence. Even Pari was going to be away.

"Did you hear about the attack by the hauries?" That was another thing he hadn't apprised her of.

"Yes, I did."

"Then you know our land is no longer safe. Wouldn't you rather stay here than travel to the forest of the mages?"

"I wouldn't rest easy knowing Raya is in the same danger. Whatever you say, if she goes, I go."

"All right." He passed a hand over his face. He would have to hand over the administration of the palace to Garim's deputy. "I suggest you rest well tonight. We will start early tomorrow."

The carriages were ready early the next morning. For the first time, Deena had slept in the palace on a bed too big for her. She would have preferred to be in the same room that she had occupied till now in the healers' residence. Gaelia and Raya, however, had insisted that she stay in the palace. She wanted to see Kran, but she couldn't ask Horace when he would release him.

Pari had not appeared after she'd left with Horace. She sent a message to Deena stating her intention to leave for Rothshire. It was accompanied by a parcel containing two identical riding outfits—black trousers and long olive-green tunics with a cinched waist and flared sleeves—which Pari wrote were gifts for a healer who had taught her the value of life. Deena wished she could have seen Pari before the latter left, but there was no time for such niceties, given what they were about to face.

Even she had much preparation to do—besides arranging for the ingredients of the antidote, she also had to carefully collect heliatin thorns. No one stopped her when she stepped into the greenhouse this time. Having Raya by her side must have helped.

The call of the exotic plants that grew there was alluring, but she had no time to roam around and inspect. She was sure that the owner of the greenhouse wouldn't appreciate it if she attempted it. That was one thing she was grateful for—not running into Lady Len during her brief stay in the palace. The lady wouldn't have welcomed her presence, whether she was innocent or not. But as she waited to board the carriages at the main entrance of the palace with Gaelia and Lady Ilyria, the said lady made her appearance.

Dressed in a brilliant red traveling gown, Lady Len looked fiercer and more determined than ever as she swept down the palace steps. Raya trailed behind her, giving a helpless shrug to the questioning looks that overtook the faces of almost everyone present. Horace was the last to join them, and he went straight to Byuton.

"Mother insists on accompanying Raya," he said. "She can stay at one of the war camps outside Bewar if you want no more visitors in your home."

"Lady Len is welcome in my home," Byuton said with a slight bow.

"Thank you," Lady Len said with her head held high. She did not spare any glance to Deena. That did not surprise her. But Lady Len did not acknowledge even Lady Ilyria or Gaelia. The former pasted a stoic expression on her face, but Gaelia rolled her eyes exaggeratedly. Deena bit back a smile.

"She's never liked me," Gaelia whispered.

Raya beckoned Deena to join her and Lady Len in the carriage.

Five days in a carriage with Lady Len? She'd rather volunteer to drink wija.

"Deena is riding with me and Mother Ilyria," Horace said to Raya. "Gaelia and Byuton will go in your carriage."

"Not fair," Gaelia mumbled. "Byuton, do you know any spell to put me to sleep?"

"Of course I know, but I will not use it."

"We have one more companion," Horace said. "Here he comes."

Deena turned to the door of the palace, where Kran stood, grinning.

"Kran will return to Alayster with you, Deena," Horace said.

"I know you didn't ask for my opinion, Lord Thian," Kran said when he reached them, "but let me make this very clear. My sister's actions were extremely foolish, and I wish to sincerely apologize for all the inconveniences she and I caused you."

Raya indicated her scar. "You mean this?"

"For that too."

Horace patted him on the back, and all clambered into their respective carriages.

Horace was seated opposite Deena, and she tried not to look at him too much, but she must have failed in her attempt, as their eyes kept meeting, which released bursts of warmth in her chest.

It must be gratitude. She wanted to tell him she was grateful to him for letting Kran return with her, but no words came out, especially not in Kran's presence. He would, no doubt, observe and record her awkwardness, only to tease her later on.

Lady Ilyria and Kran carried on a conversation—it seemed that they had met before, and the former knew about Kran's daughter. Kran was only too happy to talk about Sheila and the return of the little girl's health, for which they were indebted to Lord Thian, as Kran did not forget to mention, beaming with the genuine joy of attaining freedom. Had she returned to Alayster without him, she wouldn't have been able to face their family. That thought brought her eyes again to Horace, but his gaze was already fixed on her.

Don't blush, she warned herself, and looked out of the carriage window, wondering why her heart was galloping faster than the horses.

As they left the city walls, lush greenery enveloped them, except when they circled the famed artificial lakes of Thian, their water reflecting the cerulean-blue sky with its white puffs of clouds. The trees were both native and foreign, and the latter must be the doing of Lady Len. Now that she was not under Lady Len's scrutiny and did not have to spend hours in a carriage with her, Deena was able to think of Horace's mother with some admiration.

If not for Lady Len, they wouldn't have made the antidote for veritria or the poisonous trap for Mentra. Maybe someday she would write a note of thanks to the lady, and even hope that under Horace's persuasion, his mother would loosen her grip on the herbs.

But by the time they made their first stop in an inn at the foot of a gray-tipped hill, all amiable feelings for Lady Len slipped right from her mind. She completely ignored Deena during their lunch and an hour of rest, although she paid tender attention to Raya throughout. Lady Ilyria, on the other hand, was the epitome of grace. She showed a genuine interest in Deena's life and work.

"Someone of your knowledge and experience should not limit their work to Alayster," she said. "Come visit us in Kendrek sometime. And if you need to procure some of the rarer herbs, Healer Hian is the one who could help you. He works in the Western Frontier and has access to the hills that are prohibited to healers from the seiflands. I could write to him if you ever need anything."

"Thank you, my lady," Deena said.

"Mother Ilyria," Lady Ilyria offered.

"All assuming we survive the next few days," Gaelia said, sipping her peren mead.

"Have more faith, Gaelia," Lady Ilyria gently chided. "Let us assume we will succeed."

"I would have thought someone born under the seven constellations would not have much to fear of, Lady Gaelia," Lady Len said, addressing them for the first time.

Gaelia set down her mug and pursed her lips, probably to stop herself from retorting.

"And how is your daughter, Lady Ilyria?" Lady Len asked. "Has *her* birth chart brought her any glory recently?"

"Enough to let her survive some challenges," Lady Ilyria said calmly.

"I hope the stars will continue to guard her." Lady Len's tone belied her words.

"I was just going to tell you, Mother Len," Raya said. "Mother Ilyria chose this roundabout route back to her home only to be of service to us."

"To us?" Lady Len scoffed. "Isn't all this trouble to help the mages?"

"Who were attacked with veritria," Raya said stiffly.

Lady Len patted her hand and decided not to talk anymore. The silence spread to all the ladies who sat immersed in their individual thoughts, and when Byuton appeared to announce their departure, there was a collective sigh of relief.

As they made their way to the carriages, Gaelia wrapped her arm around Deena's waist.

"How many gold coins to swap places?" she whispered.

"You will have to drag me kicking and screaming." Deena giggled.

With a grunt of defeat, Gaelia scrambled into the carriage after Lady Len.

A hand supported Deena's elbow as she climbed into her carriage. Horace stood behind her with an inscrutable expression.

"My mother is not that bad, you know?" he said.

Whatever reply she was going to give got stuck in her throat. But he did not wait for her response as he turned to help Lady Ilyria.

Deena pretended to sleep for the rest of the way to avoid Horace's eyes. By sunset, they had reached another inn, where they were to spend their night. Horace had to visit one of his camps that was being set up near the village. He was to spend the night there but thought the ladies would be more comfortable at the inn.

It was a mild consolation that she did not have to face him after seemingly insulting his mother, who had done her no tangible harm except not treating her with kindness. She added an apology to the list of things that she would have to convey to Horace if she ever got the opportunity.

Kran accompanied Horace, but Byuton preferred to stay back with the rest of the group. Although when they lounged by the crackling fire in the inn's parlor, Byuton was nowhere to be seen. Neither were Lady Len and Raya, who had retired early after supper.

"The mage claims he is tired," Gaelia announced, yawning. "Although all he did was sleep throughout the ride."

Deena wouldn't have minded getting to her bed early that night, but inertia had gripped her once she had settled into the sunken couch by the fire. The gray fur covering the couch might not have been the cleanest she had encountered, but it was warm and soft all the same.

The inn was nestled in a valley between two hills that formed a part of the Haiga range. It meant that the night air was chilly, and the low fire was a desirable comfort. In addition, the steady thrum of conversation between Gaelia and Lady Ilyria was comforting after the stress of the previous days.

Gaelia recounted how her stepfather was helping her bring the farmers of Alayster together to meet the increased demand generated by the growing prosperity in their economy. She had moved her family to a new farmland that she managed.

"Is that why we have heard nothing of the wedding?" Lady Ilyria asked. "Because you and Malion are busy setting Alayster on its feet?"

Gaelia smiled. "More than that, we are still getting to know each other. Malion agrees that there is no hurry for a wedding."

"I would have thought he would be in a hurry to ensure the continuity of his line." Lady Ilyria loosened her pristine white shawl as the toastiness of the room increased.

Gaelia gave a surprised laugh. "We have talked about that. Malion thinks it is time the seiflands elected their leader and did not depend so much on heirs. Look at what happened to Easther.

Just because they did not have an heir, Athora could take control of them."

"Lord Kendrek would be scandalized if he was told that the next lord of Kendrek would be elected. And King Monrae would have a fit. He even wants to control who Tyren marries to ensure Athora has the support of the next Lady Kendrek. He is trying to persuade Leonara to marry one of his erstwhile valiant warriors, but I cannot figure out the logic behind that. There is nothing that irritates Leonara more than being told what to do."

"So has the king stopped looking for a bride for Prince Aethan?" Deena asked.

Lady Ilyria's daughter and Gaelia had been the two girls whom King Monrae had wanted his son to marry to fulfill some prophecy based on their birth charts. That was what Kran had told her. But both girls had refused to obey the king's orders.

"He has spread his search to Izakura and beyond," Lady Ilyria said, "since no girl on the continent seems willing to marry the crown prince."

"And what is this valiant warrior like?" Gaelia asked. "The one he is trying to fix Leo with? If he is anything like Tandon, I can understand her reluctance."

"Oh, I don't think she is reluctant," Lady Ilyria smiled fondly, "even though she would never admit that to the king. Armand keeps to himself, at least in front of me, and since he joined Prince Coraen's troop, he is no longer a valiant warrior of Monrae. But he admires Leo. That much, I am sure."

Lady Ilyria continued to talk about her experience in the Western Frontier and how she, too, had worked with Prince Coraen for the past few months. Deena leaned back on the couch, taking in the lingering smell of the spicy soup they'd had for supper and the chirping of the crickets outside the window. She must have succumbed to the tiredness and the warmth of the room, for the next thing she knew, Gaelia was gently shaking her awake.

"We are all going to bed," she said. "You will have better rest there."

Raya was also in the room with them. She let out a wide yawn. "Mother Len is already asleep, but she suspects we are up to something."

"And is her guess close to the truth?" Lady Ilyria asked.

"She did not tell me what she guessed, but she is sure that I am hiding something from her, which is the truth. I told her she was needlessly worrying. If it were not for Byuton's binding oath, I would have told her everything. I have never kept any secret from her."

"She is safer not knowing it," Lady Ilyria said.

On that ominous note, they headed off to their rooms.

20

The next morning, Deena woke up with the wish to put things right with Horace. The breakfast with everyone gathered around the wide wooden table in the center of the dining room gave her no opportunity to express an apology for insulting his mother. He and Kran had returned in the early hours of the morning and now sat at one end of the table, deep in conversation.

"I can swap with you on the carriage today," Deena told Gaelia, and the latter accepted with no qualms.

"I warn you, the ride will be deadly silent."

Deena did not mind that. It would give her more time to think if she did not have to spend the journey struggling to keep her eyes averted from Horace. And she had a lot to think about. Not just about her budding attraction to Horace, which she hoped she could successfully nip in the bud, as there was nothing as futile as expecting him to return the same feelings. But she also had to ponder about the trap she was about to set for the enchantress.

No one had said what they would do once they trapped the enchantress. Would they opt to kill her when she was in a state of paralysis? A shudder passed through Deena as she went toward the carriage.

"Is that from the thought of riding with my mother?" a low voice asked behind her.

She jerked back. Horace gave her a twisted smile.

"No. No. Not at all. I offered to swap with Gaelia."

"So I heard." He did not sound annoyed. "I offered the same to Byuton."

"And is that to keep your mother safe from me?" Deena regretted the words as soon as they'd come out. It was not her intent to goad him.

"Yes. With all the poisons you are carrying, I have to be wary." He indicated her leather bag.

"Not when your mother could kill with her looks." She huffed and hurried to the carriage.

His gentle laughter followed her.

She sat opposite Raya, which made things slightly easier, and her thoughts returned to the enchantress. It would go against her oath as a healer if she stood by and let them kill a helpless person—magical being or not. But would they have any other option to defeat someone who held powers they couldn't even imagine? It would always haunt her that she was the one to suggest the use of heliatin thorns.

Their stop for lunch gave her an inkling of what to expect in the coming days. The inn had nothing but cold bread and bland soup, and the terrain from thenceforth got rougher, with hills crowding in around them. Horace warned them to expect even fewer comforts during their nightly stop. They were to lodge in the camp set up outside the village of Veiga that did not have a suitable inn. He had sent a horseman ahead of them to arrange for their stay, but a war camp would have its limitations.

As he had warned, the journey after lunch jolted them around the carriage. Deena, in her forward-facing seat beside Horace, faced the brunt of it as she got thrown toward him repeatedly, earning derisive glances from Lady Len and sympathetic nods from Raya. It wasn't her fault that she didn't have Horace's core strength that allowed him to sit unmoving. Eventually, he laid out a hand near her arms to steady her whenever the path became rough.

It was with great relief that Deena stepped out of the carriage that evening. War camp or not, she was grateful to be on firm ground. Gaelia appeared pale, as though she wanted to throw up.

"Byuton used one of his charms to help me hold it in," she groaned. "But I still feel nauseous."

"Here, smell this." Deena handed her a leaf of maraya from her bag. "The feeling will subside."

The clanking of hammers and iron poles welcomed them to the camp. Huge tents were being erected and crude structures constructed to give some comfort to the soldiers. A tree came crashing down behind them, scaring the squawking birds from their nests. It was not just humans who had to pay for a war.

The crystal-clear lake of Semere stretched in front of them, the opposite shore not even visible. That would be Rothshire, and it was very much possible that a war camp was being set up there too.

Lady Len did not enter her tent and walked toward the lake. Deena didn't blame her. The alluring expanse of water was tempting after the long, uncomfortable ride, and she herself wished to take a stroll by the lake, enjoying the shade of the row of trees that lined its side, but not when Lady Len was doing the same. Deena had a tent to share with Gaelia and Lady Ilyria. That was some consolation, and she looked forward to a restful, even enjoyable evening.

Hence, she was disgruntled when Kran came to fetch her before she could even get out of her traveling gear.

"What do you want now?" She did not bother to hide her displeasure at having been dragged out of the tent.

"Ha! That is no way to welcome your brother who is suffering this journey just because of you."

"Don't tell me you are not enjoying being shown special favors by Lord Thian—riding off with him to inspect camps and all."

"Why do you sound jealous? Were you interested in riding off with him?"

"Shut up."

"Try to make me." He folded his hands and took a challenging stance. "Well, if you wished to ride with him, then my message will be welcome to you. Lord Thian wants you to accompany him to the village."

She scrutinized Kran to ensure he was not pulling her leg. His forced, innocent expression did not reassure her.

"I do not believe you," she said.

"Shall I tell that to him?"

"But why would he want me to accompany him?"

"Maybe the same reason he got into the carriage with you."

She gave him an impatient wave. "Where is he now?"

Kran bounced his eyebrows and coughed.

"Are you looking for me?" Horace spoke from behind her.

Deena swiveled to face him. "Er . . . yes."

She would have to kill Kran if she found out that Horace was behind her all this while.

"I would like you to ride to Veiga with me. It is Pari's village, and I intend to visit her family."

Kran mumbled some excuse and left them alone.

"Sure."

"But you have a question?"

"Yes. Why me?"

"Because you knew Pari, and you could be my excuse to visit her family without scaring them. She has gone to Rothshire without being able to visit her home, and she left a message for them." He took out a parchment from his vest pocket. "If I deliver it, they might worry that the mission she is on is life-threatening, prompting the lord of the seifland to personally visit them. They wouldn't be wrong, but I don't want them to sense that. Also, it wouldn't do to send it through a messenger, as I hope to report back to Pari that I saw them myself. It is only right. You are my solution. Here, you can give them the letter. I would only be bringing you there to see your *friend's* family."

"She *is* my friend."

"Then you shouldn't have any problem meeting them. Come on." He led her to the waiting horses and helped her up onto the glistening white mare.

"I am not the only one here who knows Pari, though. Why didn't you ask Raya to accompany you?"

He did not answer immediately and urged his horse forward. Once they exited the war camp, he slowed down, waiting for her to ride alongside.

"I wouldn't feel comfortable taking Raya. Not just because Mother will have a thousand questions, but we—Raya and I—have not interacted much before these incidents happened."

"That is a pity. She is a sweet girl."

"I don't doubt it. But I've already had my fill of sweet sisters." He bent low to avoid a branch that extended over their path.

It barely brushed Deena's head, depositing a few drops of evening dew.

"You have two, don't you? Where are they?"

"One is with her husband in Heneria, and the other was in Izakura the last I heard. She is never in the same place for long."

"So no one is currently in Thian to claim your brotherly affection other than Raya."

"You will not let it go until I admit I am in the wrong, will you?"

"Oh, I don't wish that. It is just . . . Raya was speaking to me about how she would have liked to have a sibling. Maybe what she did, the brewing of veritria, that is, was to get some attention."

"That could be true, although my mother gives her more attention than one person can handle. Nothing the girl did was ever wrong, and all her mischievous antics went unpunished."

Deena couldn't help but laugh out loud. "That is exactly what Kran would say if you asked him how his mother treated me."

"And he would be right, considering you as well as Raya have a propensity to do forbidden acts, no doubt due to the encouragement from your foster mothers."

That sobered her up. "Maybe our foster mothers felt the need to overcompensate to make up for the absence of a real family."

"Look at you—justifying my mother's actions. You have grown in a day."

Deena was determined to maintain a huffy silence for the rest of the way, but Horace had other plans. He asked her about her training and her life in Alayster, and she told him how she had visited the passes between the Haiga range with her uncle in the past when skirmishes were common between Thian and Rothshire.

"Healers were always in demand in this region, and we would travel here and set up camp to assist the healers of Thian or Rothshire."

"You mean you helped both sides?"

"We are healers. We don't have sides. Even if you were fighting Alayster, we would have helped you."

"I am sure my father would have executed any healer in his camp if he had found they were helping soldiers of Rothshire. What else did you do behind my father's back?"

"I know little about it," she said hastily. What was she doing giving this vital piece of information to the current lord of Thian? It could make him clamp down on his healers when the upcoming battles started. "I was young, and they did not tell me many details about the logistics."

"How old were you?"

"Around Raya's age. Listen, if a battle starts, you wouldn't prosecute healers who help the injured from the other camp, would you?"

"I am not my father." His voice hardened. "If you haven't noticed, my focus is on preventing the war, but it would be sorely irresponsible of me not to set up all the pieces in place in preparation for one."

"If only there had to be no loss of life."

"Sometimes that is not possible. Let me ask you this. Would you take a life if by doing so you could save ten others?"

Deena grasped the reins tighter and chewed her lips. No straightforward answer came to her. "I could never think like a warrior," she said.

"You already do. You were the one who came up with the plan we are executing now."

The whistling of the breeze intensified, and Deena pressed a hand to her ear. "Ouch, what is it?"

"Byuton's spell warning us. It happened once before when I started talking to Kran about our business with the mages. The wind picked up after that, so Kran noticed nothing out of place."

She couldn't talk about the plan, but she must convey something to him.

"Let me ask you a hypothetical question like the one you asked me."

"Go ahead."

"If you are ever faced with an enemy who has no means of attacking you, would you choose to kill them or spare them?"

"Can I assume that the said enemy could eventually cause the destruction of our land and people if set free?"

"You don't have to set them free, maybe find a way to hold them prisoner forever."

"Some would say that is a worse punishment. Look, Deena, I can't promise you what I'd do or what anyone would do if we got to that point. Our end goal must be to save innocent lives. As a soldier, I have taken lives before and probably would do so again, but I would like to think my act saved more lives."

Yes, she could never think like a soldier, even if the idea of trapping the enchantress was hers. That certainly was her plan, and she would have to live her entire life with that sick feeling.

The village gate was visible a few yards ahead of them. The wooden gate was closed and a tall palisade ran on either side of it, but neither would stop anyone determined to enter the village in case the armies reached there.

Horace dismounted and tapped the gate with the latch hanging from it.

A head peeped out through a small gap between the gate and the palisade. "Who goes there? All the citizens are in. Do not lie."

"I am Lord Thian." He pooled his senria onto his hand and shaped it into his insignia—a bow nocked with a lightning arrow.

Someone pushed the sentry aside and looked at them. "Yes, it is Lord Thian. We are sorry, my lord."

The gate swung wide open.

"All the activities in the woods made us nervous, and we decided to secure the village against any aliens. Normally, we get a steady stream of visitors from Rothshire who use this village as a stop on their way to Alayster."

"Freedom of movement is not as of yet entirely curbed," Lord Thian said as the gates opened wide before them. "There are checks instituted at the border, and merchant caravans are being allowed to pass."

After asking the sentries about the direction to Pari's house, Horace led his and Deena's horses into the village. They crossed the empty marketplace and the deserted village pond to reach a stretch of houses.

At Pari's house, her mother and sister welcomed them in, sharing confused glances. The front room was littered with fabrics of all kinds, some hanging from the roof and layers of them spilling out of cupboards. But instead of the sterile scent of textile, the house was filled with the sweet smell of fried ghee.

Deena gave them Pari's letter. "I am a friend of Pari's."

Pari's mother took the letter and let her eyes sweep over Deena. "I made this tunic." She smiled.

"Pari gifted it to me."

"Ah, then you must be a really close friend of hers." Her mother tucked a strand of black hair into her graying bun.

"We hadn't expected a visit from Lord Thian himself." Pari's sister looked flustered. She was the spitting image of Pari, except for lacking the straight-backed soldier's stance that Pari always maintained.

"Don't mind me," Horace said. "I am only escorting Deena, but I would be happy to take back any message you have for Pari."

"We had one written for her and were planning to send it to the palace through a courier runner," her sister said.

"It will reach her faster through me," Horace said. "My courier will take a message to the palace tonight."

Pari's sister nodded and went inside the house and brought back a wrapped packet.

"It also contains her favorite ghee sweet," her mother said uncertainly.

"Of course." Horace smiled.

After they were offered the same powdery sweet, which Deena gratefully gobbled up and Horace munched on thoughtfully, they bid farewell to Pari's family and returned to their horses tied to a pillar outside the house.

As Horace approached her to lift her up to the horse, his eyes fell on her lips. Deena consciously rubbed a hand over her mouth to remove any remnants of the sweet that might have lingered there.

"Is it the sugar?" Deena asked.

"What?" Horace looked at her quizzically, then shook his head and lifted her onto the horse.

The ride back to the village gate earned them some curious on-lookers. Word must have spread that the lord of Thian was in the village. The gate was left open for them to leave, but it groaned shut behind them. The villagers of Veiga were not taking any chances.

"I wish they wouldn't have to live in fear for long," Deena said.

Horace sighed. "Things seldom go as we wish. Wasn't it just two days ago that we thought you'd be able to continue living in Thian and simplify our herbal distribution?"

"That would have irked Lady Len to no end."

He laughed. "Most of my actions do. So, this needn't be any different."

"Maybe someday, when all this is over, I can return."

"Do you wish to?"

His horse nuzzled against her thigh as he moved closer to her.

"I don't want to think that I'd never see you again." Her voice sounded garbled and breathless to her own ears, and she hoped he did not notice it.

But his expression was inscrutable as he leaned toward her and brushed something off the tip of her mouth.

Her breath caught in her chest as his finger seemed reluctant to move away from her face. She shut her eyes. He mustn't see how he affected her. For a moment she felt his breath fanning her face, and in the next there was an explosion that shook the trees around them and showered them with twigs and leaves.

21

Horace swung around to see smoke swirling through the trees.

"Stay here," he shouted, and galloped toward the village. The gate was splintered, and the two sentries who had greeted them lay motionless, covered in blood.

Through the smoke that still had not dissipated, a slim, furry figure with pointed teeth trailed a sword on the ground. Someone screamed in the distance.

Two sentar swords appeared in Horace's hands, one of which he sent to the haurie, piercing the smoke.

The creature fell but revealed another of its kind some feet away. A woman struggled against its grip on her hair, screaming all the while. Mercifully, the haurie's hand had not turned to fire. Horace rode toward it.

The rat-like face widened with glee as it left the woman and scrambled toward Horace on all fours. When it was a few feet away from him, its limb extended forward and curled around the horse's front leg, pulling it to the ground.

Horace flew through the air, rolling as he reached the ground to lessen the impact.

The soil trembled under him as the earth splintered, and four more hauries appeared in a shower of soil and bits of roots. Horace jumped to his feet and instinctively manifested a shield around himself. It was a mistake. The hauries would take the exhibition of his sentar powers as a challenge and counter it with their fire.

He paused as one of the hauries stretched its hand longer and prodded the shield. Nothing happened. Fire blazed in its palm and spread through its hand. The claws penetrated the shield, and the hand reached Horace's neck. He swiveled around and exited his shield, which was useless against the fiery limb.

Dodging another hand of flames that swayed toward him, he pirouetted and slashed through the neck of a haurie that still had not blazed up. It collapsed to the ground, halting the progress of the rest. At that moment, hooves approached them from the gate.

Help was coming. Three horses rode in, their riders holding torches. They wore black armor, not the silver armor of Thian, and visors hid their faces. They went straight to the huts and laid their torches on the thatched roofs, setting them on fire. A sharp pain in his thigh distracted him from the screams of the villagers. One of the hauries had successfully wrapped its limb around his leg. The scalding-hot limb pulled him down and dragged him on the ground, the jutting stones on the path tearing his tunic and cutting his skin.

The jolt made him lose his sword. He manifested an arrow and pushed it with his senria to the haurie without looking. It missed the chest of the creature but struck its shoulder. The limb loosened, and Horace released his leg.

"Fool," someone yelled—a human voice, a familiar one. "Aim for his hands and then neck."

Before the haurie could act on the command, Horace somersaulted and kicked the creature in its chest, sending it sprawling on the ground.

Fire had spread through the closely packed houses, the orange flames intermingling with the dusk sky. Chaos reigned as villagers ran for their lives, carrying children and hastily grabbed bundles. A few rushed to the village pond with buckets to fetch water, but on seeing the screeching hauries approaching them, they dropped their intention and fled.

He needed to get to the horse riders and stop them before the entire village turned to ashes. As he ran to them, the hauries let out a cackling laughter and called him in their chillingly hoarse voices.

"Lord of Thian. Lord of Thian. Look at what is happening to your subjects."

He couldn't help but look behind him as the hauries wrapped their long, flailing arms around the necks of two panicked villagers.

"Stop!" Horace yelled. But their necks snapped. An uncontrollable shudder passed through his entire body.

"A shame." One of the horse riders now faced him and removed his visor, revealing the jeering face of Val Tandon.

Tandon was here. He'd dared to creep into the territory of Thian and hurt the people. A fury he had strived to keep under check burst out of Horace in the form of a spear.

He faltered slightly as the manifestation of the weapon took a large chunk of his energy, but he threw it at Tandon. If that coward died here tonight, that would be an end to the havoc he had been wreaking around the continent.

But the spear stopped midair as the hand of a haurie took it in its grasp and handed it to Tandon.

At the same moment, the searing limbs of two other hauries bound Horace's wrists. At least his people would be free to make their escape now. The appendages jerked him to his knees and pulled his arms backward, almost straining them out of their sockets. An involuntary scream left his throat.

Horace struggled as pain misted his eyes. Through the blur, he saw Tandon dismounting his horse—the valiant warrior's look of glee matching the rat faces.

"I don't want to get too close to you, *my lord*," he said tauntingly, "or else you might spit sentar weapons at me. So instead, I will use your spear for the purpose." He aimed the spear. "Rothshire was always mine. Now Thian is too."

The spear left Tandon's hand, but it did not reach Horace. First, he thought a haurie had taken hold of it again, but it was not a fiery hand that held the spear; it was a fiery whip. It flew over Horace's head, and a howl erupted behind him. His wrists were suddenly free. Twisting around, he saw the spear strike the forehead of a fallen haurie.

The whip returned to him and floated midair. He took hold of it and lashed it at the three remaining hauries, keeping them at bay.

A lone rider on a horse entered the gate of the village. Tandon's sword had come out of its sheath, and he backed up toward his men, who now joined him. Before they could act, three sentar arrows came flying toward them.

Two arrows found their mark on the throat and forehead of Tandon's companions. Tandon struck the third arrow down with his sword and kicked it away. The arrow flew around him and attacked him from behind even as he tried to flick it away with his sword.

Horace smiled. If there was anyone he would have wanted to see at that moment, it was her—Lady Ilyria.

With a grunt of relief, Horace lashed the whip at one of the hauries and wound it around its neck. Fire erupted from its neck, countering the fire on the whip.

"Let it go," Lady Ilyria shouted.

Horace let go of the handle of the whip, and the weapon moved up to the face of the creature, burning the furry head. The creature screamed and ran helter-skelter before falling to the ground, dead.

Horace turned to the remaining hauries, but they had leaped toward Tandon, who was still fighting Lady Ilyria's arrow. One of the hauries grabbed Tandon by his waist while the other burned a hole in the ground. Together, they dragged a screaming Tandon underground.

Ilyria jumped down from her horse and ran to Horace. "Are there any more of them?"

The crater that the hauries had left on the ground was eerily empty. Horace looked around at the burning houses and the scattered bodies on the winding road, running a hand over his face. The seared skin around his wrist still smelled of scalded flesh, although the smoke from all around him was more overpowering.

"We have to check," he said.

He took control of a horse that Tandon had brought in, and together they rode through the village paths. Dead bodies were strewn on the path. The rest of the villagers had fled, although some might be trapped in the burning houses. The fire was still spreading from one house to the next, aided by the wooden outer structure and thatched roofs.

"We must put out the fire before it spreads further." Horace turned to the village pond, ignoring the ache in his chest. Did he tempt the hauries here by visiting the village?

"It will take much time to carry water from the pond, but we can do what we can." Lady Ilyria crafted a pail from her senria and sent it whooshing to the pond. It filled with water and returned to the scene of fire before Horace reached the pond.

"We need twenty more of you, Mother Ilyria." He manually took water from the pond in a bucket left there by the villagers and ran with it to the houses, the splash doing nothing much to quench the fire.

"I think we will get four more pairs of hands, one of which could speed things up more than the rest."

Four horses galloped into the village and stopped by the pond. It was Byuton, Gaelia, Kran, and Deena.

Seeing what Horace and Lady Ilyria were doing, they headed straight to the pond.

"Byuton," Lady Ilyria called, "can't you work some of your magic to move the pond water to the houses?"

"All the water in this pond won't suffice," Byuton said, hesitating by the pond. "Oh, all right, I will try something, on two conditions. One, none of you must tell my parents I did this spell, and two, one of you must ensure I reach the camp again, because I won't be able to do that on my own, and all of you get on the floor before this spell makes you dizzy."

They obeyed. Byuton closed his eyes and placed his left hand on his abdomen. He rotated his right palm to the left in a continuous motion. No spell was uttered, and his lips were clenched, nearly white.

Deena, who was kneeling closest to Byuton, made a choking gesture, and in a few more moments, Horace realized why. All breathable air was sucked out from the surroundings. He gasped like someone had pushed him to the depths of the ocean.

He put his head between his knees, fighting the dizziness, but before he lost consciousness, the air returned, and with it, life. A shiver trembled down his spine as everything went cold first before returning to a normal temperature. Horace stood up with the others, all coughing and gagging.

The fire had died down, but the young mage collapsed to the ground.

22

Deena ran to Byuton and checked his pulse, not finding it easily. His face was clammy and his breathing shallow. She tried to shift his bracelet away from his wrist, where it had a hold tight enough to restrict blood flow. It did not have a link or clasp. He must have gotten it on his wrist as a child and then never realized he outgrew it.

"Can I get some water?"

A pail constituted of golden light flew to her and landed next to her, splashing water on her lap. She dipped the hem of her tunic into the water and wiped Byuton's face. Blood seeped from under his bracelet.

"I need something to remove this bracelet. It is cutting into his skin."

"No," Byuton whimpered. "Please don't." His eyes fluttered open. "It will return to normal soon. I did some advanced magic that I shouldn't have. The bracelet stopped me before the magic could kill me."

"Magic can kill?" Gaelia kneeled by him, raising his head onto her lap.

"If performed by someone who can't handle it. Anyway, did I succeed?"

"The fire is out," Horace said. "I would say that is a success. There will be something to rebuild because of what you did."

Kran ran to the houses, probably to check if the fire was indeed completely out.

Byuton leaned on his elbow and surveyed his work. "Not quite successful. I had wanted the houses to cool down so that the fire doesn't restart, but there is not a drop of snow or ice anywhere."

"Was that what you were trying?" The voice came from above their heads. A tiny bird with a blue tail circled over them before swooping down to perch on Byuton's knee. Deena jerked back, her skin tingling until goosebumps erupted under her flowy sleeves, but Byuton did not react, as if this was not the first time a talking bird had landed on him.

"Thili," Gaelia said. "You are back."

So this was the enchantress that was Mentra's twin. Even Kran's description of her had not prepared Deena for seeing a bird that talked as easily as a human, even though its beak did not move as human lips would. Also, it was hard to imagine that this bird, as small as a nightingale, was an alluring beauty of Thisaur. The blast of colors on her feathers, however, would put a nightingale to shame.

"Yes, I got Byuton's message, and it looks like I arrived just in time," the bird said.

"Does *just in time* mean when others have done everything there was to do?" Byuton said.

"I wouldn't say *everything*." She rose from his knee and spread her wings, between which a rainbow appeared. Light expanded under the rainbow as a rectangular door and icy wind rushed through it.

Deena hugged herself as the chilly wind made her shiver to her bones, her tunic doing barely anything to protect her. A layer of white, powdery snow covered the rooftops and village paths and even the hairs of those present. The piney scent of mountains replaced the smell of all-pervading smoke.

Thili clapped her wings, and the light and rainbow disappeared.

"You overdid it," Byuton said.

"Huh, speaking of overdoing things"—Thili returned to the ground—"wait till I tell your parents what you did here tonight."

"You wouldn't." Byuton looked genuinely scared.

"I would. Imagine ignoring the warning of the bracelet just like that."

The bracelet now hung loosely around Byuton's wrist, although it had left an angry welt where it had tightened. So Byuton had not outgrown it. It must be a magical restraint of some sort.

"It was exceptional circumstances," Byuton argued.

"It very nearly was," Thili said. "The very exceptional circumstances that would have made your parents childless. Never overstep your limits again. Do you hear me, child?" Her squawky voice rose in pitch.

"Yes." Byuton made a disgruntled face, which conveyed that he thought hearing and listening were two different things.

"We must find the people a safe place to stay for the night," Horace said. "I am going to search for them and bring them back to the war camp. And by the way, for those who don't know, Tandon was here, and he was responsible for all that happened. So, I have to guess your sister was behind it too, Thili."

"Oh, you know. That means she has been up to something." The bird turned to Lady Ilyria.

"Yes, we have to fill you in on what happened."

"Why didn't you bring my soldiers with you?" Horace asked. "The four of you shouldn't have rushed in here without backup. And Deena, you shouldn't have come here since you are defenseless."

"I wanted to know you were all right." Her answer sounded weak even to herself. It was true she couldn't fight any sort of enemies, but she was not going to wait on the outskirts while her friends met an uncertain fate. She had even gone halfway back to the camp for help when she'd encountered Lady Ilyria and the rest of them.

"When we heard the explosion," Lady Ilyria said, "we wanted to ride to you with your soldiers, but in your absence, your commander would obey only Lady Len, and she claimed it was just rogue thunder." Lady Ilyria's face showed what she thought about that. "So we all rode in the direction you took and met Deena on the way. We thought we could be more helpful by coming straightaway rather than going back for the soldiers."

"And you certainly were right in doing that. I would be dead by now if you hadn't come," Horace said.

A shudder passed through Deena. The fear she had felt while waiting for him was not meaningless, and she did not want to think what his fate would have been if Lady Ilyria hadn't reached him in time.

The bodies of the dead villagers and enemies around them painted a gruesome picture. Horace could have been one of them. Deena walked to the bodies, checking that they were indeed dead, that there was nothing she could do to revive any of them.

Soldiers injured or dead in battle were not an unfamiliar sight for her, but the helpless bodies of the villagers screamed murder rather than death in battle. Kran joined her as she returned to the group of people who were watching her curiously.

"We also have to check if there are any more hauries left," Horace told Lady Ilyria.

"I will come with you," Kran said.

Horace nodded. "The rest of you must take Byuton to the camp and let them know what happened. Command them to send soldiers, horses, and carriages to the village. We will need help transporting the villagers to the camp. Here, take this." He removed his ring and extended it to Deena. "This gives you the authority to issue the command if anyone prevents you from doing so."

Deena took the ring and rubbed her thumb on his insignia carved on it. Lady Len would not like it if she issued such a command, but she could not pander to the ego of the lady who had not even thought of sending soldiers to check on her son. She slid the ring onto her middle finger, the only one it was not too loose for.

They completed their ride back to the camp in silence, and as soon as she arrived, she asked around for the tent of the commander of the camp and went to him to convey Horace's message.

The man twirled his mustache and looked doubtful. "I don't even know who you are."

She extended Horace's ring again. "But you know the message comes directly from Lord Thian."

His eyes fixed on the ring. "Does Lady Len know about this?"

"Lord Thian's words were to bring this ring to you. I did not go to Lady Len."

The soldier who stood behind the commander said, "Lady Len is walking by the lakeside with Lady Raya."

"All right," the commander said with a sigh. "I will send the troops and carriages to the village and the hills. That must be where the scattered villagers are hiding."

Deena agreed. There was nothing much left for her to do as the commander rushed to act. She retreated to her tent, where she found Byuton lying on a bed in the darkness, the only light being the one from the torches burning outside that filtered in through the flaps. Gaelia sat by his feet, warming them with her hands or sending him nourishing energy.

"He is still clammy but insists on speaking," Gaelia said. "Is there something you can give him to make him feel better?"

"Nothing will work," Thili said from a stool near his head. "Herbs cannot counter the reaction of using too much magic. He must weather it, but don't worry. He will survive. This isn't the first time he has stepped out of line, despite being warned not to do so."

"Getting back to where we were," Byuton said, "once the trap is set, we want you to be there to ensure we can bind her."

"How are you able to tell everything to her?" Deena asked. "Didn't your solemn oath apply to you?"

"Why would it? I trust myself."

"And if he can't trust me," Thili said, "there is no one he can."

"Well, trusting you is not an option," Byuton said. "Even if Mentra shifts into your form, no one could tell the difference because you are one and the same."

"Oh, she could never shift into a bird," Thili said. "In fact, she cannot shift into anything or anybody. The things I will tell you now will make you wish you were nowhere near this conflict."

"Some of us already wish that, Thili," Gaelia said with exhaustion dripping from her words.

Deena sat on the empty bed opposite them, acknowledging the tiredness of her body. She circled the ring around her finger, hoping Horace hadn't come across any more hauries. He had not been in good shape when he'd gone to look for them, but it was a relief that Lady Ilyria and Kran were with him. And whatever Thili was going to tell them, Deena resolved she would help to stop the enchantress Mentra, who did not care that innocents got hurt in her quest for revenge.

"Well, then listen to this. My travel to Thisaur has been to try to track the powers my sister possesses. There is only one way an enchantress can gain powers. That is by being sexually intimate with someone who holds the same power, and my sister never had physical relations with any of the known shifters of Thisaur."

"So . . . er . . . were you with a shifter who was a bird?" Gaelia asked.

"Yes," Thili answered without blinking. "Alantria. She was a shifter and a messenger in the court of Edri. But in that case—in that case alone—I did not steal the power. It was freely given. In most other cases, me, my sister, and other enchantresses follow Niferon's command and steal powers from his enemies and give it to him." She bobbed her little head and did not talk for a while.

A maid entered with an earthen pot filled with glowing embers. She laid it on the ground at the center of the tent and lit the candles on the tall stands by the four corners.

Thili continued when she left. "I don't enjoy remembering those times. Coming to our current issue, my sister is not a shape shifter. She did not change into another species like a shifter or into another person like the pisharas. What she did was take over the body of another human. Possession. That is what it is."

"You mean like a demon?" Byuton asked.

"Exactly like a demon. To be precise, it is a specialty of the demon king, Ryegor. Or was. Until my sister stole it. I learned as much from my trip to Thisaur. The body of Mentra might have belonged to some unfortunate human whom my sister killed before possessing her body. I am sure she took it after ensuring Monrae would find her attractive, and it wouldn't have been an easy task for my sister, because when I knew her, she was no killer."

"But she is now," Deena couldn't help but say.

"It must have gotten easier with each kill." Thili sighed.

"So you mean all Byuton's needle pricking was useless?" Gaelia asked.

"Yes, a body possessed can't be retrieved with a prick of silver," Thili said.

"That means one of us could still be her." Gaelia looked at Deena and Byuton and then shook her head like she wanted to dismiss the idea.

"Very much possible until the moment I came in," Thili said. "That brings me to the second thing I wanted to say. If anyone didn't know it, we are twins, Mentra and I, and we can recognize each other's energy. So I know for sure she has not possessed any of you. But, when I flew into this camp, I sensed her energy trail. She has been here, but now she has left. She might have been watching the camp or had some other plan to attack the camp."

"But we just sent a large chunk of the army to the hills," Deena exclaimed.

"Don't worry. The reason she fled is that she sensed me. She won't act when I am around."

"Then you mustn't accompany us to Bewar," Byuton said, "or our plan of luring her to the scroll won't work."

"Be very careful. I will not stop you from doing anything and everything to protect your land, but the net you cast might end up being too small for her."

It sounded like Thili still admired her sister. All that they knew about Mentra was from Thili, but how much of that could they trust? The two enchantresses were, after all, of one blood.

Deena tried to imagine what she'd do had Kran been the one destroying the lives of people. Would she ally herself with his enemies to help bring him down?

Gaelia and Byuton seemed to implicitly trust Thili, but someone had to acknowledge the possibility that the enchantress would have some desire to help her sister. Deena decided it had to be her. She would keep her eyes and ears open where the enchantress sisters were concerned.

"What other choice do we have?" Gaelia asked.

"Unfortunately, none," Thili said. "I made discreet queries without appearing in front of Niferon or his cohorts. He is not hunting Mentra anymore, and even if I told him she is plotting against him, he would laugh it off after locking me up, for he still has a price on my head."

"Why is that? Why only on your head when both of you abandoned his service?" Gaelia asked.

"I don't know the reason for his decision, but she might already know that Niferon is not hunting her. She would have heard it from the hauries. That takes away an advantage I had over her. I'd threatened her, saying I would turn myself in and disclose her location to him."

"I am kind of glad you don't have to give up yourself to Niferon," Gaelia said.

"But what will we do once we trap Mentra?" Deena voiced the question that had been disturbing her for days now. Horace had not given her a satisfying answer, although he must have thought of ending the enchantress's life once she was a captive.

"The very thing Gaelia wouldn't be glad about. I will create a portal and take her to Niferon's court."

"No!" Gaelia exclaimed.

"He won't just let her walk out again even if he is not actively hunting her," Thili said. "That could be the only way to contain her."

"But you would be imprisoned too," Deena said.

"Yes, but I don't want to give her a fate that I am unwilling to share. We shared the same womb. I will feel her pain even if I am not with her. Maybe the rest of our lives will be spent in Kalantra's dungeons together. I won't regret that."

Deena blinked. An eternity in the prison of the goddess of death was not something she would have voluntarily chosen.

"You don't trust me, child, do you?" Thili asked.

"Er . . . I just met you."

"Wise answer." Thili let out a tinkling laughter.

"It will be an uphill journey," Gaelia said. "But once she saves your life a couple of times, you can't help but trust her."

"Aww, such a sweet thing to say, Gaelia. The thought will warm me in Kalantra's prison."

"Won't her fires do enough to warm you?" Byuton snorted. "Come on, Thili. There should be something else that you can do to restrict Mentra. Aren't you a powerful being yourself? Think of something."

"We had similar powers once, me and Mentra, but if I am honest, she is a tad more powerful now that she has the scrolls of Varys and Zesta. Tad? No. With the powers of both the gods, she could easily annihilate me. And now she has the backing of the hauries. They are mercenaries and will protect the ones who pay them, even if they have to blow themselves up for it. More blood will be spilled in the coming days."

23

It was almost daybreak when Horace returned to the war camp. Three enormous tents had been erected to accommodate the hundred or so villagers who were led there by his soldiers. Food was also being prepared for them, which was a relief, as most of the villagers were down in spirits. The unexpected attack had left them in shambles, and he had been the reason it happened. He was Tandon's target. The hauries wouldn't have attacked the village had he not gone there the previous evening. And Pari's family would still be alive.

He tried to smother the frothing guilt and focus on the task at hand. Mobilizing his soldiers to rebuild the village was his first task, and even if there was no danger of another imminent attack, he would allocate two sentar warriors to their protection. He had scoured the area with Kran and Lady Ilyria. No more hauries were left in the region—at least, not above ground.

Sleep was nowhere in his mind as he walked toward the smaller tents that were allocated to him and his co-travelers. Lady Ilyria and Kran had already proceeded to their tents, and he wanted to check in on Deena and the others, but the one he wanted to see first was his mother.

If she had immediately dispatched their soldiers, the loss could have been limited. If she hadn't delayed Lady Ilyria by arguing with her, a few innocent lives could have been spared. If she hadn't given in to her vanity and had remembered to act like a leader, their people would have suffered a smidge less.

"Mother," he called from outside the tent she shared with Raya, his voice louder than necessary. There was no reply. They might not be awake yet, and he would have to give them time to be decent before barging in, but he couldn't rest without having this talk.

"Mother," he called again.

There was no movement inside the tent.

"Mother, do you hear me?"

Nothing.

"Raya, are you in there? I am coming in." After a pause with no reply, he pushed the flap and went inside. No one was present. He flinched at the smoke that had filled the tent. For a moment, his mind raced to the hauries as he swirled around, making sure nothing was on fire.

The cinders in a small earthen pot that must have been lit to keep the tent warm were smoldering. The beds were made as though no one had used them. Perhaps they'd left the tent earlier, and the beds were made after that. But whoever did that would have removed the smoking pot from the tent.

Raya could have dragged his mother to the other tent to learn what happened, and they could have spent the night with the other ladies. With that in mind, he rushed to Deena's tent, pausing to hastily call out a warning. This time there was a response as Lady Ilyria poked her head out.

"Is Mother here?" Horace asked.

"No, but come in. All the others are in, and none of them are sleeping, except for Byuton."

"What about Raya?" he asked.

"She is also not here," Lady Ilyria said.

"We figured she was with Lady Len." Gaelia came forth.

"They both are not in their tent."

"They must be receiving the villagers," Lady Ilyria suggested.

"We might as well check." Thili hovered over her. "Given what is going on around here."

The others spread through the camp, while Horace went straight to the large tent where the meal for the villagers was arranged. His mother could be there, trying to make amends. The anger he had been feeling for her melted slightly. No one knew his mother like he did. She might have a sharp tongue and an inflated ego, but she was not a bad person. She would be the first one to correct her mistake, especially without letting others know she had corrected it.

But she was not in that tent, nor in the second one filled with the mint-like smell of ajinthya. The healers were treating the injured villagers. Deena was among them. Their eyes met, and she acknowledged him with a nod, but she was dressing up the scraped knee of a child and carried on with that task.

He went to her. "Have you seen Mother?"

"No. Not since I returned."

"We are looking for her since she is not in the tent."

"Ah! Did you look by the lake? She was seen walking there yesterday."

"No, I will go there now."

"I hope you find her soon." She handed him his ring. "And when you do, please remember to dress those wounds of yours."

"I will come back to you." He tried to give her a reassuring smile and failed. "There is one more thing." He wanted to get it off his chest. "A few succumbed to the fire in the burning huts."

Deena's eyes widened in horror. "Pari's hut?"

He nodded, unable to form the words. With a sigh, he left for the third and final tent.

Lady Len and Raya were not in there either. Villagers sat in circles, unharmed but shaken. The buzz of their voices filled the structure with the reassuring vibrancy of life. When he exited the tent, Lady Ilyria and Gaelia came running to him with Thili soaring over them.

"Did you find her?" Ilyria asked.

"No . . . no." Horace ran a hand over his chest. "No, I couldn't find them."

"I flew all over the place," Thili said, "including by the lake. Some soldiers mentioned seeing her there last evening, but there was no sign of her or Raya. They wouldn't go anywhere without telling others, would they? I mean, Lady Len has a mind of her own, which often disregards others."

"No," Horace said with more harshness than he'd intended. He knew his mother had a will that did not bend to the convenience of others, but he did not want to hear anybody else say that. "She is not irresponsible." He ended in a calmer voice.

"I should have checked the tents when I arrived," Thili said, "since my sister's energy trail was present all over the camp."

"You mean..."

"Yes," Thili said, "she could have taken them. But why? She already has the scroll that was in your possession. What would she want with Lady Len?"

Horace shut his eyes tightly. The initial attack of the hauries had been to capture Raya. He should have given her more protection, but he had thought that a camp full of soldiers was safe enough.

"Or it could be Raya who was the target, and my mother was just the collateral damage."

"Why Raya?" Thili asked.

"Because of who she is—Zesta's daughter and heir," Lady Ilyria replied.

"Oh! Even then, why would Mentra want Zesta's heir?" Thili landed on the ground.

"I don't know," Horace mumbled before repeating it louder for the sake of the others. "But I must arrange for a search party."

"It won't serve any purpose," Thili said. "Mentra could have shifted them far away through her portal."

"What can I do now?" What kind of lord was he if he couldn't protect his own mother and sister, let alone the village on his land?

"You need rest and recuperation, Lord Thian," Thili said. "Running through these hills and collapsing with exhaustion won't serve any purpose. Here comes the healer. Deena, you'd do well to tend to Lord Thian's wounds and see he revives his energy before setting off again. And if you are setting off to anywhere, I suggest carrying out the plan you already started. Trapping her might be the only way to rescue your mother and Raya."

In the healers' tent, Deena applied a cooling balm to his wrist and ankles where the limbs of the hauries had seared off the skin through his clothes, the edge of which she had cut off. He had not noticed the exposed flesh or the stench it emitted.

"It will stop hurting, but the healing will take time," Deena said, focused on his wounds.

"Will it ever stop hurting?"

She looked up.

"The last few days were difficult," he said. "We talked little to each other."

Deena's hands gripped his fingers. "You can talk all you want when you see her again."

"Will I see her again?"

Deena's throat moved, but she had no reply. He was grateful to her for not giving him false assurances—ones he was giving himself at that moment. It was only a matter of time before they trapped the enchantress. He would make her reveal where she had hidden his mother. Then things would return to normal with regular debates and arguments with her, which he would never shy away from again.

"For her sake, you must believe you will see her again," Deena finally said. "And also, I am going to give you a sleeping draught, like the other day."

"No, no. There is so much to do. We must set off for Bewar at once. It is imperative that we succeed."

"We will succeed, but you need to regain your energy before travel."

"It is not safe to sleep." He hated the way he sounded like a child, but when he closed his eyes, he saw the burning village and the screaming people, and he imagined his mother and Raya suffering a similar fate somewhere. Also, another attack was imminent. He had to be vigilant.

"Horace, we need you at your full strength," Deena said. "When you sleep, I am going to stay awake and alert. And at the first sign of any disturbance, I will wake you up. I know exactly which dried leaf you have to smell to wake up from the deepest of sleeps."

Something loosened up inside him upon seeing her grim determination, and the sense of having to carry the entire weight of the world lessened. "You also had a sleepless night, didn't you?"

"Yes, but I don't need to manifest senria. I can sleep on our ride to Bewar. Byuton has taken over my bed anyway."

Horace knew Deena had kept her word, because when he opened his eyes, the first thing he saw was the sheath of leaves that she had clutched in her hands as she sat on the ground beside his bed, her eyes open, alert, and fixed on the opening of the tent that was covered by a layer of material darker than the normal flap. The light outside was still bright. It must be midday.

He sat upright, startling her.

She recovered quickly and gave him a shy, self-conscious smile. "So this was not necessary." She waved the leaves. "Kran just informed me that everything is ready for our journey. His sound must have woken you up, but you had a good rest. I will let them know you would like something to eat."

She left the tent before he could even thank her.

He dressed and ate as fast as possible before finding everyone gathered near the carriages prepared for their travel. He had to tell them about a slight change of plans. They would not stay overnight in any of the villages while crossing the Haiga range. Instead, they would travel as much as possible and set up camp when the horses needed rest. There was no point in endangering another village with his presence. So a third carriage was loaded with enough material to set up camp.

No one spoke of the two empty seats, but Horace reminded the soldiers to load Lady Len's and Raya's belongings onto the carriages.

Everyone was on edge as the journey began, expecting the ground to break open with hauries jumping out from underneath. Thili flitted in and out of the carriages, reassuring them that if a great number of hauries did come, they would get enough warning ahead of time, as the ground would rumble with their movement. That information did not particularly reassure the traveling party, but they were indeed grateful to have Thili's company for part of the way.

When they stopped for food and rest, she regaled them with tales of Thisaur and of how she was once almost eaten by a dragon that was left biting down on its own tongue as she disappeared from its mouth using a portal.

"You might wonder why I am not creating a portal for you to travel to Bewar," she said, even though no one put forth that question. "Each jump through a portal costs me a feather. I will regain them in time, but I have to be careful how and when I use them. Also, even if I sacrifice six feathers for the lot of you, a large perimeter around the Bewar forest does not allow the creation of portals."

"How did your sister get into their vault, then?" Gaelia asked, ensuring that Kran was out of earshot. He was the only one who still didn't know what they were up against.

"Hauries. Easy non-magical transport and undetectable if only one or two pop up behind a hill, where nobody ever checks for craters. Here, take this."

A leather-bound book fell on Byuton's lap, from which a blue feather stuck out.

"Write in this when you want to send me a message. When it is time for me to come and pick her up, I'll be there. Once I bind her, we can question her about Len and Raya before I take her to her final destination."

"You didn't really mean you're going to Niferon with her, did you?" Byuton scowled. "You can't get trapped in Kalantra's fire pits for an eternity. I was too weak to contest that idea when you first suggested it, but we need you here, Thili. Even if there is no Mentra."

"You don't know how long an eternity is, my child. All of you will be long gone by then. It wouldn't matter if I was flying free here or trapped in Kalantra's underworld if none of my family remain. You do not know how many families I found and lost to time. This way, at least I'll have my sister with me. I am being selfish here, choosing to trap her with me. Fire doesn't scare me. I am no syrelin."

Thili remained uncharacteristically silent after that, although she warned she would leave them during the night so as not to alert Mentra of her presence.

The journey continued in silence as the previous evening's exhaustion took its toll, and Thili was in no mood to cheer them up. She was with them when they changed horses and drivers in the village and bought food from the inn at night, but with the arrival of light, Thili had vanished.

24

Rehela was the last village they encountered before entering the forest of Bewar. That was where their carriages and drivers would wait until their task was done, when they would go their separate ways. Deena was looking forward to getting back home, but she knew it wouldn't be a peaceful journey without knowing that Raya and Lady Len were safe.

She had not spoken much to Horace during their travel to Rehela, almost forgetting how close he had come to kissing her. But every time their eyes met, that memory came rushing back. She also sensed the despair he was restraining as he put on a brave face to lead them. When they'd camped, she'd found him pacing outside the tents, hands tightly clasped behind him, and once, when he thought no one was watching, he wiped his eyes with unnecessary harshness.

They were now outside the borders of Thian, and nobody recognized the party as belonging to Lord Thian. The villagers present in the breakfast room of the inn that morning asked them whether they had witnessed anything of the strife between Thian and Rothshire. They politely replied in the negative. When the villagers learned about their intended destination, they were left alone with their sickly-sweet porridge and dry bread. Worried glances were frequently cast at them, and the innkeeper even went as far as giving each of them a piece of dried ginger, which he said would ward off mages. Byuton pocketed it with a grin.

The last stretch of their journey through the forest was made on horseback, their few essentials packed into small bags. Deena wore her leather bag with herbs across her chest, as it contained her most valuable possessions.

Horace's stiff shoulders did not relax even when they were traversing the lush green terrain or trotting across sparkling brooks. His neck strained to look behind him, and his eyes darted between trees whenever a fox disturbed from its sleep or a musk deer distracted from its foraging scrambled through the undergrowth.

"We are closer to Rothshire than to Thian." Kran slowed his horse to trot alongside her at the end of the group.

"No wonder he is on edge," Deena said.

"Is that the only reason? Who would have thought hauries would pop up on the continent? And under the command of Tandon when it was not long ago that syrelins made a similar appearance."

Deena wetted her lips. There was much that Kran did not know, and she was not at liberty to tell him most of it. But the enchantress's identity was no longer a secret. Wasn't that what Lady Ilyria had said?

"Come on, tell me," Kran said.

"What?"

"The thing you are hiding. I can feel it. You and everyone else whispering once my back is turned." He gave a crooked smile. "It is only fair that I know what I am walking into."

"You aren't walking into anything. I will administer the antidote to the mages, and then we will return to Alayster."

Kran did not seem convinced, but he rode on in silence without pushing her for further information. More than anything else, the frustrated look on his face made her want to tell him the truth.

"And Tandon is commanding the hauries because he has the blessing of the queen of Athora, who also happens to be an enchantress."

Kran choked on whatever he was going to say. Then he recovered and whistled. "Enchantress. Do you mean Queen Mentra? How? I wouldn't call her very enchanting."

"It is not her actual form."

"That makes sense. As does Tandon's involvement. He has always been her lackey."

"But you and I aren't getting involved in whatever they are brewing."

"Easy for you to say. You forget I am a soldier."

"But not of Thian. You must return to Alayster with me. This is much bigger than you or I can handle."

"What if the danger comes to Alayster?"

Deena had no reply. The idea was that the danger would be stopped in Bewar when the enchantress attempted to get her hands on Edri's scroll, but she couldn't tell that to Kran. So, she did not further the argument. If all went well, he would be safely home without having to encounter powers beyond his abilities.

"There is a clear patch coming ahead," Kran said. "Let me go and check it before you ride in."

He rode ahead, ignoring her protest, but when Horace held up a hand to stop him, he reined in. The group slowed down as they approached the circular ground devoid of trees. Giant multicolored cuboidal stones of different sizes—some standing as tall as a human and some lying horizontally—bordered this brown patch. There was enough space between the stones for them to ride in, but an unnatural stillness pervaded the circle, as if not even air was present inside it. Outside it, the forest continued as before, with chittering birds returning to their nests and a gentle breeze swaying the branches. Every eye turned to Byuton.

"What?" He shrugged.

"It is your area," Horace said. "Tell us what it is."

Byuton shrugged again. "What do you want me to tell?"

"Oof, Byuton." Gaelia snorted. "Just tell us if it is safe to enter."

"You all have the dried ginger, don't you?" Byuton smiled.

"Couldn't we round the circle and avoid it completely?" Lady Ilyria asked.

"I wouldn't suggest that," Byuton said.

"You are being too cryptic for your own good," Gaelia said.

"I think he wants us to enter it but cannot tell that to us," Horace suggested.

"You are very intelligent, Lord Thian." Byuton smiled.

"Enough of this." Kran urged his horse forward.

Why did he have to be the one to go headfirst into unknown territory? Before the others could act, Deena followed him, but as soon as Kran passed between two stones, he ceased to exist. Not quite. The tail of his mare that was still outside the circle swished in the air, seemingly disconnected from its body, until it, too, was pulled into the circle away from their sight.

Deena hurried ahead, bracing herself for the unknown. The moment she passed between the stones felt like plunging into an icy storm. Her breath hitched, and then she emerged into a room with floors and walls of gleaming sea-green marbles. She blinked slowly to make sense of her surroundings. The air carried the faint fruity aroma of a perfume rather than the earthy scent of the forest.

There was a ringing in her ears, and someone's words reached her as though from a long distance away. She looked around, rubbing her eyes and pressing her ears. She was no longer on her horse. Neither was Kran or the rest of the group who had by then joined them.

The room was windowless, with a bolted door at one end and another open at the other. The latter led to a seemingly endless corridor. Byuton's sudden laughter jarred her back to the present.

"Welcome to Xylera," he said, his eyes twinkling with amusement. "Now that we have entered it, I can tell you we are in the town of the mages. This is the official quarters of the master of the mages and also the gateway to Xylera." He paused, allowing the group time to absorb their surroundings. "The stone circle is part of our protection, and the magic wouldn't let me tell this to you while we were outside the circle."

"You said mages cannot open portals," Horace said, his eyebrows smashed together. For a weird instance, Deena felt the urge to throw herself between Byuton and Horace, but the former's voice was calm when he replied.

"That we cannot, my lord. But there are things we can do. For instance, it has been several minutes since all of us stepped into that circle."

"No way," Gaelia said. "I remember everything that happened. First Kran and Deena went in, and then we immediately followed, and here we are."

"Then where are the horses?" Byuton asked.

"The horses . . ." Gaelia's voice trailed off.

"Fires of Kalantra," Kran exclaimed. "Where are the horses?"

"They have been transported to the stables and your belongings to the place of your residence."

Lady Ilyria was hugging herself and turning around to take in the full view of the room. Deena did not know what everyone had expected while riding to the area of the mages, but it was certainly not this. She had envisioned a small settlement among the trees, with staff-bearing mages standing on guard. Instead, they had walked into a pristine chamber straight from the forest.

"After the guards ensured that you were friends," Byuton said, "which my presence assured them, they sent the horses to the stables and we came here. If you weren't our friends, you'd be at the other end of the forest by now, with no memory of what happened and with an intense desire never to return to the stone circle.

"Now that you are here, let me introduce you to my father. Come."

He led them out of the empty room through the long corridor, which, too, had green marble floors and walls. Carved wooden doors led off from the corridor—doors that were closed and bolted, and each of them were punctuated by sculptures representing humans and animals engaged in various activities. Dancing humans were interspersed with hunting animals. While a deer grazed, a woman was halfway through unsheathing her sword.

Byuton paused and opened a door. Then he looked back at the sculptures. "They are cursed to remain like this for eternity."

"Byuton," a stern voice called from the room. A giant of a man stood in front of a circular platform that seemed to float in the air. The room itself was circular, with the same green marble floor, but the wall was covered all around with what looked like a blackened mirror that showed no reflection. "Curses should not be spoken of so lightly. And you mustn't diminish the handiwork of our sculptors by assigning magical origin to their work."

"This is my father, Densyus Tantas." Byuton said resignedly. "And the master of the mages of Bewar."

Densyus stood before them in a flowing black robe embroidered with silver stars, like the night sky itself. His short reddish-brown hair streaked with gray sharply contrasted with the black mop sported by Byuton. He towered over even Kran and Horace. And Deena, like Byuton, had to crane up her neck to meet his gaze.

"I am grateful to you for making this journey," Densyus said to them all, but his eyes rested on Deena. "I know you deserve to rest after your travails. When you have done that, I will take you to those awaiting the antidote."

"I don't require any rest before doing that." Deena stopped herself from addressing him as "my lord." His bearing gave the impression of a man holding power—like the lord of a land. But the power he held was different.

He gave a grateful nod. "Then I will ask Byuton to take everyone else to our abode."

"I will come with you." Horace stepped up.

Kran gave her a wink, which Deena hoped nobody else saw. She had expected Kran to insist on accompanying her, reluctant as always to let her wander into unknown territory, but he gladly left with Byuton, Gaelia, and Lady Ilyria.

When Deena accompanied Densyus and Horace back to the corridor, the others were already out of sight. The only explanation was that they had entered another room, but they were in a land where magic was blatantly used. She mustn't look for logical explanations.

"I hope the travel onto our land did not disorient you," Densyus said. "The illusion of the stone circle is a part of our security system. We couldn't let you in without going through it."

"We made it through all right," Horace said. "How were your guards attacked even with such strong security?"

Densyus stepped out of a door onto a cobblestone street, a cool breeze caressing them. The saffron tint of the setting sun swathed the colorful box-shaped buildings lining the steeply climbing street that appeared to be carved into a hill. Through the gaps between the buildings, similar streets ran above and below them. And at the very bottom of the hill, a mighty river meandered toward the setting sun.

"Xylera is hidden by the shroud spell and oblivion spell, but our magic does not work near Edri's scroll." Densyus indicated with his hand that they could cross the street. The people who passed them bowed to him, confirming that *master of the mages* was indeed an elevated position, although Deena wasn't sure what it entailed.

"That made the place we hid the scroll an easy target for Mentra," Densyus continued. "So when Thili warned us, we removed the illusion from a few more sites to confuse anyone hunting for the scrolls in our region. All those locations had powerful guards, but the poison took them unawares. Here." He knocked on a door painted in a rich red shade. A hanging balcony overhead had baskets with ruby-colored lobelia cascading out of them.

"They are housed here—the victims, that is—waiting for your arrival."

"How many were injured?" Deena asked.

"Six."

And one of them was his wife. Even though he didn't mention it, the strain around his mouth spoke about the worry he had been holding in.

"The antidote worked on our soldier," Horace said confidently, perhaps spotting the strain.

"May it have the same effect on our warriors," Densyus said.

The door was opened by a woman wrapped in a scarlet robe. She stood aside as they stepped into a small hallway that, after all the colors they had witnessed, was rather plain. There were only a couple of rooms within, one of which was a wide chamber with a string of windows on one side overlooking a backyard. The room was lined with beds separated by curtains. Six beds currently had curtains drawn around them.

"They were put into an enchanted sleep," Densyus said, "so that their suffering is minimized."

"Were they given aziril?" Deena asked.

"Yes, though in an enchanted sleep, they don't need sustenance. But we didn't want to take any chances. We obeyed your instructions."

Deena took the vials of antidote from her bag and the syringes to administer them with. There was surely enough for six patients. The man on the first bed was in a much better condition than Jianther. His skin had a similar scorched look, but to a lesser extent. The same was the case with the others—three more men and two women. She gave the antidote to everyone and paused at the final bed to check the burns of the woman. Her face had marks of having been touched with veritria—the brown patch on her right temple and cheek indicated that she'd turned her face just before being splashed with the poison.

"Tisila was at the forefront." Densyus moved a black curl of hair from her scarred skin. "The others must have used the tarshish spell against the poison, but her sentar shield was too late to stop it."

"I am sorry," Deena said softly. "But I assure you she will recover."

25

Horace had never in his life slept more comfortably than he did that night. He had taken no sleeping draught, and the bed in which he lay was a simple mattress covered in a sterile gray sheet. The room itself had no provisions to remove the chillness of the night. The only addition it had other than the bed was a wooden cupboard in which his belongings were neatly arranged. There was not even a blanket on the mattress or in the cupboard.

Throughout the night, however, he felt like the mattress was holding him in a warm embrace, emitting scents of a fully bloomed rose garden that transported him into a dream in which he had a deep, long conversation with his mother. She told him how much she trusted him and that she was waiting for him to rescue her.

When he walked to breakfast the next morning, he uttered a promise to his mother to leave no stone unturned in finding her. He would be the first to reach the trapped enchantress and the first to question her, albeit with Thili's help. Only with his mother and Raya would he return home. He stood for a moment to take a deep breath to calm himself before he met his companions. He could hear their voices from further ahead in the house.

Byuton's house, on a cursory glance, looked like any other building one would find in Thian or Rothshire. The tiled floors and stone walls were simple enough, although they had a sparkling look like they were freshly scrubbed. But in no house in his seifland would the door open of its own accord when one stood before it. Nor would a warm breeze waft through the rooms if one shivered.

Horace had no difficulty finding the dining area. On the previous night, the meal was provided to their separate rooms so that they could relax. But this morning everyone had gathered in the open courtyard at the center of the house around a long, rough-hewn table. White puffs of clouds floating through the sky rendered the open ceiling the quality of a painting that would be a credit to even the castle of Athora. From the middle of the table rose the bare trunk of an old oak, on which was built small shelves to hold pots of honey and bowls of cream.

The rest of the group was present, looking refreshed. Byuton was not with them, as he had spent the night monitoring his mother's condition. The mages had removed the sleeping enchantment from the injured warriors, and two among them had stirred during the night, awake long enough to assure those present that their pain had subsided. So Deena's antidote was not a onetime wonder.

Horace sat in the empty seat beside her. The bowl in front of him immediately filled with thick porridge, and the plate next to it was simultaneously stacked with piping-hot steamed rice cakes.

"Not a moment passes here without something magical happening," Deena said, digging into her porridge.

"You saving the lives of those mages was pure magic too," Horace said, earning a delighted smile from her, which took him back to that moment in the forest before the haurie attack. He had wanted to kiss her then. He did even now. He wanted to find out whether her kiss would give him the same relief that her elixirs and balms gave the wounded.

"Lord Thian." Byuton arrived, distracting him from pleasant thoughts.

He bit into a rice cake to hide his confusion, the heat scalding his tongue.

"Yes," he choked out.

Deena extended a glass of cool water, which he gratefully drank to soothe his mouth.

"Father wishes to meet you whenever you are ready."

They had agreed to set up the trap for Mentra that day. Horace had offered to be there and also to be a part of the watch team that would observe the location from a distance. Once the trap was set, Densyus's network of spies would surreptitiously reveal the secret location of the scroll, hoping the information would reach Tandon or Mentra.

"What news of your mother?" Deena got up to greet Byuton.

Byuton smiled, his eyes softening. "She just woke up."

He gave Deena a hug that made her stumble back into her chair. Byuton stabilized her. "The mage community will never forget what you did for us, and I will never forget what you did for her."

"It is my job, Byuton. Any healer would have helped you."

"Yet you can't escape our gratitude." He beamed.

"Don't refuse a mage's gratitude, Deena," Gaelia said. "You never know when they could save your life."

"It doesn't always need to be lifesaving." Byuton took the chair Deena had vacated. "Mages can repay in a lot of other ways too. For instance, the dreams you all saw last night were gifts from us."

Gaelia dropped her spoon, her eyes widening. "You mean you know what each of us dreamed last night?"

"No, I have no idea of any of your scandalous dreams, but you should have seen your deepest wishes."

"I have no qualms in admitting that I dreamed of my beautiful wife," Kran said, "and I can't wait to get back to her."

"That can be arranged as soon as you feel rested," Horace said.

Deena had already handed over the heliatin thorns to Densyus. She had embedded them carefully in a parchment, which they were to wrap around the scroll of Edri. One touch on the parchment by the enchantress and the poison would paralyze her. The purpose of her travel was complete. She could leave with Kran and Gaelia to Alayster. He did not want her anywhere near the enchantress or the hauries she would send.

"You must go back to Rehela and take one of the carriages to Alayster. I left instructions with the drivers. Mother Ilyria will be given transportation by the mages to the port of Easther, from where she can get to Kendrek."

Byuton nodded. "That can be easily arranged."

"But . . . but what if you need us here?" Deena said.

"We can't foresee that," Byuton said, "but there is no point in endangering your lives. You must return here and spend days with us once this danger has passed. Until then, you are better off on your own lands."

Lady Ilyria cleared her throat. "I don't want to impose on you, Byuton, but . . ."

"It won't be an imposition, Mother Ilyria," Byuton said. "The transport will be ready whenever you are."

"I meant I don't want to impose on you and continue staying here, but I believe I can be useful if she brings on the hauries. The only way to deal with those creatures is by manipulating weapons from a distance."

"And you are the only one who can do that," Horace said.

"The only one here," Lady Ilyria corrected with a graceful smile.

"I, for one, would be grateful for your help," Horace said. But he left the final decision to Byuton, as he was the host.

Byuton remained silent for a while until it seemed like he would not provide a reply. The clattering of spoons in bowls continued, and Deena walked around the table to sit by Gaelia.

"The tarshish spell can push enemies from a distance," Byuton said slowly as though musing to himself. "The chilling spell can also be used on the hauries without getting close to them. But yes, we don't have any spells that could take them out. That is another thing that I shouldn't be revealing, as the fear of the alleged killing spell is what keeps our enemies away. But that is the truth. There is no killing spell, and we have to use weapons like anyone else. You will be a welcome addition to our team, Mother Ilyria."

So that was settled. Kran, Deena, and Gaelia were to depart for Rehela after a rest of two days and take the carriage from there to

Alayster, while Horace and Lady Ilyria would help the mages until the enchantress was trapped.

Horace had to admit that kidnapping his mother was an excellent strategy by Tandon or Mentra. It had successfully diverted his attention from the frontier. And if the enchantress did not target the scroll soon, he would be stuck here for a long time. That wouldn't prove beneficial to his land or his people.

But he knew his mother would be counting on him. Until he found her, he would abandon everything else. Even Deena. The yearning to spend more time with her did not dissipate, but at this moment, there was nothing he could offer her. Maybe someday she would return to Thian.

Lady Ilyria accompanied him and Byuton as they went to see Densyus. Byuton's house was near the center of the town, where stood the small temple of Edri, with its spiral roof and arched doorway. It was enclosed within a wooden fence. Music from a flute floated out of the temple from which people were streaming in and out. Some sat around the multitiered ivory fountain placed outside the fence. The water in the fountain danced in rhythm with the music.

"The morning rituals would be in full swing now," Byuton said as Horace breathed in the scents of sandalwood and camphor. "Once upon a time, Edri's scroll was placed in the temple, until we had to hide the town with magic."

They went up the steeply climbing path that led to the official quarters of Densyus. Cartwheels clattered from the street above, and shops along their way were opening for business.

"It is strange to think mages live life almost like us," Lady Ilyria commented. "Look at that. Is that a sweet shop?"

"Ah yes! The finest sweets available in your seiflands come from our town," Byuton said. "We disguise ourselves as citizens of Alayster or Easther to do the trading."

Horace took in the bustling roads, the running children, and the smell of freshly baked bread wafting out of houses. He'd been foolish to think that mages never left the Bewar forest. They would need to trade for all the necessities of life, and for that they'd have to travel to the other seiflands. He couldn't help but admire how they preserved their secret by never exhibiting their powers while in other lands. If his situation had been different, Horace would have liked to help them establish trade links with Thian. Maybe he'd get a chance to discuss it with Densyus once the danger was averted.

Densyus was waiting for them in the room where they had met him the day before. Two other mages were with him. One was introduced as Heyar Setreki, a combat mage, and the other was Byuton's grandfather, Muryt Tantas.

"The thorns are in place." Densyus walked to the mirror-covered wall and knocked on it. A section of the blackened mirror shimmered and cleared to show a cluster of rocks in front of a fast-flowing river. "That is where Edri's scroll currently lies. Our watchers are extending their vision for us to see the location."

"But Father, Mentra can manipulate water with Varys's power. We mustn't lead her to a water body."

"The scroll will suppress all magic and power," Heyar said. "Like the curb circle does to our power."

"But the curb circle does not suppress the power of gods." Byuton rubbed the back of his neck, his silver bracelet gleaming on his wrist.

"The scroll does," Muryt said. "Also, she doesn't need to be close to a river to summon water if she has Varys's powers."

Byuton made an impatient clicking sound with his tongue.

"Have faith in our research," Densyus told him.

"How can we help?" Horace asked.

"For now, there is nothing to be done but wait," Densyus said. "Eight of our folks are watching the place and transmitting to us what they are seeing. We could use your skills if Mentra brings Tandon or the hauries along with her. We also have three more sentar warriors in our midst who were trained by Tisila."

"We are pleased to hear your wife is on the path to recovery," Lady Ilyria said at the mention of Tisila.

Densyus looked at her, confusion marring his features. Muryt coughed and turned his attention to a parchment he was holding. Heyar returned to the circular platform at the center of the room on which lay several more parchments. Densyus's glance flittered to Byuton and back to Lady Ilyria.

"Thank you. Tisila is not my wife," he said ruefully. "She is . . . she is a part of my family nevertheless, and a valued member of our security team."

Behind him, Byuton rolled his eyes. Horace could sense that Lady Ilyria was bursting to ask follow-up questions, but to her credit, she reined all of them in.

"Byuton will lead you to the watchers," Densyus said, recovering quickly, "but I suggest that after seeing the location, you two take turns on the watch with the three sentar warriors on our team, as it could be a long wait. Whispers will soon reach Tandon and Mentra about the real location of the scroll, but we can't say when they will act."

They agreed to take turns and left Densyus, Muryt, and Heyar to their discussions. Byuton took them to the corridor and opened another door. This time they exited to the forest, outside the circle of stones.

"I will never get used to this." Lady Ilyria paused and shook her head.

"We try to keep it all disorienting," Byuton said. "Only someone who has lived here for years can go in and out through these doors and know exactly where they will land."

Three horses were ready for them. They rode through the forest as they had done during their journey from Rehela, but this time, they headed north. Emerald hills loomed to their left, and the sound of a babbling river seemed to be their guide stone, but even amidst the trees, sections of paved path appeared. The stones were old and not as well laid as in Xylera, but it was possible that the town had extended to this region once.

They followed the sound of the river until the steadily streaming water body became visible, flowing down from the hills. A rickety wooden bridge hung in the air above the river with no pillars or ropes to support it. Horace had no intention of testing its stability.

"The river Laryshia marks the border of our lands," Byuton said. "The bridge is a warning for anyone wandering unknowingly to this area to stay away, for a magically floating bridge is a clear sign of mages being present around here."

"Do we have to cross the river?" Lady Ilyria, too, did not sound happy with that idea.

"The watchers are present behind that small hill on this side"—he pointed to the distance—"and also in those trees that line the river by the other side. Those are not actual trees, by the way. You can choose to remain on this side, but if you ever have to cross Laryshia, know that the bridge is rock solid. It will be neither swayed by a wind nor washed away by a flood. Don't hesitate to cross it. I can show you right now."

He trotted his black mare forth, but it stopped when it reached the water, probably wondering like them how it was supposed to get onto the bridge that was not connected to the ground. Byuton gently encouraged it to move ahead, and it relented, stepping on an invisible path and finally reaching the bridge. Once there, it trotted with more confidence and reached the opposite end.

"I will die before admitting that the horse is braver than me," Horace muttered.

Lady Ilyria laughed. Together, they coaxed their horses up the invisible path to the hanging bridge. The bridge did not sway or even budge under the hooves. The wooden planks with considerable gaps between them stayed stronger than iron. Having demonstrated the strength of the bridge, Byuton led them back to the other side and went upriver, toward the hills, till they reached the one Byuton had earlier pointed out.

"When you join the watchers," Byuton said, "they will hide your horses with a shroud spell."

The river was wider here, with a group of rocks heaped by its side, forming a tall mound. One side of it was open, leading to the hollow space within. On a raised platform at the center of it lay a rolled-up parchment with golden knobs at either end.

"This seems too easy a target," Horace said. "Won't she be suspicious?"

"Suspicion won't keep her away from the scroll that she badly needs. The outer layer has the thorns," Byuton said. "If what Deena says is true, the effect should be immediate, and our work thereafter is very easy. So, which of you wants to join the watchers first?"

26

Deena, along with Kran and Gaelia, left Xylera early in the morning. Densyus and Byuton saw them away, accompanying them far beyond the exterior of the stone circle. Lady Ilyria was with the watchers at that hour, and Horace was sleeping after being on duty during the night.

But both had said their farewells at different times on the previous day. Horace had come to her room as she was wrapping a packet of herbs to leave with Byuton as a gift, tucking in the single dose of antidote that remained. It was her most valued possession, but the mages might need it if Mentra attacked again with the same batch of veritria.

"I don't know how long I'll be here or at the borders," Horace said, leaning on the doorframe, "but if you write to the palace, the letter will eventually find me."

Deena could only nod and gulp as she recollected the dream that she'd seen the previous night of him standing so close to her until she could feel his breath fanning her cheeks. She refused to believe Byuton's words that it was the deepest desire of her heart to have Horace so close to her. It was only a memory from the time he had almost kissed her on their ride back from Veiga. He must have forgotten about that momentary attraction and had more important things vying for his attention. She chided herself for feeling awkward in his presence.

"I will," she said with more composure than she felt. "And if you ever need my service, you only need to write to Lord Alayster."

"Can't I write directly to you?"

The fluttering in her stomach restarted at the earnestness in his tone. "Certainly," she managed to say. "It is... My village is Trilin. Anything addressed to Healer Deena will reach me."

He stepped forward, took her hand, and pressed it to his lips. "I will wait to hear from you."

With those words, he left, leaving the imprint of his warm lips on her hand that she held close to her chest for a long while.

Kran's voice brought her back to the present, although she did not hear what he'd said. He repeated. "How long will you both need to rest once we are in Rehela?"

Deena craned her neck to look at Gaelia, who was behind them. She seemed to be engrossed in the richness of the verdure and the fragrance of the wildflowers that enclosed them from either side. The canopy weaved by the branches overhead filtered the harsh sunlight to a soft green glow. Even the forest floor did not escape from the greenery, as ferns that thrived in the shadow and logs swathed in moss fought for space with the thick undergrowth. It was a wonder that Kran could find the return path through this area, considering he had traversed it only once under Byuton's guidance.

Deena slowed down for Gaelia to join them. "Not much time. We'll have some refreshment and start immediately."

"I agree," Gaelia said.

"I wonder what Mother and Hena make of my absence." Kran pushed away a low-hanging branch on their path. "Last they heard I was going to Thian to get you."

"Malion wrote to them," Gaelia said, "saying you are away on official business."

Kran's face relaxed. "That was kind of him."

"It was the least he could do."

"He did more than he should have." Kran gave a stern look to Deena, as though still chiding her for her foolishness that had dragged him to Thian in the first place.

"They needn't know all the details," Deena said. "Don't you think?"

Kran did not answer her. Twigs snapped somewhere ahead.

"Stay here," he said, before galloping his horse forward. His hand reached for his sword and drew it.

Gaelia looked at Deena. "I rather not hang back here."

"Me neither," Deena said. And they rode behind him. Kran's horse came to a sudden halt in front of a thick growth of underbrush.

The shrubs shook like something was struggling to get out of it. It could just be a deer that had gotten its antlers stuck in the bramble.

As harmless as that would be, a cold fear gripped Deena. She wanted to turn the horse and ride back to the mage colony. Kran, however, didn't budge.

Twigs broke away from the net of overlapping plants, and a figure in black stumbled out, bloodied and covered in dirt. Lady Len. She fell face-first on the path and tried to crawl forward as another figure emerged out of the bushes. This time a figure Deena hadn't been looking forward to meeting—a haurie.

The giant rat-faced creature ignored the riders and lunged forward to grab Lady Len's ankles. Kran jumped down from his horse and ran to the haurie, slashing through its hairy arm. Blood gushed from the stump, and the haurie's wide mouth gaped in a screech of anger or pain, exposing its serrated teeth. Lady Len lay unmoving on the ground, temporarily saved from the haurie.

Deena felt her hands go cold around the reins that she clasped tighter than necessary. She must help in some way. Gaelia had dismounted before she could.

"I need help to get her out of the way," Gaelia said, looking warily at the haurie that was still screeching. Its throat vibrated violently until a flame built up around its neck.

Kran struck the haurie again, but this time, before the blade hit the target, which was its other arm, it had wrapped that arm like a vine around Kran's wrist, squeezing it.

Deena was unable to see what happened next because she had to help Gaelia carry an unconscious Lady Len to the horses. Hearing a strangled grunt, she craned her neck to look at Kran and the haurie. He had somehow extricated himself from the limb that had wound around his wrist. His sword was now in his left hand, and the haurie's second arm also lay amputated on the ground. This time it didn't screech. Instead, its whole body burst into flame.

"Get away, Kran!" Deena yelled.

She and Gaelia heaved Lady Len onto the horse, with Gaelia climbing behind the elder woman to prevent her from falling down.

Boom.

The forest floor shook, and smoke and fire filled her vision as Deena tried to catch a glimpse of Kran, but there was nothing left of him. The fire caught on to the dry branches of the shrub and formed a scarlet background, against which she saw the scattered remains of Kran and the haurie.

She heard a scream, realizing too late that it was her own.

"No." This time it was Gaelia who screamed.

Deena ran to the fire as the horses neighed and tried to bolt. Birds squawked, trying to escape the flaming trees, and a couple of deer sprinted out of the bushes. They brushed past Deena, who stopped before the scene of disaster. She kneeled and slapped her hand to her face to block out the vision and to wake herself up from the nightmare. There was no waking up.

"We must go," Gaelia said as if from far, far away.

"Deena," she called again, this time pulling her arm. She had come to get her.

She somehow got Deena onto her horse and climbed back onto her own, behind Lady Len, who was still unconscious. Kran's horse had gotten away. Together they rode back the way they'd come, Gaelia leading the way, as Deena had no idea of her whereabouts.

Why were they riding away without Kran? Leaving him alone in the forest? They were so close to getting back home, weren't they? If he had made it through this day, he would have been on a carriage to Alayster.

Maybe this day never happened. Maybe this was just a nightmare, and she was still sleeping in her bed in Byuton's house. But that bed only showed dreams that one truly desired. This was her greatest fear, not her desire. This was no dream.

The tears dampening her cheeks and neck were very real. They blurred her vision and made her feel impotent. She had no memory of returning to the circle of stones or of stepping into the green marble hallway. Hands led her on as a sharp ache compressed her chest. The only man she could have called a brother was no more in this world. No one would stop her again from making foolish mistakes, no one would look out for her now, and worst of all, a little girl would no longer see her doting father—all because she'd dragged him into this disaster.

She vaguely recognized the bedroom that she had occupied earlier and collapsed onto the bed, pressing her face to the pillow. At one point, she felt a hand on her back, trying to soothe her, but it didn't stop the tears. She didn't care who witnessed her despair.

Her next conscious thought was of someone gently shaking her awake. She must have fallen into a sleep of exhaustion.

Lady Ilyria sat beside her. "Deena, you must drink something. It is night, and you didn't drink or eat anything the whole day."

Deena sat up, blinking rapidly as reality slammed into her, pulling her out of the dream world in which she'd been back home with Mother Sheila and Hena, and Kran was playing with his child, Sheila.

"I can't..." Deena began.

"Strength, my dear," Lady Ilyria laid an arm around her.

Deena hugged her knees and rocked back and forth. Strength. She was left with none. Death was not new to her. There had been lives that she couldn't save, but Kran was different. He was so full of life one moment and gone the next. If not for the chance encounter with the haurie, they could have been on their way home now. But then...

"Lady Len," she said. "How is she?"

"She is fine." It was Horace who spoke. She hadn't seen him in the room.

"I will bring you some food." Lady Ilyria excused herself, and Horace took her spot.

Deena wished she'd stay. It was easier to cry in front of her, or that was what she'd thought until he took hold of her hands and squeezed them.

"I..." she began.

"Come here," he said.

And then she was sobbing into his chest with him holding her like he would never let her go.

When the sobs subsided, she distanced herself from him and wiped her face with the hem of her riding dress. He gave her a scarf.

"How can I ever return home?" She took it. "What will I tell Mother Sheila?"

"That Kran is not just a hero in Alayster but also in Thian. He saved my mother's life. I never thought I'd see her again. And I wouldn't have if not for him."

She looked into his twinkling dark eyes and saw he meant every word.

"Densyus and I went to . . . the site with some mages. We brought him back to Xylera and gave him an honorable cremation according to the rituals followed in Alayster."

She nodded, moistening her lips, recognizing the thirst she had been ignoring until then. Lady Ilyria was right in advising her to drink something. She couldn't hide in bed for the rest of her life. It would serve no purpose. There was much to be done.

"I should see to Lady Len. She was injured."

"Not badly. Gaelia used some of your pastes and balms on her and cleaned up her wounds."

"I should still see to her."

"Do it tomorrow."

"I can't sleep. Not now."

"Don't sleep. You can talk all you want. Neither me nor Lady Ilyria are going to be on watch duty tonight. We will be with you."

"But *she* can attack any moment now. The hauries are on these premises."

"At least for tonight, you are our priority. Tomorrow, Gaelia will be with you and Lady Ilyria, and I will join the watchers."

"For the first time, I wish I were a warrior and not a healer. For once I want to kill instead of save." A rage she had never known before filled her heart. She could destroy. She could kill. If only she could get her hands on them. On Mentra. Or Tandon. Or even a haurie.

He took her hands again. "The one who saves life is greater than the one who takes it. Never underestimate who you are."

27

Deena was not left alone even for a moment during the night. Horace and Lady Ilyria sat with her, listening to her reminisce about Kran or accompanying her in long intervals of silence. Lady Ilyria fed her twice, although Deena didn't realize what she was eating or drinking. And during some hour of the night, she fell asleep again—this time dreaming of Kran chiding her for moping around.

When she woke in the morning, it was Gaelia who sat at her bedside.

"I sent a message to Malion," Gaelia told her. "He went to Kran's home yesterday. They are grieving but being very brave."

"Thank you." Deena wished she could be there with them at this time, sharing in the grief. But it might be better to return home and tell them that the person who caused Kran's death was being punished. It might be good that their journey back home was postponed.

After a wash and a simple breakfast that Gaelia provided for her in her room, Deena decided it was time to get her act together.

"How is Lady Len?" she asked.

"She was troubled and injured. The mages put her into an enchanted sleep to calm her down."

"Was that wise? She might have a lot to say about her captors or Raya."

"Nothing coherent. She kept repeating that Raya was alive. Seemingly the hauries kept them captive somewhere underground. She wasn't quite clear with her words. I have never seen her like this."

"It is understandable after all the shock."

"To be honest, I felt sorry for her for the first time in my life. She was despairing when she tried to say how she was separated from Raya. The haurie dragged her above the ground and brought her to the forest. We think they wanted to leave her dead body in the forest for Horace to find. That was when she made a run for it."

"I will check her . . . make sure everything is all right. Also, the injured mages. I can see to their well-being."

"Are you feeling up to it?"

"I will once I start doing it."

Gaelia didn't argue. She accompanied Deena to the house where the mages were recovering. The infirmary was livelier than during her previous visit. The curtains were removed from around the beds, except for one. The patients sat reading or talking to loved ones who visited them.

Byuton's mother, Tisila, was up and about. The burn on her face had diminished to a scar that was well on its way to healing. Magic must have been used in its mending. She was helping a woman with bandaged hands to eat.

Once she recognized Deena, Tisila came up to her to express her gratitude for the antidote and to commiserate on her loss, while Gaelia continued the task of feeding the woman.

"Byuton has told me plenty about Kran with much admiration." Tisila handed over the packet of herbs that Deena had packed two days ago for Byuton. "You must keep this while you stay with us, for you know how best to use its contents."

Deena accepted the kind words and the packet with a watery smile. "Is there something I can do for you or for the others who are recovering?"

Tisila took her to a couple of mages who were complaining about an ache in their stomach that spells could not relieve. Deena advised a liquid diet, as their system needed time to get back into action after the long enchanted sleep.

"Can I also check on Lady Len?" Deena asked Tisila. "How long will her enchanted sleep last?"

"Until they put an end to it, but if you want to examine her, someone here can wake her up. I am no mage."

Tisila spoke to a lean bearded man who had come in to visit a wounded mage. He moved to Lady Len's bed, kneeled beside it, and uttered some words under his breath.

Lady Len stirred.

"Give her a few moments to be fully conscious." The man rose and returned to the bedside that he was visiting.

"Byuton mentioned you are a sentar warrior," Deena told Tisila.

If Byuton had not told her that Tisila was not his birth mother, Deena wouldn't have known. Both had the same twinkling eyes and raven black hair. Lady Ilyria had also informed her and Gaelia that Tisila was not married to Densyus. They had not figured out how the three were connected to each other but had decided against posing any further questions.

"And to think I could have shielded myself against the poison, but I underestimated her—Mentra. Or maybe I was mesmerized by her beauty like everyone else was."

"You saw her real form?"

"Oh yes! I have come across the queen in my life, and I wouldn't have believed she was an enchantress had Thili not informed us about it. Yet, I was not prepared to see her alluring form. It was blinding."

A grunt alerted them to Lady Len returning to consciousness. She lifted a shaking hand to her face and laid it over her eyes.

"Raya," she whimpered.

"Everything is going to be fine." Deena went to her.

Lady Len's hand was cold and shaking when Deena took it. She was still in shock. "I will bring you some tea steeped with eela. It is an excellent remedy to settle your nerves. Where can I make some?" Deena asked Tisila.

She showed Deena to a platform at the end of the room where several pots sat steaming—just pots with no fire underneath. Some of them had plain water that boiled with sizzling bubbles, while others had thick sweet-and-sour smelling soups. The marble platform was cold to the touch. Jars with tea leaves and plates of corn breads were also arranged there.

Tisila handed her a teapot. From her bag, Deena took out a bottle with powdered eela flower—grown and nourished by Lady Len herself. There was some justice in it becoming useful to the lady.

After she drank the hot cup of tea, Lady Len began breathing more easily and her hands became steadier. She sat up, immersed in thought.

Deena did not disturb her. She prepared different types of herbal teas for the recuperating people and occasionally visited Lady Len's bed to check if she needed something.

On her fifth visit, the lady spoke. "Horace told me your brother died saving me."

"Yes."

"Will you believe me if I say I am sorry?" A single tear flowed down Lady Len's cheek.

"Please don't trouble yourself with that." Something fell off from Deena, something that had made her dislike this lady even before she had set eyes on her. In its place trickled in warmth and empathy for Lady Len.

"It will never stop troubling me—lives lost unnecessarily. He was a soldier, wasn't he?"

"Yes."

"So he knew what he was signing up for." Lady Len sighed. "Still, an unnecessary loss like many others."

Deena had no response. Dwelling on Kran's death would bring back all the despair that she was fighting to keep at bay. She sat beside Lady Len, not wanting to give in to the impulse to walk away.

"Did you see her? The one who captured you?" Deena asked.

Lady Len had not been told anything about Queen Mentra's real identity. Seeing the enchantress and knowing the extent of the danger they were facing would have been another shock she had to endure after her capture.

"All I ever saw were the hauries."

She closed her eyes as though she didn't want to speak more about it. Deena understood the feeling. Lady Len, like herself, might be hoping that the memories would go away if she did not heed them.

After a period of silence, Lady Len said, "Would you tell those mages not to enchant me to sleep?"

"Would you prefer a sleeping draught?"

"No, I want to sleep when I am ready."

"As you wish, my lady." Deena sat by her bed until Gaelia came to get her.

They returned to their accommodations and talked for a few hours while lounging in armchairs in the dining courtyard. It was lit by lanterns with dancing flames not made up of fire. The magical light in the lanterns grew brighter and brighter as the sky above them dimmed to a pale orange shade. It was late in the evening when Horace and Lady Ilyria returned from their watch duty.

They went to their rooms to rest for an hour before joining Deena and Gaelia.

There was still no attempt made for the scroll, but the tension was palpable on the faces of both sentar warriors, as if they expected it to happen at any moment. After all, the hauries were in the region. It was only a matter of time before the enchantress made her next move.

"I met Mother on my way back," Horace told Deena. "She was grateful for your attention and administrations."

"It helped me as much as it helped her."

"She said it was the tea you prepared with eela leaves that returned her strength."

They all sat around the table, looking at it expectantly for food to appear as it always did. An unexplainable restlessness gripped Deena. Something was wrong. Something she couldn't quite put her finger on.

"Why is the food taking so long to come?" Gaelia tapped impatiently on the table. "It is odd. It always appears as soon as we sit down."

Yes, it was odd. But something else was odd, too. What was it? She shifted in her chair as memories swirled around in her head—Kran dying, Kran coming to Thian to save her, her getting captured, her being questioned by Lady Len in Thian's court.

"Maybe we are early today," Lady Ilyria said. "But I was famished and didn't want to wait."

"Wait," Deena said as the thoughts clicked into place. She turned to Horace. "What did Lady Len say about the tea I made for her?"

"That it cured her."

"No, what did she say I made the tea with?"

"Eela leaves."

"Did she say leaves? Are you sure she said leaves?" Even to her ears, her voice sounded shrill and shaky.

Horace looked at her with concern. "You are shivering. Are you quite all right?"

"Yes, but think carefully. Did she say leaves? Or something else?"

"I am sure she said leaves. She also picked one of those 'wonderful leaves,' as she called it, from the bottom of the cup and showed it to me."

Gaelia and Lady Ilyria looked as clueless as Horace, but Deena's heart pounded faster. Words did not come out with ease as her mouth went dry. Then with effort she said, "Lady Len would never mistake the flower of eela for its leaf."

"Maybe she was too shaken to know the difference," Lady Ilyria suggested.

"The tea calmed her down," Deena said. "It was not nerves. It was ignorance. Leaves are the most useless part of an eela plant, and they resemble thorns more than leaves—"

"While its flowers disguise themselves as leaves." Understanding dawned in Horace's eyes. Understanding that turned into horror.

Lady Len's knowledge about eela was second to none. If it wasn't Lady Len in the mage's infirmary, it could be only one other person—the one with the power to possess another's body. And a body could only be possessed after murder.

Horace got up from his chair, faltering as he pushed it away from the table.

"What? What happened?" Gaelia frowned.

"It was not my mother who was brought in here yesterday."

"You mean?" Lady Ilyria stood up.

"Deena is right. My mother would never mistake her plants."

"Let us not be hasty," Lady Ilyria said. "Can we be sure? It could just be the trauma that didn't let her remember such a tiny detail."

"It wasn't a tiny detail for her," Horace said.

For a moment, it seemed like none of them could move or speak. And then Byuton walked into the courtyard, rubbing his hands and muttering something. "Sheesh, this is frustrating. Why can't I do this simple spell?"

"Byuton," Horace said. "We must hasten. She is here. Mentra."

Byuton stopped as though someone had punched him. "It is not possible with all the protections."

The lanterns around them flickered.

"It is possible if we let her in when she was in the body of my mother," Horace said.

The lights died.

28

For the time being, Horace had to suppress one vital bit of information that had struck his chest like the shard of a sword—his mother was dead. That was the only way the enchantress could have possessed her body. It could mean that Raya, too, had been killed, for they only had the masquerading Lady Len's words that Raya was alive. But if he let that realization sink in, he would be rendered incapable of acting. And act he must.

Byuton was running around the courtyard, checking the lanterns, uttering spells to them. But the only light that pierced the darkness was the small ball of senria that Gaelia had manifested. It floated over them, casting a golden glow that mingled with the milky light of the moon that came in through the open roof.

"The magic has been curbed," Byuton announced. "Spells are not working. Question is, how far is the extent of the curb and where does it begin? Nothing can be done within the curb circle without destroying its origin. We need to reach my father soon. But before that . . ."

He took out a small book from within his vest and jotted something in it quickly with a blue feather. "I hope she can read my handwriting."

It must be his message to Thili. They had not yet captured Mentra, but it surely wouldn't be long now. Outside the house, they found the whole town submerged in darkness. Doors clicked open and people stepped out to the street to check what was happening. The cold night air had an added chillness to it, probably because of the non-functioning warming spells that the town employed.

"Why can't we just use fires in our lanterns?" Byuton muttered as he ran up the street, panting as the ascending path slowed him down. "It is not looking good. The circle is not tiny. The whole town seems to be covered. Stay indoors, everyone."

But the curious men, women, and children gathered in groups to discuss what was going on. Lady Ilyria sent a ball of senria to hover over them so that they had some respite from the darkness.

"There is a curb circle around us," Byuton shouted again. "Get in and stay in."

His voice had grown squeaky, which ensured that it did not reach too far. Horace was now ahead of Byuton and took the turn that led to Densyus's official quarters. Mentra could even now have reached the scroll. That was not a matter of worry, as the trap laid for her would surely ensnare her. And once she was in their clutches, he wouldn't fail to extract the price of his mother's life. His muscles tensed up before the tightness passed to his chest. Revenge would not bring her back, though. He would never again walk into her chambers and see her regally reposed at her desk, jotting in her book. She wouldn't remonstrate with him or challenge his every decision.

With a mighty attempt, he shifted his focus back to the present. His revenge could wait. There could be more deaths if he didn't focus, for he could sense an attack coming. Mentra might have used the curb circle to make the mages vulnerable before an attack. The only question was how it would come.

Densyus and Muryt were already exiting their building.

"How could this be?" Muryt said. "They would have to surpass the stone circle to curb our magic so effectively."

"Horace, what is happening?" Densyus came up to him, taking in the flustered group that included Deena, Gaelia, and Lady Ilyria. Byuton ran up to them, clutching his stomach and panting.

"We believe Mentra has possessed my mother's body," Horace said in a steady voice.

"That would account for the curb," the older mage said.

"She was in the infirmary," Deena said. "The others there could be in danger."

"Tisila." Densyus set off for the red building on the opposite side of the street.

"We could not contact the watchers because of the curb," Muryt said. "Anything could be happening now."

"Let us check if Mentra is still in the infirmary." Horace manifested a sword with a serrated blade.

But the infirmary was empty, not just of the impostor Lady Len, but also of all the other inhabitants who had been there. An eerie silence hung in the room where the beds lay deserted and food lay uneaten on side tables. It seemed like the occupants had left in haste.

"What do we do now?" Byuton and Muryt asked at the same time.

The decision was taken out of their hands as the ground rumbled and the building shook, toppling the curtain stands and water-filled pots with a loud crash. Horace held on to the doorjamb to steady himself while others found similar supports.

"Is she causing the earthquake?" Gaelia's voice shivered.

"More like her minions are," Horace said.

The root of this disturbance could only be the hauries. It was time to fight, perhaps a losing battle. The rumbling did not stop, and he could only guess at the number of those rat-faced creatures that would need to move under the ground to cause this much turbulence. And soon they would emerge to a land filled with mages who couldn't do magic.

"We need to lead them outside of whatever curb she has accomplished." Horace left the doorjamb and stumbled toward Lady Ilyria, who was clutching the railing of a bed. "And it must be us who do it."

Her mouth set in a determined line.

"I can come too." Gaelia manifested a sword of her own.

Horace couldn't deny her support. The sentar warriors were outnumbered as it was. "But don't tempt them with a sentar shield. They will counter it with fire, and things get ugly when their whole body turns into fire. Sentar swords and metal swords will be useless then. In such a case, only their face is a possible target, which will remain of flesh and bone." He turned to Densyus. "You must follow with your mage warriors and join the attack when we are outside the curb circle."

"Father and Byuton can do that. I am coming with you." Densyus unsheathed his sword. "Trust me. My sword will not fail me even within the curb circle."

"He is right," Byuton said. "That sword won't fail him."

Muryt patted Densyus on the back. "I would like to think the curb applies only to our town and does not extend to the forest. If so, you must lead them up the hill, into the trees. All our magical protections are down, so it won't be difficult to exit the town. I will collect our combat mages and join you there."

"Father, let me remove my bracelet," Byuton said in a hurried whisper.

"No." Densyus's answer was harsh, but he didn't elaborate as a scream sounded outside. "Let's go."

He was the first one to exit. Horace looked back at Deena. "Stay away from everything. Hide."

"Don't worry about me," Deena said grimly.

He gave her a long glance before going out into the dark night, which was not so dark after all. In the distance, streaks of fire cut through the air. The hauries had not waited to use their fire power. Smoke swirled up from the center of the town, the burning smell reminding him of the disaster in Veiga. Such large-scale destruction had to be prevented at least here, even though the enemies had now come in more numbers.

"How do we draw them out?" Gaelia asked.

Lady Ilyria stepped in front of them. With a deft movement of her fingers, she manifested ten silvery arrows that hovered in front of her, their polished tips shining in the moonlight. Then they flew down to the town center, becoming tiny dots of light.

She stared at them with intense focus as they flew around, eliciting screeches from hauries. Then she flicked her palm toward herself. The arrows shot back to her.

"They will follow," Lady Ilyria said. "We must make our move now."

Byuton, Muryt, and Deena backed off into the infirmary as Horace, Densyus, Lady Ilyria, and Gaelia ran further up the street. Horace kept looking back at the arrows that obediently followed Lady Ilyria. The stooped figures of the hauries were scrambling not far behind. Some were on all fours, but the ones who had already had flames for their arms ran on their hind legs.

The humans would have been at a disadvantage had the hauries chosen to overtake them underground, but the creatures were madly following the arrows, which even now swerved back to pierce through their skin.

Lady Ilyria did not even have to look to hit her target, as the hauries were packed close to each other. They crossed street after street, climbing higher and higher. The cobblestone streets slowly turned into pebble-covered paths. Fear-filled faces peered out of houses.

"Stay inside," Densyus shouted as he ran.

One of the hauries in the forefront veered to a house and grabbed the knob of the door that slammed shut in its face.

Horace skidded to a stop. Things could quickly go wrong if the other hauries followed suit. The creatures had to stay focused on them and not the civilians. He slid down the path, reaching the haurie as it pushed the door open and forcefully threw off whoever was on the other side.

Horace thrust his blade into the stomach of the haurie. It extended its arm toward him. An arrow struck the haurie's forehead before extricating itself with a squelching sound and flying back to Lady Ilyria. The haurie fell like a deadweight, but the closely following creatures dashed at Horace. It was too late to get away. He heard his companions calling out warnings. Lady Ilyria's arrows swooshed toward the hauries, but before they could strike the creatures, a shield of senria extended between Horace and the hauries, originating from a perpendicular street.

A man and a woman ran toward them within the shield and stood in front of the hauries, their swords ready.

"Get back, Horace," Lady Ilyria yelled.

He did not have to be told twice, but the sentar warriors within the shield were in more danger than they realized.

"Run!" he yelled at them. The shield wouldn't stop the hauries. And in a moment, they saw why. The monsters extended palms laced with fire and penetrated the shield, reaching for the warriors.

The man within the shield pushed the woman outside to the other side before one of the haurie's arms swirled around his torso and dragged him into their midst. He screamed, and so did the woman, who made to return to the hauries.

Densyus, however, had reached her and pulled her backward. "Tisila, it won't work. Shields don't work on them."

"But Yesh . . ."

"We can't save him now," Densyus said.

It was true. The man's screams died down. Densyus dragged Tisila along with him as the hauries threw the dead warrior's corpse at them through the sentar shield that now had giant holes in it. Aflame hands of the hauries rapidly snaked toward them. Tisila slashed the arms, but to no effect, as her sentar sword passed through the flames, leaving the limbs intact. Horace wanted to yell at them to run without attacking.

But Densyus swiveled on his ankle and dealt a blow to the fiery hand. A severed furry hand fell to the ground. The haurie was stunned for a moment, and Tisila slashed through its head. Densyus again cut off a hand of fire that loomed toward them, his sword somehow accomplishing that impossible task, but he couldn't afford to stop and continue the attack. He was outnumbered.

They had to get away quicker. Horace, Gaelia, and Lady Ilyria were ahead and not in immediate danger, but Densyus and Tisila were moments from being grasped by those vile arms, even with Densyus's sword cutting them off at regular intervals.

Lady Ilyria slowed down and sent her arrows to the hauries, but there were too many of those creatures.

"I don't have the energy to manifest more arrows," she panted.

"Here. Use mine," Gaelia said.

Lady Ilyria's eyes widened as Gaelia took hold of her hands.

"You mustn't."

"Please use it."

Lady Ilyria looked at the determined eyes of Gaelia and turned to the hauries, ten more arrows shooting out of her palms. These distracted the hauries enough to give Densyus and Tisila time to get to the others. Together, they continued running up the hill, leaving the houses behind.

That was some consolation. The people living in the town would not be the major target of the hauries now, even though the running party was not anywhere near victory. The twenty arrows belonging to Lady Ilyria found their targets among the hauries, but not all the time. Once they entered the wooded area, the branches obstructed the flight of the arrows.

"We are outside the border of our town," Densyus said. "The curb should have ended."

"Can't you do some spell to check it?" Horace asked amidst panting.

Densyus picked up a stone on his path and clasped it in his hand.

"Do something minor," Tisila said.

"You keep telling me that," Densyus said. Then he dropped the stone. "It did not work. We can't predict the extent of the curb. Running is useless now."

"Then we must turn and fight these creatures," Horace said. They had reached a plateau top overlooking the river. Laryshia glistened like a bejeweled silk mantle under the moonlight. The black mound that held Edri's scroll was visible in the distance, but calmness prevailed around it—the calm before a storm. If Mentra approached it, it would certainly be with an army of hauries. The watchers would be sorely tested.

"Then let us do that right here," Densyus said, and he stood in front of everyone else, his sword at the ready.

29

Deena remained in the infirmary, peering out of the window, as Byuton and his grandfather sneaked out to gather more mages to follow the hauries. They had initially waited for all the creatures to pass, but some of those monsters lingered in the town, attacking people. So, they had ventured out through the back door to an alleyway that led to the town center.

Another scream rent the night air. Deena pressed her hand to her ear and kneeled. An explosion somewhere up or down the street drowned out the shouts of terror. A wave of helplessness and impotency swamped her as she remembered how Kran was blown up. That would be the fate of many of the people down there. She was no warrior to go out and help those unfortunate mages on whom danger was unleashed the moment their power was snatched away. She was only a healer who could mend broken people after a war, but the rampage of the hauries made her doubt whether there would be survivors left to be healed.

Something banged against the infirmary door. "Don't hide in there," a grating voice said. "You can't escape."

Then the smell of burning wood filled the hallway as the haurie burned a hole in the door.

Deena frantically looked in her bag for a knife or something sharp to defend herself. The penknife she found was pathetically small, and the vials and boxes would be useless. She tore open the packet of herbs. The bristly bunch of dried leaves could only cure and not harm. Unless . . . She took out a three-pronged leaf from the stack and thrust it into the burning hole, simultaneously crawling away and covering her nose with the hem of her dress.

The door continued to burn, but a thump outside told her something huge had toppled down. Deena scrambled up to the window in time to see the haurie rolling down the street, unconscious.

The oaflin leaf had done its trick, and there was one less menace on the streets for the time being. She was not completely helpless as long as she had a bunch of oaflin leaves and hauries who provided the fire for smoking it.

She pushed away from the window and went to the dark bedchamber to get a piece of clean cloth. After stumbling through to the end of the room where the pots and plates were scattered, she found a stack of dishcloths on a table.

One of these she wound around her mouth and nose and then took the back exit that led to a narrow street with entrances to the backyard of houses. It ran parallel to the main street from where she could glimpse sparks of fire and running bodies, but importantly the hauries had not yet discovered the backstreet. People, though, were running hither and thither, possibly to find regions where the curb on the magic wouldn't work.

"What are you doing here?" It was Byuton. He was shepherding some mages through the backyard of a house to another parallel street that went up the hill.

"I have a plan."

Byuton might not agree with her action, but he might be able to show her a shortcut to reach the center of the attack without attracting much attention from the rat-like creatures.

"What?" He let the last of the mages go to the opposite street and turned to her as another explosion sounded somewhere far away.

"I have oaflin leaves with me. Their smoke could put the hauries to sleep."

"Are you sure?"

"I tried it on one. If you show me how to get to the town center without being seen, I could spread these leaves to where they are rampaging. Their fire will do the rest."

He looked around to see whether the street was empty.

"You are going to do a very dangerous thing, but I will help you, as it could save lives. You must help me in return, though. Don't tell anyone this happened."

He slipped his silver bracelet off his hand and put it in his vest pocket.

"What is the use of removing your restraint? Magic is pretty much useless now."

"Not my kind of magic."

"What kind is that?"

If it was the kind he used to put off the fire in Veiga, it couldn't do him any good to use it. Wasn't it the very purpose of his bracelet? To restrain him from doing things beyond his limit?

Byuton did not answer. Instead, he took her to the lowest part of the street and turned to the right, which would lead them straight to the town center.

"Maybe you shouldn't do anything you are forbidden to do."

"Scores of my people have died tonight. There is nothing wrong if I become one of them. My parents might want to save me from harm, but you, for one, should realize all lives are equally special. Also, I will not suddenly fall dead. My action will only decrease my life expectancy." He said it like it was not a huge concern to him.

Deena was not sure he understood what a decreased life expectancy meant. Maybe she could even now dissuade him from cutting his life short.

They reached one edge of the fence around Edri's temple and rounded it until the fountain was in view. A group of hauries rampaged near the fountain that was now lifeless due to the curb. Its two top tiers lay shattered on the ground, and the central pillar leaned to one side. Carts lay overturned around it, going up in smoke.

"I could sneak out there and deposit the leaves." She gulped at the prospect, and the pungent smell of the smoke brought tears to her eyes. "You needn't endanger—"

A body crashed into the fountain before crumpling down lifelessly. The long-extended arm of the haurie who had thrown it retreated without spotting Byuton and Deena's presence.

"Do you still want to go into their midst?" Byuton asked, putting out his hand for the leaves. "The important fact here is not that you will die. It is that you will fail. I can guarantee you success."

Deena gave him the bunch of leaves, unable to deny the truth of his words. Her sacrifice wouldn't mean anything if she failed. "Don't take unnecessary risks with your magic."

"Only the necessary ones."

He took the leaves and blew on them. A swirling wind lifted and carried the leaves over to the fountain. They floated above the heads of the hauries at a uniform distance without attracting attention. Then they dropped.

"Cover your nose," Deena said, observing Byuton. His lips had grown pale, but he was steady and not on the verge of fainting as he had done in Veiga. Still, if he breathed in the oaflin smoke, he would faint.

He removed his vest and pressed it over his nose just in time as the oaflin was scorched in the fire of the hauries, releasing a thick white smoke that mingled with the darker fumes from the other sources.

The hauries dropped down one by one. Not just them. A man in the clasp of one of the hauries also fainted, as did many other mages who were running through the street. By the time the smoke slowly dissipated, the hauries and humans in the vicinity had been rendered unconscious.

"How long will this effect last?" Byuton asked.

"For my peace of mind, could you wear your bracelet again?"

"That can wait. It is a useless restraint."

"I will tell your mother that when I see her next."

He gave her a disgruntled look before sliding the bracelet back on.

"The effect will last for an hour in the humans. I am not sure how long it will be for the hauries."

"Then we shouldn't waste any more time. The hauries have to be killed before they wake up."

"In their sleep?" Deena shuddered.

"Would you prefer to wake them up and kill them?"

No. She wouldn't want that. "I guess you are right."

Byuton's eyes softened. "Go and wait inside the temple. I will gather up the survivors and do what's needed."

Deena removed her mask and breathed deeply now that the oaflin smoke had dissipated. "What about the hauries that were following Horace and others?" She silently prayed that their friends were still unharmed, but seeing the scene of death and destruction around her sank her heart. Houses had warped and were on the verge of collapse, and bodies—dead or unconscious—littered the street.

"Grandfather is leading combat mages after them. Once out of the curb circle, they should be able to help our sentar warriors," Byuton said hurriedly before running off to the sleeping hauries.

Deena turned to the spiral-roofed temple and entered through its arched doorway. The inside was dimly lit by lamps that threw giant shadows of the pillars that lined either end of the chamber.

These lamps must be of actual fire. The smell of seel oil that permeated from the stone walls confirmed this.

She had been in temples dedicated to Edri before. But this one was different. There was no separate sanctum, but one gigantic chamber with an altar in the middle. Idols or vessels of offerings were absent as well. Instead, on the altar swirled a whirlpool of air, carrying with it fresh-looking rose petals and yellow hibiscuses that might have been the offering of the day.

She clasped her hands together and closed her eyes. "If you are seeing any of this destruction, please make it stop."

"They can do zilch to stop it," someone said from the shadows. "Your gods."

Deena backed away from the whirling air. "Who is there?"

"It is me." Lady Len emerged into the light cast by the lamp on the wall. No, not Lady Len. *Her.* The enchantress in the guise of Horace's mother, who was no longer in this world.

30

"I am sorry I startled you."

Deena clutched her bag close to her body. There was nothing in there that could save her now. No oaflin leaf to smoke the enchantress to sleep or heliatin thorn to prick her. She was all alone with the person who was the root cause of this plague. A chill ran through her spine when she looked into *Lady Len's* eyes with the knowledge that the lady had died.

"Tisila warned us when the magic died down and we ran in different directions," the enchantress said, still maintaining her guise. "And when those creatures erupted, I hid in here."

"Oh!" That was the sound Deena had intended to make, trying her best not to reveal that she knew the reality of her companion, but all she heard was a choked gasp.

"You appear to be in shock."

"There is so much death and destruction outside," she said in a shivering voice.

"Deena, you are barely hiding the hatred in your eyes. You know who I am, don't you?"

"Yes, Lady Len."

"No. Not her. You looked at me with a mixture of dislike and respect during our journey here. That was your feelings for Lady Len. But now I see fear and hatred. That could only be reserved for me. The real me."

During the journey? "How long have you been . . . her?"

"Ah! So you haven't figured out when I started this masquerade, have you? I have been with you since the beginning of this journey. I like you, Deena. Lady Len wrote highly about you in her diary—even calling you a successor of sorts. I don't know whether that referred to your vast knowledge of herbs or her son's growing interest in you, but I respect what you do. It is a noble profession. I don't want to harm you."

"You are harming a lot of others, though." She would be a fool to believe that the enchantress would spare her just because she was a healer or because Lady Len admired her, which she found hard to believe. Mentra was playing at something—she was not in here without reason. Did she think the scroll would be here? Their plan wouldn't work if Mentra didn't get to the actual location where the poisonous thorns awaited her.

"It is the hauries' doing." Mentra walked carelessly around the whirling air representing Edri. She flicked a hand into the air, plucking a bloom out of it and smelling it.

"And who brought them here? The same way you brought them to Kran." A blind white fury threatened to engulf Deena as Kran's smiling face flashed in her mind. He had been so full of hope of returning home, and the enchantress had put an end to those dreams in a moment.

"Tandon had ordered that haurie to blow up so that you would get the opportunity to *rescue* me. But he didn't command it to take down someone with it. Your brother chose his fate, I would say. He was a soldier who knew what he was doing, but I meant it when I said I am sorry for your loss." She looked around distractedly, like she was waiting for someone.

"As sorry as you are for murdering Lady Len and taking her body?"

Mentra dropped the flower. Her lips quivered for a moment before she clasped them tightly against each other.

"She possessed a truth serum that I tried on her."

"No!" Deena gasped. If it was wija, then it would have been enough to torture the life out of Lady Len. She hadn't deserved that.

"She had once boasted to me about it. How was I supposed to know that it would drive her to her death? I only wanted to know the identity of Zesta's heir, but unfortunately, the serum broke the indomitable Lady Len. It seemed too good an opportunity to pass up. So here I am, wearing her. If nothing else, this body helped me bind the mages within the curb circle." She looked at the ground where concentric circles were drawn with chalk. Words were also scribbled in the space between the circles.

How did one break the curb circle?

"Oh, you cannot break the curb by wiping this drawing," Mentra scoffed as though reading her mind. "You need to have the knowledge of a mage to do that, and if you are planning to run out and get one, do not hesitate. I will be long gone before the curb is removed. I will also leave you with this body. Get her properly cremated."

A shimmering figure stepped out of Lady Len's body, and the latter collapsed to the floor. The light solidified into a woman in a white dress with a stole wrapped around her neck. Her face was perfectly symmetrical, as though an artist had taken great pains to get the measurements right, and silky black hair cascaded to her ankles. But it was neither that nor her luminescent, dusky skin that accounted for her allure.

It was how she looked at Deena with her wide eyes. She had poise like a divine sculpture, and her full blood-red lips parted in a charming smile. Deena felt an irrational wish to be in the enchantress's good books. But then Kran's face flashed through her mind, and she shook herself out of the daze.

"What did you do to the heir of Zesta?" Deena asked, struggling to keep a grip on the fact that she was dealing with a dangerous entity.

"She is alive and has proven to be quite useless in deciphering her mother's scroll." She looked around again. "After I leave here tonight, I will send you a message to let you know where she is. Retrieve her if you want."

"If a haurie hasn't already blown up beside her," Deena said in a trembling voice. "Wearing a mantle of benevolence doesn't absolve you of cruelty. Do you believe you can evade consequences with this pretense?"

"Then bring on the consequences," Mentra sneered. "I am waiting."

"If we can't oppose you, it is because you hold more power than us. Like Niferon, who evades you because of his power. You're just like him."

A dangerous light flashed across Mentra's face, illuminating her gray-flecked eyes. "Don't you dare take my name along with his. We are nothing alike."

"From where I stand, there is no difference between the both of you."

A thundering sound filled her ears. The next thing she knew, she was drowning in a column of water. She tried to fight her way out of it, but the water trapped her in as though it were a brick wall. In another moment, the water disappeared. If she hadn't been drenched, she would have thought that she had imagined it.

"Like I said, I don't want to kill you," Mentra said, drawing the last drop of water into her palm.

"How?" Deena choked. "How did you do it? Magic is curbed here."

"Human magic is. But not of the gods." Mentra tapped the twirling air as if to prove a point.

"What are you waiting for, then? Take what you came here for and leave, and take your rat servants with you."

Mentra had to touch the poisoned scroll. Deena would take her there if she had to lead the enchantress by her hand.

"Oh, I will. I will. Any moment now. It is only a matter of time before Tandon sets up my portal and the army of hauries near the scroll. Isn't it strange that the mages slyly publicized where they were hiding the scroll? It is almost as if they have a trap ready for me. I am sure my sister had something to do with it. So, I couldn't walk in without curbing their magic or bringing in the hauries."

This was not good. Tandon could remove Mentra's immobilized body before the mages or Horace reached there, if they could even get there with more hauries present around the scroll. How many more lives would be lost tonight? She had to blink hard to dispel the image of death and devastation that filled her mind.

At first she thought it was because of that action that specks of light appeared in her vision. But then the specks coagulated with each other to form a door within a golden rectangle. Light streamed through it until dimming to reveal a man standing outside a cave. A rapidly flowing river circled behind him, reflecting dancing flames. The man turned to enter the cave.

"We part ways here," Mentra said. "Don't be an obstacle in my path if you know what is good for you."

She stepped through the door at the same moment in which the man picked up something from a raised platform within the cave.

Deena did not have to think twice. If the poison affected him, Mentra would find out about their trap and wouldn't fall for it. She would escape with the scroll, only to wrought such misery yet again.

She lunged after Mentra, getting hold of the white stole that floated behind the enchantress. She was dragged in through the portal, feeling as though her whole skin had turned inside out and back again. The portal closed behind her, and she was in the forest lit by trees on fire, both around her and on the hill overlooking the river. Humans and hauries were clashing against each other, the latter outnumbering the former. Battle cries and pained screeches filled the air, along with an occasional mighty blast.

Mentra turned angry eyes at her, but at the same moment, the man who had entered the cave fell in a lump.

"Tandon." Mentra ran to him.

Tandon was lying supine on the ground, his eyes open, reflecting the light from the fires raging outside. Tears streamed from them.

"What . . . what happened to you, son?" Mentra kneeled by him, feeling his face with her hands and wiping away his tears.

A strange caustic smell seeped through the cave. It couldn't be from the heliatin thorn. That poison was odorless. Deena sniffed again. The smell had an underlying peppery tinge to it, like cloves gone bad—which texts said was the distinctive odor of veritria.

"You are in pain, aren't you?" Mentra's voice was soft and caressing. "Why can't you respond?"

Deena stepped up to them. Tears were still streaming down Tandon's face. She could imagine his eyes had a pleading look, even though the paralyzing poison wouldn't let him show any emotion. He had somehow come into contact with not only the poison of heliatin but also veritria. He must have carried it with him and broken the vial during his fall. The shards of glass below his knee indicated this was what had happened—a just punishment for the one who had orchestrated Kran's death.

"Your body is burning," Mentra murmured.

"You sent him with veritria, didn't you? He doused himself with it."

The enchantress didn't respond, but her hand on Tandon's forehead froze.

The same pain that had tortured Jianther must be consuming him now. It wouldn't be long before it squeezed out his consciousness. Soon he would scorch to death like the heirs of Rothshire without even being able to scream in pain, while she, a healer, watched.

A shiver passed through her, not just because of her damp clothes. Her hand extended toward her bag, wherein lay the antidote to veritria. Then she paused. This was Tandon. He was the reason Kran was dead. He was the one who had helped Mentra execute all her evil plans. He deserved to die. She could stand by and watch as his life faded away in the most painful way possible, couldn't she?

No, you can't. The voice in her head sounded almost like Kran.

"Move," Deena said harshly, startling Mentra. She had to do it before she changed her mind. This was not the moment to think whether he deserved to be saved. All her training went against such a debate.

The enchantress obeyed and gave her space to examine Tandon, although still kneeling on the ground close by, watching her with shrewd eyes. Deena took out the syringe of antidote and injected it into his elbow.

"It acts fast," she said.

"Why isn't he moving, though? That was never an effect of that poison."

"You would know, wouldn't you?"

"Is it an enchanted sleep?" Mentra trilled a mournful tune and then let out a string of angry words in an alien tongue. "It won't work when the scrolls are here. I must remove them."

Mentra fished into a pocket on Tandon's cloak and took out a scroll. "Where is Edri's scroll?"

The scroll Mentra held must be Zesta's or Varys's, because Tandon wouldn't have had the time to pocket Edri's scroll. It was then that Deena noticed a golden knob sticking out from under Tandon's leg. He had dropped the scroll before he fell.

Mentra pulled it out, holding the knob. She didn't touch the parchment, not because she saw the minute thorns embedded in the outer cover, but because the scroll was soaked in veritria. The poison had scorched Edri's scroll into a crumpled brown mess. Mentra screamed in fury and threw it out of the cave. She also threw the other scroll, although not with equal force. It unraveled from its stick as it landed at Deena's feet.

Elegantly carved golden letters glowed on it and floated above the parchment to form a single sentence in Cele.

De zin haird te'zakt il vid vin te'ria de vayi dit.

And then the letters changed to the common tongue.

From the day you read this, you will wield the power of life.

31

Deena was sucked into a blinding light before comforting darkness wrapped her in its folds. But then she could see again. A seed germinated in front of her eyes, rapidly elongating into a tree, only to fall and decay as fast as it had grown.

Then it was a tiny embryo that went through the same process—of birth, growth, and decay.

Breath life, a woman's voice whispered in her ears. The ground she stood on shook, or maybe her body was shivering. An intense urge to throw up brought a trembling hand to her mouth, and with that touch, she became aware of her surroundings.

She was still in the cave with Mentra and an unconscious Tandon. The enchantress gaped at her and the parchment from which the words were still projecting.

"Impossible," Mentra hissed.

The glow from the letters died, and the parchment burst into a flurry of particles over and over again until none of those particles were visible.

"You are not the heir." Mentra gave her an incredulous look, arching her perfect eyebrows.

No, she wasn't. She was someone who was trying to hold in the contents of her stomach.

"You cannot take Zesta's power. You are a human."

"I don't want . . . any power," Deena managed to say while fighting the metallic taste in her mouth.

"It is not a matter of not wanting it," Mentra said scornfully, even the disgust not marring her beauty. "Only Thisaurians or half-bloods can handle that much power. It will kill you. But"—she stood up slowly with the grace of executing a dance maneuver— "you could give it to me. I can handle the power. I can save you. Give the power to me."

Deena badly wanted to oblige. She would do anything to please this lady—enchantress or not. An earth-shattering blast outside the cave brought her back to her senses. No. The enchantress would destroy the world with this power.

"I don't have any power. You are mistaken."

Deena stepped back as Mentra's eyes became icy cold. It was not just her eyes. Ice crusted on Deena's skin, causing tiny painful pricks, although not deep enough to draw blood.

Her skin might be turning blue for all she knew, but she couldn't take her focus away from Mentra, who was now floating closer to her like an ethereal being. The destruction of the scrolls must have removed the protections around them. Mentra could now summon water, or its other forms.

"Pass the power onto me. You only have to speak those words. Your intention will make it happen. It was the only thing I would have made Raya do." She circled around Deena like a dancer.

"Then I would have let her go. But the scroll didn't respond to her like it did to you. Say the words and I will let you go."

Deena trembled, the icy shards on her skin biting sharply, mirroring the fear Mentra's words instilled. For a fleeting moment, she considered obeying the enchantress. It would be so easy to say those words. Whatever was coursing through her veins felt so alien and wrong. It did not belong to her. She would be a thief if she held it. It was Zesta's power—the power of life. That much she was sure.

Her lips half opened to speak out the words that would relinquish whatever she held to Mentra—to the enchantress who would use it to pit her continent against the land of gods—causing death and devastation on a much larger scale than she was doing now with the burning and exploding hauries.

She pursed her lips and vehemently shook her head.

"Now, I will have to force you to do it," Mentra said.

The ice on her skin thickened until it became a wall that entombed her. Her breath became a foggy layer on the ice crystals that masked her face. It wouldn't last for long. Soon the ice would expand into her nose and mouth, suffocating her.

Breath life, the voice in her head said.

Her heart raced, and her breath came in quick, shallow gasps. Nothing changed.

Create life.

Life. Power of life. She breathed again, willing the power of life, whatever it was, to take control of the ice and save her. And it did.

The wall of ice splintered into tiny shards and reformed into two blobs. These hovered in front of her as though awaiting her command. What was she supposed to do? Create life? How? Mentra had told her to speak the words. So that was what she did.

"Be mighty animals," she commanded. "Hold her back."

The blobs reshaped into two giant elephants with magnificently sharp-edged tusks and sinewy muscles that flexed and moved even though they were crafted out of ice. The ice elephants pushed Mentra to the edge of the cave. The enchantress slowed their progress using a sentar shield, but it did not stop them. She let out a stream of chants that Deena did not understand except for the word 'haurie' that kept repeating.

Deena ran out of the cave. She had to get away before Mentra escaped. It did not take long to understand what the chants meant. Three hauries came howling through the trees and toward the cave as though they had been summoned. The one at the back missed its two arms, and its body was on fire, like the time another of its kind had exploded near Kran.

Deena turned to the cave. "One of you, get the hauries," she shouted at the elephants, wondering when she had gone crazy enough to hope they'd obey her. But they obeyed.

One of the elephants left Mentra and galloped out of the cave, crashing through the rocks that blocked its way and thus widening the opening of the cave. It barreled into the hauries, butting one with its head and twirling its trunk around another, only to throw it into the river. The third haurie that was on fire froze at this sight and turned tail, running back to the scene of battle that was raging further ahead. But it could only move a few steps before, with a bang, it exploded into pieces. The elephant shielded Deena from the blast, the intense heat causing its body to melt away into a deluge of water. Within the cave, Mentra had managed to push the other ice elephant away with multiple layers of sentar shields, like Deena had never witnessed before. Radiant blue hexagonal crystals made up the shields, and they not only pushed the elephant but also enveloped it, slowly turning into a block of ice, blocking its movement.

There was not much time to waste. When would Thili come? Would she heed Byuton's call and come?

The mages could fight Mentra, but for that, the curb circle must be broken. Even then, all their focus would have to go into defeating the hauries.

She must help. The power of life was coursing through her veins, and she had already used it once. Maybe she could yet again breathe life into something. She ran to the river and stepped down the bank, slipping and sliding on the pebble-covered waterfront.

"If I hold any power of Zesta's, I use it to give you life." She didn't know if the words would work on water, but it had worked on ice. And water was the only weapon that could disarm the hauries. Bending down, she touched the river and breathed with the same intention.

The flow of the water stilled before an immense wave rose above her head, threatening to slap her away. Mentra might be taking control over the element with Varys's power, but in another instance, the water reshaped into a creature with four legs. Not one, but several. Some with claws and sharp teeth. Some with razor-sharp antlers. Others had horns or tusks. And all were more enormous than their real-world counterparts.

"Go, stop the hauries." Deena's voice trembled, unlike a god's would. But she was no god. She did not know what these creatures of water that had taken the shapes of tigers, lions, stags, bulls, and elephants would do. Her mind couldn't comprehend the enormity of commanding the actions of each of them or whether they would harm the very people she wanted to protect.

The rippling bodies, however, moved to either side of the river, galloping into the areas where the hauries were lighting up trees and destroying life. They scattered the hauries or splattered them with water. An explosion greeted the mighty lioness, but it leaped straight through the blackened air, quenching the fire by losing its form in a splash of water. The noble stag charged into the fiery body of another haurie, dousing it and returning it to its rat-like form. The fires were similarly put out in many areas, punctuated by cheers from the warriors.

Deena had another task for these animals she had created, but didn't know how to summon them back to her. She breathed again, willing life to form from whatever was around her. Nothing moved.

"I need you to find Byuton," she said to no one in particular. "Find him and tell him the curb starts at Edri's temple." What if her creation got destroyed before finding Byuton? "And do not get destroyed," she added.

The pebbles around her feet clattered. She squinted into the dark, imagining that she saw a small weasel-like animal, but it was gone before she could repeat her instructions.

Mentra exited the cave and was now advancing toward her with a whirlpool of water swirling in front of her. A similar formation arose from the river too, both of which dashed toward Deena. She dropped to the ground and lay flat on her stomach. The water bodies crashed into each other above her and splashed on her.

"You won't last long," Mentra shouted, her shrill voice grating on Deena's nerves. "Can't you feel the power draining the life out of you?"

Deena coughed the water out of her nose and mouth and tried to raise herself to her knees. Her palms, that were pressed to the rocky ground, shivered, not giving her the force to push herself up. Mentra was right. Strength was abandoning her. She blinked as dots formed in front of her eyes. A shudder passed through her chest and stomach.

"Give the power to me now and save yourself."

No. The voice did not leave her throat. She clutched a stone, hung her head, and breathed. "Come alive. Capture her."

The clattering could be her teeth chattering or the pebbles around her coming together again. She raised her head. It was the latter. A stone giant stood between her and Mentra. The latter raised her hand as if to strike it down, but the giant lunged forward and held the enchantress in a tight embrace.

"No." Mentra's sound was muffled.

At the same moment, the night sky was lit by an arc of rainbow, and it was the last thing Deena saw.

32

Deena wanted to remove the moist cloth from her face. Who put it there? And why? She didn't have a fever. She was only sleeping. Someone must be playing a prank on her. Most probably, it was Kran. He had always scorned her need for a daytime nap. When she woke up, she was going to upturn a pot of water on his head as revenge.

But then she slipped into a deeper sleep, where she did not feel the coldness of the damp cloth on her forehead. She ran behind Kran along the canal behind their house in Trilin. Her scruffy knees and the pigtails bouncing on two sides of her head somehow seemed unreal. She wasn't that young, was she? Kran, too, did not look any older than ten. His head was closely shaved, and the insignia of his school was emblazoned on the back of his shirt. They were indeed children. It felt good to be a child again. So she played with Kran the whole evening until night came as a dreamless sleep.

Her lashes felt too heavy as she tried to open her eyes. Raya sat beside her, reading a book bound in green leather. She must indeed be dreaming. Raya was lost to them. As was Lady Len. And

Kran. Everything came flooding back to her befuddled mind, and she struggled to widen her eyes, but they drooped again, and she returned to the side of the canal along with Kran.

Birds chirped somewhere far, urging her to wake up. Or it could just be a single bird. Her eyes flew open. She was no longer in Trilin, nor was she a child. This was Xylera, and she was in the infirmary of the mages, the creepers that covered the backyard visible through the windows.

When she was last in the infirmary, it was in disarray because of the havoc caused by the hauries underground. The chamber was still empty of people, but everything had been tidied. She was the only occupant of the room. No, she wasn't alone. A bird with multicolored feathers and a long blue tail perched on top of the curtain stand that stood beside her bed. It flew down to her side.

"Look who is awake," Thili said.

Deena did not have much energy to react, but it all came back. Mentra had gone for the scroll, and Tandon had been poisoned with veritria. Then a scroll did something strange to her. It let her animate non-living things. She had had Mentra in a trap, and then there came a rainbow out of nowhere and . . . She couldn't remember anything else.

"Do we have her?" she asked, her voice sounding croaky. Her mouth was parched, and her head pounded.

"You might want to drink some water," Thili said.

Deena tried to raise herself onto her elbow but collapsed back into bed.

"Of all the times to wake up, you chose to do it when I am your bystander." Thili ruffled her feathers, and a blue light flashed in the room, blinding Deena for a moment and worsening the pounding in her head.

When the light dimmed, a woman stood by her bed and the bird had disappeared.

Deena recoiled in a mixture of horror and revulsion. It was Mentra—the same eyes, lips, and figure, but the hair was a deep pink and bounced around her shoulders instead of trailing to her ankles, and she wore a flowing blue gown.

"Rest assured"—Thili's voice remained the same as when she had been the bird—"I am the good sister. We are twins, didn't you know?"

Thili lifted Deena with an arm under her shoulders as though she were a child and sat behind her. Leaning on Thili, she took sips of water, clarity returning to her with each sip.

"What happened to me?" Deena asked when she felt she could do so without sounding like a haurie.

"Ah! You survived." Thili summoned pillows from the nearby beds and gently placed Deena on top of them so that she was in an upright position. Then, in a flurry of colors, she zapped back into the form of the bird.

"Don't tell anyone you had the privilege of seeing that." She perched on the chair by her bed.

"You didn't give a proper answer to any of the questions I asked." Deena did not hide her annoyance. Each word she spoke was taking their toll, and any moment she could slip back into unconsciousness.

"Ask away, child. What do you want to know?"

"Did we get Mentra?"

Even as she asked it, she knew the answer. No, they didn't. If they had, Thili would have taken her to Thisaur and both sisters would be trapped there. Unless Thili didn't keep her word.

"No, she escaped," Thili said, "but not before she was thoroughly defeated by you."

Deena snorted. "I don't believe that." The memory of sending a stone creature after Mentra came back to her, and also ice elephants. Then there had been animals that rose out of the water. Did all that really happen, or was she dreaming? "What happened to me? How was I able to do . . . magic? Was it magic?"

"It was a sort of magic, but not of this world," Thili said. "I was not there, so I don't know what exactly happened."

"The scroll. I think it was Zesta's scroll. Words appeared out of it."

"And were you able to read it?"

"Yes."

Thili bobbed her head. "That makes sense. The scroll considered you worthy of reading it and gave you its secrets. You hold Zesta's powers. That much was evident by what you did. The only thing we didn't realize was how you got it."

We? Where was the rest of their group? Horace. Where was he? Gaelia and Lady Ilyria. Did they make it? So many questions waited to burst out of her.

"Tell me everything that happened."

"Your water creatures defeated the hauries and sent them—the ones that were not killed by the warriors—scurrying back to their holes. And the messenger you created with stones took the message to Byuton. He removed the curb circle, and the combat mages descended on Mentra. That and your rock giant must have made her realize her game was up. And once I was there, she took Tandon's body and fled into a portal."

Their plan had not worked. But at least Mentra did not get the scroll of Edri—and she lost Zesta's scroll to boot. That was something.

"I believe Edri's scroll was destroyed by veritria that Tandon was carrying," Deena said. "He was also poisoned by it."

"Ah! His death will be a major setback for my sister. She depended on him for most of her schemes. She also loved him like a son." Thili's words were not victorious, but had a tinge of sadness in them.

"He didn't die. At least, not due to veritria. I gave him the antidote."

Thili's small head snapped back to her. "You mean . . . you saved his life?"

Heat tingled her face. She averted her gaze and fixed it on the window opposite her bed, starting at the vines that grew outside it. The act of giving him the antidote had almost been instinctive. Arguments that should have prevented her did not have any chance to interfere, and in giving into that instinct, she might have done more harm than good. Now, the enchantress would have the continued support of her most faithful follower.

"No wonder the scroll considered you worthy," Thili exclaimed. "You valued life, and it valued you, not even considering you wouldn't be able to hold the power."

Deena emerged from her self-doubts with another memory. "Mentra, too, said that the power would kill me."

"It very nearly did," Thili said kindly. "You are a healer, so I needn't lie to you. That night has taken several years off your life. But as someone who has lived many years, I can assure you a long life is grossly overestimated."

"But I feel better after a sleep."

"A sleep that lasted a month."

"What? It can't be."

"Oh yes. Ask the people who have been sitting by your bedside all these days and nights."

Deena ran a trembling hand over her face. A month! How was she asleep for that long? She remembered dreaming, though. Long, happy dreams of Kran and her childhood home.

Something silver flashed across her eyes. She brought her hand up again. A silver bracelet adorned her wrist, with seven charms shaped like various flowers and leaves dangling from it. She felt the cool metal between her fingers and looked at Thili questioningly. But she had some idea what it was—a magical restraint, like the one Byuton possessed.

"That is a gift from Densyus. His magic is a bit different from the others in that he can render magical properties to things. Have you seen his sword?"

Deena shook her head.

"It's a rare ability. A dangerous ability. But he has used it to give you that bracelet. It will remind you not to wield the power of life because any more blatant usage and your life will be severely cut short."

A lowered life expectancy.

"Does Byuton also hold similar powers?"

Thili pecked at her wings for a while, like any other bird, and Deena doubted whether she would reply. When she seemed satisfied with the state of her feathers, she spoke. "It is a long story, but yes. When Byuton was an infant, Densyus accidentally gave him magical powers belonging to the ancient god that were too much for him to handle. The bracelet keeps him in check."

Not always.

"He might occasionally break the restraint," Thili said, "but I must warn you against doing the same. You have already ensured you won't live to see your lush black hair turn gray."

Thili remained silent for a while, giving her time to take in the implications of a shortened life. Strangely, it did not scare her, although a heaviness settled over her heart. Maybe she would miss some things in life, but after Kran's loss, after all that she had witnessed in the past months, death did not seem to be a stranger, especially if that fate was for a worthy cause.

"If she comes back—" Deena began.

"There will be a lot of us ready to face her before your life is endangered," Thili said firmly.

"I don't understand why she didn't already kill us with the power of water that she holds."

"She had nothing to gain," Thili said with a faraway look. "The scrolls were destroyed, and once the curb circle was removed, the mages and I could have done things to stop her."

"But does she still have Varys's power?"

"I believe so. And there is a good reason for that. After our last meeting, I learned the reason Niferon stopped hunting Mentra. It was because Varys had declared her as his heir. He's always liked her, and he must have taken pity on her after what she suffered. His is the only power she can rightfully hold.

"I hear eager footsteps coming this way. But before I leave, I want to commend you on one thing. Even when using the power of life, you didn't seek to animate the dead. Many would have found it tempting to do so. Now I will leave you in the hands of a most anxious friend."

Thili took flight from the chair and went out through a window into the cloudless blue sky.

Some of the tightness in her chest eased when Horace stopped at the door, pausing to look at her with a surprised expression.

"You are awake," he said in an unsteady voice before slowly advancing to her bedside.

She tried to smile, but her cheeks shivered, and she had to purse her lips to stop it.

"Why is no one with you? Who left you alone?"

"Thili was here till now," Deena said.

He looked haggard, with sunken eyes and a fully grown beard. But when he took her hand, a smile lit up his features. "I thought I'd lose you too."

The image of Lady Len's lifeless body left by Mentra in Edri's temple flashed through her mind. He must have found what was left of his mother, and if what Thili had said was correct, he had been grieving for a month.

"Seems like I slept for a very long time." Deena sought to lighten the mood, but even then, she couldn't smile.

"A really long time." He raised her hand to his forehead, then clasped it and sat by her.

"Did everyone survive?"

"From our team? Yes. We all suffered injuries, but nothing serious. The same cannot be said about the mages. Many gave up their lives. Byuton's grandfather was one of them."

"I am sorry to hear that."

Horace did not carry any signs of injury as far as she could see. Any minor wounds must have healed by now, but his gaunt appearance suggested the anguish he had undergone in the past days.

"We were lucky to have Lady Ilyria with us," he said. "Two weeks ago, she escorted Gaelia back to Alayster. They took Kran's ashes to your family."

Yet again, she wasn't with them to share in their sorrow, but as soon as she could get up, she would go to them.

There was another person who would have been cremated. "Lady Len..."

"We found her. Although I will never know how it happened or when it happened. Some of her writings suggest she was alive before our journey to Bewar."

Deena wished to touch his face, to comfort him and tell him healing would come. But she did not. At least there was one comfort she could render. "I can tell you something about that."

Then she related what Mentra had told her about using wija on Lady Len and its effect on her. Horace's knuckles became white as he painfully gripped her hand, but she didn't budge.

"If so, I treated her cruelly during her last few days." His voice wavered. "I know she looked at me for comfort, but I was unable to give it to her."

"I am sure she understood your state of mind, Horace. She was your mother. Who could have known you better?"

When he seemed to have regained some control over his emotions, she spoke again. "I am sorry for your loss. She didn't deserve it. Also I am sorry we couldn't find Raya."

"Oh! Didn't Thili tell you? We found her." His face cleared with a look of relief. "Alive. And she has been by your bedside every single day since then."

"So that wasn't a dream! I saw her here, or thought I did. How did you find her?"

From his vest, he took out a book bound with greenish leather. "After the events here, a parcel arrived in the palace of Thian, addressed to you. My administrator forwarded it to the war camp near Semera, where I had been visiting at that moment."

"What is it?"

"It was my mother's. She seemingly started writing in it after the scrolls were stolen, to put to words the knowledge she still remembered from them so that they weren't lost forever. Read the final page."

Deena took the book. It was thick, and most of the pages were filled with tidy handwritten letters in blue ink. She turned to the last page.

He trusts her. If she is willing, I could work with her to complete the information in this book. There are a lot of details of the herbs that I might have forgotten. Maybe someday he will want her to take my position in the palace. I can sense his interest in her. At least my plants will be well taken care of. And Raya will have a mentor closer to her age.

The writing stopped there, but toward the end of the page, an elegant hand had scrawled a few words in red ink that had dried to the color of blood. Deena couldn't read it because her eyes had grown blurry. Lady Len had not hated her. Lady Len had considered her knowledge worthy enough to add to the book. As for Horace's interest in her, his mother might have misunderstood him.

"It seems my mother knew me better than I understood myself," Horace said softly, tightening his hold on her hand, this time not painfully. "Whenever you want to return to Thian, everything my mother left behind and I will be waiting for you."

Her tears did not stop flowing for quite some time. Finally, she felt too weak to cry and gave him a smile.

"Thili says I might not have many years left to—"

She could not finish her sentence because he kissed her. His beard grazed her skin in a pleasurable tingle, and her hand tangled in his hair, drawing him closer. It was almost like the years of life she had lost in the battle were being returned to her, like her heart was racing to recover lost ground. When his lips parted from hers, she felt rejuvenated, like she had finally woken up from a deep, restful sleep.

"Even I don't know how many years I have left," Horace said. "But there is no one else I want to spend them with—for however short or long a time that is."

He gazed at her for a long moment before returning her attention to the book she held. "Did you read the writing in red?"

She shook her head and proceeded to do so, the pounding in her heart slowing down to a bearable beat.

Under Semere, find Raya.

"Do you think Mentra . . .?" Deena gasped.

"She must have had this book. It is not my mother's writing."

Mentra's voice rang in her ears.

After I leave here tonight, I will send you a message to let you know where she is. Retrieve her if you want.

She kept her word. Why?

"Raya was under the lake, cocooned in a bubble of some kind," Horace said. "When the soldiers and I approached it, the bubble burst to release her. She had not been harmed, fortunately."

As if on cue, Raya came hurrying into the room with Byuton, Tisila, and Densyus. A small four-legged creature followed them, and above their heads swooped in Thili.

"Deena." Raya took Horace's place and hugged her while the others stood smiling around her bed.

"You must do something about this creation of yours," Byuton said as the animal climbed his trousers using wide paws. A marten. Pebbles and stones made up its body, moving with the flexibility of flesh, bone, and fur.

"It is your only creation that survived the night," Thili said as she settled back to her spot on the bed.

"And Stone Marten delivered your message," the stone marten said, now proudly lounging on Byuton's arm.

"It can talk," Deena said slowly.

"It talks quite a lot." Byuton sighed. "My parents are unwilling to adopt again, and I don't want a pet. Someone must take it."

"I like it," Raya said. The marten pricked up its ear and jumped to Raya's lap. She welcomed it with a giggle.

"We have matching bracelets now." Byuton grinned at Deena.

"Bracelets that shouldn't be removed," Densyus said seriously. The lines around his eyes were deeper than when she had last seen him.

Byuton winked at her.

Tisila hurried to the table at the end of the room to prepare her a refreshing cup of brewed herbs.

"I wish to take off the bracelet once," Deena said. "To write a scroll, leaving what was intended for Raya to her."

Densyus studied her for a moment. "You may do that, as it won't be a huge drain. But in no other case must it be removed, come what may."

"And what might be coming could be severe," Thili said. "Especially for Thian."

Deena looked at Horace with concern filling her heart. The war would still be a threat, if it had not already begun.

"Pari keeps us well-informed," Horace told them. "Tandon is back at the palace of Rothshire. Mentra managed to somehow revive him from the paralysis, although he is still bedridden."

"She must have gotten the knowledge from the scrolls she stole," Deena said.

"Possible," Horace said. "And now Rothshire suspects us of attacking their new heir, although no one can quite say how it happened. Their troops are ready at the border, as are ours."

"So the pieces are set," Thili said. "Let us see who makes the next move."

FALL OF EASTHER

When the seifland of Easther falls after the tragic demise of Lord and Lady Easther, Tisila the sentar warrior and Densyus the mage must unite to shield the infant heir from evil forces. Download the complete prequel novella for free from the author's website. https://jroshni.com/

READ ABOUT MENTRA'S FINAL MOVE IN RUIN OF ROTHSHIRE

Pari has only one target in the seifland of Rothshire – Tandon. Killing him would not only avenge her family but also set back the enchantress's plans. But she cannot stand aside and watch when people are attacked by mysterious sea creatures. Little does she know that the man who fights alongside her is her enemy's brother and that he will pave her path to Tandon.

www.ingramcontent.com/pod-product-compliance
Lightning Source LLC
LaVergne TN
LVHW091621070526
838199LV00044B/885